WILDFLOWER

Falls

Center Point
Large Print

Also by Denise Hunter and available from
Center Point Large Print:

Honeysuckle Dreams
On Magnolia Lane
Summer by the Tides
Lake Season
Carolina Breeze
Autumn Skies
Bookshop by the Sea
Riverbend Gap
Mulberry Hollow
Harvest Moon
A Novel Proposal

**This Large Print Book carries the
Seal of Approval of N.A.V.H.**

WILDFLOWER

Falls

A RIVERBEND ROMANCE

Denise Hunter

CENTER POINT LARGE PRINT
THORNDIKE, MAINE

This Center Point Large Print edition
is published in the year 2023 by arrangement with
Thomas Nelson.

The text of this Large Print edition is unabridged.
In other aspects, this book may vary
from the original edition.
Printed in the United States of America
on permanent paper sourced using
environmentally responsible foresting methods.
Set in 16-point Times New Roman type.

ISBN: 978-1-63808-888-2

The Library of Congress has cataloged this record
under Library of Congress Control Number: 2023940405

WILDFLOWER

Falls

Robinson Family Tree

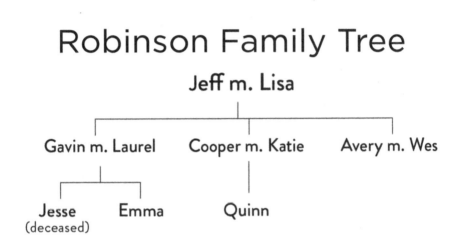

Jeff m. Lisa

Gavin m. Laurel　　Cooper m. Katie　　Avery m. Wes

Jesse　　Emma　　　　Quinn
(deceased)

One

Charlotte Simpson had never stalked a man before.

She freely admitted to the social media stalking of an ex-boyfriend or two. In high school she'd once sat outside her boyfriend's home to see if Mindy Miller really was only dropping off brownies for his sick mother. (She wasn't.)

But Charlotte had never stooped to peeping out a barn window, the rubber rings of the binoculars pressing into her eye sockets.

She turned the Focus knob. Gavin Robinson walked toward the leveled rectangle of land that would soon support her new stable. His jeans were faded and speckled with . . . She fine-tuned the focus. Paint? Drywall mud? Something construction-y? He squatted, inspecting one of the footers on the western edge of the space.

Rogue nickered from the pasture outside the window, wanting her attention. But she couldn't pull her gaze from the man a hundred yards away. She adjusted the eyepieces for a better fit. Gavin had aged a little since she'd seen him last. But then, he hadn't had an easy life.

He'd been way ahead of her in school—eight years maybe? That would make him . . . thirty-fiveish. Charlotte was closer in age to his sister,

Avery. She'd been a senior when Charlotte was a freshman. Their brother, Cooper, had also already graduated by then.

They'd never run in the same circles, but everyone knew the Robinsons. They had a good name in the community. They stuck together like paint on a barn and were always willing to lend a hand.

Avery ran Riverbend Gap's medical clinic, Cooper was the county sheriff, and Gavin owned the construction company she'd hired to build her stable. When she'd entered his office on Jell-O legs that warm April afternoon, she hoped to work with him personally. But his business partner and brother-in-law, Wes Garrett, was working the office that day, so he'd taken the project himself.

Thus, this was her first real glimpse of Gavin since the "Big News."

He stood, seemingly satisfied with the subcontractor's work, and did nothing more interesting than trek around the dirt rectangle. But since this was her first chance to observe him up close . . .

Observe. Yes, she liked that word much better.

As soon as she got up the nerve, she would go out there and chat with him about the project. Her heart palpitated in her chest like a foaling mare's. She would tell him the footers of the foundation looked good (as if she knew). She would ask him what came next and what the schedule would be like, even though Wes had thoroughly covered that.

It was hard to tell in that big, open space with the mountains rising behind him, but Gavin was tall—at least six feet. He was tanned from hours in the sun and built like a man of his trade. His black hair was shorter than she remembered, though the top was long enough that the warm May breeze toyed with it.

She squinted as she homed in on his face, wishing she could remember his eye color as, even with the binoculars, she was too far away to tell. They were set deep beneath the dark slashes of his brows. A clean-shaven jawline revealed sharp turns.

He would be considered handsome by anyone's yardstick with his well-placed, rugged features and athletic physique. But she didn't care about all that. After all, it wasn't Gavin's good looks that had her studying him like a scientist with a microscope. It was his genetics.

Welcome to Riverbend Gap! Best little town on the Appalachian Trail!

Gunner Dawson roared past the welcome sign on his Harley-Davidson, then leaned into a curve. He followed the two-lane road that led him across a bridge spanning the French Broad River and immediately into the town proper.

He slowed his Harley to a crawl. Old storefronts lined Main Street: a hardware store, a coffee shop, the Beauty Barn, the Iron Skillet, the Grab 'n' Go Deli. The latter brought back a fond memory of fresh-toasted bread piled high with salami and melted cheese so thick it made his mouth water.

Locals meandered up and down sidewalks on the sunny Saturday afternoon, dined alfresco on sidewalk patios, and rested on shade-drenched benches. Hikers, obvious by their backpacks and sweat-stained T-shirts, entered Appalachian Out-fitters, no doubt to grab supplies and restock their food packs.

In short, the town appeared exactly as it had last time he'd been here. A year ago he'd come off the trail seeking a home-cooked meal and a decent bed. Ideas he could get behind today after his four-hour trip turned into six due to extensive road construction on 75 and an accident on 40.

When he reached the other side of town, he accelerated, following the road that ran alongside the meandering river. He passed the campground and a few more businesses: a clinic, a mercantile, a flower shop, all housed in old homes. He continued, heading to the far side of town where the houses thinned and properties stretched out, low and hilly.

He was a day early for his interview, but he couldn't resist another peek at the quaint horse ranch where he hoped to hire on. After being one of many trainers on a large operation, he was eager for the challenge of something new. Something smaller.

And this pretty little town, nestled in the Appalachian Mountains, fit the bill. The smell of pine and mowed grass teased his senses as his eyes feasted on the sweeping panorama of majestic blue-green mountains. Yep, he could settle here for a while.

Up ahead the modest wooden sign came into view: *The Stables at Wildflower Falls*. When he came to the gravel drive, he turned. Wouldn't hurt to check in. Maybe he could even get the interview over with, and then he could start searching for a place to rent. He wouldn't need much. A bed and a small kitchen. Plumbing would be a plus.

The driveway wound between fenced-in pastures toward a two-story farmhouse. A red barn sat behind the house, to the left. A bay mare watched him pass by while her foal wandered off toward a copse of trees.

A moment later he pulled up behind a beige Tahoe and turned off his motorcycle. His back muscles protested as he dismounted the bike and removed his helmet. He stretched. He wasn't twenty-five anymore. In fact, he'd passed that milestone almost a decade ago, though it hardly seemed possible.

A squirrel nattered in the sudden quiet. A

breeze whispered through the treetops and cooled the back of his neck. He glanced down at his attire: gray tee, worn jeans, boots. A little grungy, but he'd be riding horses, not sitting behind a desk.

Two quick leaps had him up on the big front porch. He rapped on the screen door's wooden frame and waited. Nice house, if old. Someone had kept it up. The porch rails had a fresh coat of white paint and the chairs were clean and ready for occupants.

When a second knock proved ineffective, he headed back down the steps and turned toward the barn. A Denali sat way off in the distance, beyond the red barn. Ms. Simpson, whom he'd met the summer before and recently exchanged several emails with, was likely tending to her horses.

He followed the well-worn path, taking note of the hilly pasture behind the barn that ended at a steep-sloped mountain. A few horses grazed nearby: a chestnut, a palomino, and a bay, all sporting healthy, shiny coats. Ears forward, eyes soft, they turned his way as he neared.

Gunner slipped inside the open barn door and took a second for his eyes to adjust. Then he opened his mouth to call out, but the sight at the other end of the barn snatched the words from his tongue.

A petite woman stood at the edge of a window,

peering through a pair of binoculars. "Come on . . . turn around."

This was not the woman he'd met last summer. This one was much younger, for starters. Beyond the window a man inspected a raised piece of land that must be the new stable in the works. Not her husband, he assumed, as she'd surely have no reason to spy on him.

He cleared his throat.

The woman squeaked, bumped her head on the window frame, and whirled. The binoculars clunked to the ground. Wide green eyes fastened on him.

"Sorry. Didn't mean to startle you."

She pressed a palm to her chest as a pretty blush crawled into her cheeks. "I was just . . . checking on the, uh . . ." She kicked the binoculars aside, mashing her lips together. "There was an, um— you know. Anyway, can I help you? Are you here about boarding a horse?"

He barely kept his lips from twitching. She was pretty cute, all flustered like that. Nobody blushed like a redhead. "Gunner Dawson. I have an appointment with Ms. Simpson tomorrow, but I got into town early. Thought I'd stop by and check out the place. Is Ms. Simpson in?" And then, because he couldn't help himself, he glanced down at the binoculars. "Or is this a bad time?"

The pink in her cheeks deepened as she rubbed

her neck. "Um, no, now is fine. I should've mentioned in my email that the woman you met last summer, my mom, passed away last August. So your appointment is actually with me."

All traces of humor drained away. "Sorry to hear that. She seemed like a nice lady."

"She was." The woman scooped up the binoculars and approached, extending a hand. "You can call me Charlotte. And I can give you the tour, such as it is."

He shook her hand, noting the strength of her grip—and a barely perceptible cleft in her chin. "That'd be great if it's not a bother."

"Not at all." Auburn waves fell just past her shoulders. Those green irises featured a charcoal outer ring, and her perfectly proportioned nose sported a smattering of freckles. She was dressed in work-appropriate attire: boots, jeans, and a sleeveless black top with little ruffles at the shoulders. His eyes caught on the spray of light freckles on her sun-kissed shoulders as she led him through the barn.

Her drawl was as sweet as southern iced tea on a hot summer day. He'd never had a boss younger than him, but as he listened to her explain her operation, it was clear he'd be in good hands. She asked relevant questions and found they agreed on horse-training philosophy. In the past he'd used traditional methods when requested by his employers, but he favored natural horsemanship, which relied on psychology, communication, and understanding.

As they talked she glanced over her shoulder a couple of times toward the man in the distance. Employee? Lover? Stalking victim?

He nodded toward the patch of ground. "Your new stable?"

"It'll be finished in early July."

"A good deal larger than what you've currently got, by the looks of it."

"Almost twice the size. Concrete floors, twelve-by-twelve stalls. That's the owner of the construction company out there."

Another flush. Interesting.

A while later they ended the tour at the paddock ring where Gunner hitched a boot heel on the bottom fence rail as they continued their conversation. The ranch's boarding business had been part-time work for twenty-two years, and she was planning to expand into horse training and trail rides, making it a full working ranch.

"We need to turn this place into a moneymaker if we're going to keep it—and we definitely are. The website's almost up and running. A lot of people around here own horses, and we've already got a list of clients whose horses need training. Also some of our boarders have minor issues to work out. There's good money in training, as I'm sure you know. And no one else in the valley offers trail rides, so I think that'll be a hit. We get a lot of tourists here to hike and river raft and otherwise enjoy the great outdoors. Ranches in other tourist towns make a good living off trail rides."

"Sounds like a feasible plan."

Her hair glistened like burnished copper under the sun as she turned to him. "So, just to clarify, you basically travel the country training horses?"

"That's the gist of it."

"Your résumé is impressive and you come highly recommended. But I'm sure you're aware this place runs at a slower pace than what you're used to. And comes with a lot less money."

"That's true." But the ranch was everything he'd hoped for. Some operations didn't treat their horses humanely. The animals were just a means to an end. But Charlotte's concern for their health and happiness was obvious in the animals themselves. The horses were relaxed and bright-eyed, their tails swinging loosely. They groomed each other in the field and nickered when Charlotte came around. All good signs.

"But not a problem for you?"

She had a detailed plan for this place's growth and the passion required to take it to the next level. This was a place he'd love to work and the kind of person he'd enjoy working for. "I've been employed by outfits of all sizes, and I don't need much to get by. I'm a simple man. Ready to

18

take on a new challenge—and happy to ditch the uniform."

Her eyes twinkled. "Did I forget to mention the white polos?"

He turned as if to go. "Well, it was nice knowing you."

Her laughter stopped him in his tracks. Gripped him. She laughed with such abandon.

"But the shirts are so nice, with the logo and everything. And the tan riding breeches are really comfortable."

He couldn't help but return her smile. Heat sparked between them as the moment stretched out. Horse smart, cute as a button, and a sense of humor too. If that wasn't the perfect trifecta in a woman, he didn't know what was.

The attraction was unfortunate, as she would be his boss. But he could handle the temptation. He was a man of discipline. Anyway, she apparently had a thing for a certain construction worker.

She tilted her head, still studying him. "The owner of Four Winds called you their horse whisperer."

"Nah. I just pay attention. Horses have plenty to say if you watch and listen." He glanced over her shoulder. Speaking of the construction guy . . . "Your contractor is heading this way. I should go now."

"No!" She glanced over her shoulder and rubbed her lips together. "I mean . . . you might as well, you know, stick around a minute. Gavin will, uh, be around a lot this summer. You should meet him."

"Sure." Gunner gave her a speculative look. Did that mean he had the job?

He didn't have time to ponder the subject as the man in question approached. He walked with the confident stride of someone who knew who he was. He wore a T-shirt with the company logo, a cordial expression—Gunner's gaze slid down his arm—and a slim silver band on his ring finger.

Two

Blue. His eyes were worn-denim blue. Charlotte scanned Gavin's face, searching for familiar features, and stopped at his lips. Aha! The upper one sported a defined Cupid's bow and the lower one was thick. The upper lip not so much.

You're staring at his mouth.

She snapped her gaze back to his eyes. Yep, he'd caught her staring. Her face went nuclear. Belatedly, she shoved the binoculars behind her back. Why was she still carrying these things around?

"Hi." She cleared the threadiness from her voice and tried again. "Um, hi."

Gavin offered a professional smile as they shook hands. "You're Charlotte, right? I'm not sure we've ever formally met. Gavin Robinson."

"Yes, uh, right. I think your little sister was a few years ahead of me in school."

"Sounds about right."

Do not look at his mouth. Her curious eyes ticked over to his ears instead. Small and slightly pointed with detached lobes, just like—

"Gavin Robinson." He held out a hand to Gunner.

"Gunner Dawson."

"Sorry, I should've introduced you. Gavin is

the owner of Robinson Construction, and Gunner is, uh . . . my new horse trainer, I guess? If he's amenable to the idea, that is." Wow, she was so smooth today.

Gunner's brows darted upward as he met her gaze. "Very much so."

"Congratulations are in order, then," Gavin said. "You must be new around here. Where you from?"

"Louisville most recently."

"He worked at a big horse farm there," Charlotte said.

Gunner gave a nod. "Came through Riverbend on the trail last summer and liked the looks of it."

"You're not the first. Welcome to town." Gavin fished a business card from his pocket and handed it to Gunner. "You won't be in need of construction, but if you need anything at all, just give me a call. I know all the best restaurants."

"That's awfully nice. Thank you."

"You'll find most folks around here are helpful and welcoming."

Charlotte found her voice. "He's right. You won't have any trouble fitting in and making friends." He'd only be here six months—had some big job opportunity come November—but no reason he couldn't settle in a bit.

"Good to know." Gunner eased away and confirmed with Charlotte that he'd be there in the morning.

And then she was alone with Gavin. She shifted awkwardly.

"I stopped by to inspect the footers. I'll be checking in regularly and doing the framing along with Wes. We're pretty hands-on with the business."

"That's what he said. That's great." Could he hear the slight quiver in her voice?

"I didn't get into this business because I liked sitting behind a desk."

"Of course. I feel the same." There were so many things she wanted to ask him—things that had nothing to do with construction—but they all jumbled up in her throat. She couldn't ask them anyway.

"Makes sense. It's a great property. Your new stable will be a real asset."

"That's what I'm hoping."

"I don't think I ever extended my condolences on the loss of your mother. I didn't really know her, but she was well-liked in town. And known for taking great care of her horses."

It had been nine months, but the mention of her mother still awakened that vacant spot inside her. "Thank you. She loved them like they were her babies, and I intend to do the same."

"You're off to a good start." He glanced back at the stable. "That'll be the Taj Mahal of barns."

Her last effort to save this ranch. "Go big or go home."

His eyes twinkled. "I like the way you think. Wes and I will be around most of next week and the one after, framing. You'll be surprised how fast it goes up. The rest will require patience. As I'm sure he mentioned, we do our best to stay on schedule, but sometimes weather interrupts our plans or there are material delays. But we'll have her up by first of July."

"He explained all that. We're good. You guys have a good name around here."

"We'll try to live up to it then. If you don't have any questions for me, I've got another job to check on."

She wished she could come up with an intelligent query because she didn't want him to leave just yet. But she didn't know a footer from a fan belt. "Nope, I think I'm good."

"All right then. We'll see you bright and early Monday."

"Sounds good."

He began walking away.

Maybe she could've said "good" one more time. And he'd caught her staring at his lips! *Great impression, Charlotte.* She covered her eyes.

He probably wanted to run screaming from her property. He'd probably go home and tell his wife about the awkward little horse rancher who had a big, fat crush on him.

She shuddered. Because he couldn't be more

wrong. If she was curious to the point of stalking and staring, it was only because she was too afraid to come out and tell him the truth. That at the age of twenty-six, her only blood relative deceased, Charlotte had just discovered she had three biological siblings—and one of them was Gavin Robinson.

"Who was the hottie on the motorcycle?" Charlotte's younger sister barged into the house a minute behind Charlotte and headed for the fridge. At twenty-one Emerson had long since lost the innocent waiflike appearance she'd had when she and her dad had come into Charlotte's life. Now she was two inches taller than Charlotte's five feet two and sported a trim, athletic build. With her blue eyes and thick blonde hair that hung to the small of her back, she put Charlotte in mind of a Disney princess.

"Hello to you too. That was our new horse trainer, Gunner. I just gave him an impromptu interview, and he passed with flying colors." From her spot at the sink, Charlotte gave Emerson a pointed look. "And he's way too old for you."

Emmie waggled her brows. "But not for you."

"Ranch employees are off-limits."

"That's never been a policy."

"We've never had a ranch employee before." Charlotte finished washing her hands and grabbed the towel. Based on Gunner's emails, she'd pictured him older somehow. In his forties at least, with a receding hairline and a saggy little paunch shadowing his belt buckle. Instead he was lean and muscular with a full head of dark hair and green eyes that seemed to see right through her somehow.

Emerson's eyes twinkled. "You realize every female horse owner in a fifty-mile radius will suddenly have a problem horse."

"Great, we could use the business."

"What are these doing out?" Emerson nodded toward the binoculars Charlotte had dropped on the island.

"Um . . . I was keeping an eye on the construction. Of the, uh, stable."

"That's a little weird. You know that, right?"

"I never claimed to be normal." So Charlotte hadn't exactly mentioned her recent discovery about her biological dad and siblings. Even though Emerson was her sister in every way that mattered, they weren't related by blood, and Charlotte didn't want to hurt her feelings. She'd have to tell her soon though. Certainly before she ever revealed the truth to the Robinsons—if she ever got up the nerve.

Emerson finished the glass of water. "I'm going to visit April for a few days."

Charlotte's shoulders sank. She had her hands full with the new trail horses, the new trainer, the stable, the upcoming open house, and her job at the Trailhead Bar and Grill. "Can't you put it off for a bit? There's so much to do around here."

"She needs help with her computer—she's trying to get her jewelry business off the ground—and it's been forever since I've gotten away."

Charlotte couldn't remember the last time *she'd* had so much as a day off. But they'd always spoiled Emerson a little. Charlotte was as guilty as her parents. "I hear you, but I rely on your help with the horses, especially since we bought the new ones."

Emerson cut her a glare. "You mean since *you* bought them."

"Since the *ranch* bought them, and you are half owner. You really shouldn't be taking off like this when there's so much to do for the expansion. I was hoping to brainstorm with you about our big open house." At least she hoped it would be big. They had to get this place in the black.

Emerson crossed her arms. "That's why I wanted to sell it. Think what we could've done with the money."

"I can't be the one to lose the ranch that's been in our family for three generations." Expansion was the only way to turn the ranch into a full-time operation. "I promised Mom." How many times had they had this same conversation?

"That's right. *You* promised her and you

shouldn't have! It's as much mine as yours, and you gave me no say."

"I thought we'd settled this."

"No, you settled it because I can't sell my half without yours. So fine, have it your way. But I won't be tied down to this stupid ranch for the rest of my life. I have things I want to do, too, you know."

As if Emerson had shown so much initiative. "Like what?"

"I don't know. Like start a coffee shop or bakery or go to college or travel."

Charlotte gave her head a shake. "This town already has a bakery, you hated school, and you don't have the money to travel."

"Well, I would've if we'd sold the ranch. I love to bake and make food. Maybe I could go to culinary school."

Charlotte blinked. This seemed to come out of left field. Then again, in middle school Emmie wanted to be a ballerina and in high school a forensic artist, an astronaut, and a professional basketball player.

"You're a great cook. We can certainly talk about that. But can we focus on the ranch for now? It's too much work for one person."

"I don't want to work with four-legged animals all the livelong day. You can't even earn a decent living on this place. Mom never made it work."

It was true that their dad's truck-driving salary

had been all that kept the place running. And after the divorce, Mom struggled to make ends meet. Dad moved to Asheville. Since Emerson had just started high school and Dad was often off driving his routes, she'd stayed here.

"We'll make it work," Charlotte said. "Why do you think we're doing all this—the stable, the open house, the expansion?"

Emerson let out a wry laugh. "Yes, let's talk about the stable—and the eighty thousand dollars from Mom's pension you're using to build it. We could've used that to pay down the loan or just put the property up for—"

"I had no idea you felt so strongly about—"

"Because you wouldn't let me get a word in edgewise. Just because you're older doesn't mean you know everything."

"I asked what you thought about it. In the living room that night after we got the pension check."

"Yes, you did. And I told you I didn't see myself at the ranch long term."

"I thought you meant in, like, ten years or something. Why didn't you speak up sooner?"

Emerson rolled her eyes. "Because you would've just steamrolled right over me like you always do."

"I don't do that."

"You're doing it right now!"

"That's not fair. The expansion is already well underway. It's too late to stop it. It's gonna bring in more money, you'll see. Once you receive half the profits, you won't be complaining anymore."

Emerson speared her with a flinty look. "I have to go." She headed for the stairs.

"Emerson, don't leave like this."

She turned with a huff. "We're fine, Charlotte. I'm gonna pack a bag and head to April's. I'm sure you'll figure it out. You always do."

Charlotte gritted her teeth. "Could you at least clean out the water tank before you go? I have to be at work at four."

"Sorry, no can do. I just stopped by to grab my things." She rushed from the room and up the creaky stairs.

Charlotte grabbed Emerson's empty glass and set it in the dishwasher. She couldn't believe her sister was just leaving at a moment's notice. But then, she didn't bear the burden of the ranch and its horses. Not that it was a burden. Charlotte loved it more than anything.

It went all the way back to the stories her grandmother had told her about the ranch's origins. The sacrifices her grandparents had made, eking out a living during the ranch's early days, how her grandfather had used his inheritance to start a breeding farm. They loved the ranch life so much, they hung on until it started making real money. Charlotte's young, adventurous heart relished the tales.

But by the time her mom took over, the

economy had slackened and the breeding business struggled. She made the difficult decision to switch to boarding instead and worked a full-time job at the bank to maintain it. Her efforts had kept the ranch alive, but it was no longer self-sustaining.

Perhaps her mom had felt the ranch slipping away when she'd extracted that promise from Charlotte two weeks before she passed.

Mom was in the makeshift office in the stable doing the bills when Charlotte popped in.

"I have to run over to the feedstore. Do we need anything besides glucosamine?"

"I don't think so." Mom didn't look up from her work. Her brows knitted and lines creased her forehead.

Charlotte set down the shovel and entered the room. "Something wrong?"

Mom leaned back in the chair, her gaze skating over the bills scattered on the desktop. She released a sigh. "I made a mistake."

"What do you mean?"

She shook her head. "I never should've switched to boarding horses. The breeding business was good—it was just going through a bad spell because of the economy. If I'd waited it out . . ."

"You can't know what might've happened. The business could've gone under entirely."

"I'm worried about its future."

"We'll be okay, Mom."

"We need to make some changes, but that costs money we don't have. I'm getting older, and I don't want to leave you girls in this situation—if I don't run it into the ground altogether. Your grandparents worked so hard to build this ranch."

Charlotte put her hand over her mom's. "We won't let that happen, Mom. Let's give it some thought."

"I've been doing that for months. I'm at my wit's end."

"Well, I'll come up with something." She squeezed Mom's hand. "It's going to be okay, I promise. I won't let this place go under."

She'd meant every word, but since her mom's death Charlotte had been struggling just to make ends meet. She didn't make the income her mom had made at the bank. The expansion was a last-ditch effort to make this ranch a full-time operation once again. Otherwise, Charlotte didn't see how she could keep up this pace.

Her sister bounded down the steps. "See you later, probably Wednesday."

"Wednesday?"

Emerson glowered.

Charlotte sighed. "Fine. Drive carefully. Tell April I said hi," she called just before the screen door slapped shut.

She wished they'd had a chance to talk things

out, but Charlotte wasn't feeling so amenable right now. It was entirely possible she might've said things she couldn't take back.

They hadn't argued like that since they were teenagers. Emerson used to complain that Charlotte bossed her around, and Charlotte insisted Emerson got away with murder—which she had. All the rules that had been written in stone for Charlotte were up for negotiation where Emerson was concerned.

Days like this she wished her mom were still alive. Or her dad, for that matter. Emerson had been adrift since they'd passed. She didn't go to church anymore, never visited the gravesites, and seemed to have no direction in her life.

Charlotte missed both her parents terribly. She'd always known Patrick Simpson was not her biological father. But she barely remembered her life before he entered it when she was seven, bringing a toddler with him. Emmie, having been recently abandoned by her mother, latched onto Charlotte like a leech to a host. Charlotte was happy to accept the big-sister role.

And having a dad around was a novelty she embraced. During the summers he sometimes took her on his truck-driving routes. She loved riding in his big rig and listening to him talk over the CB radio. Sometimes he let her talk too. She learned all the slang, and Dad laughed with pride as she conversed like a pro with the other drivers.

She was mesmerized by this secret language. But what she loved most was that, even in the wee hours of the night, she could reach out into the void and someone would always answer back. It was comforting somehow.

She only had a few memories prior to her parents' marriage. One of them was in the stable after her mom's beloved horse Luna foaled.

"Where's the baby's daddy?" Charlotte had asked her mother while watching Luna clean her spindly-legged baby, the familiar smells of straw and horseflesh filling her nose.

Mama squatted down next to her. "Filly, honey, remember? A girl foal is a filly."

"Where's the filly's daddy? Is she like me?"

Mama's green eyes fixed on her. "What do you mean?"

"Doesn't she have a daddy?"

Her mom was quiet so long, Charlotte thought she didn't hear. "Mama, doesn't she—?"

"She has a daddy. It's Rogue, the stallion who visited awhile last fall, remember?"

The black thoroughbred stallion was one of the most beautiful horses Charlotte had ever seen with his shiny coat and thick mane. He was tall and powerful, and Charlotte hadn't been allowed near him.

Mama turned Charlotte toward her and stroked her cheek. "You have a daddy, too, honey. But he can't be with us."

Charlotte thought about the big strong horse. "Like Rogue?"

Her mom's eyes went sparkly and she nodded. "Yeah, honey. Like Rogue."

Somewhere she had a strong, powerful daddy who couldn't be with her. That was enough for Charlotte. Maybe her real daddy was a superhero.

She later brought up the subject of her father during her elementary years. But her mom was always vague and quickly changed the subject. But by the time she reached fifth grade, she was old enough to know superheroes weren't real. But maybe he was an FBI agent or an astronaut or a Navy SEAL. They had secret missions too. His work was important and he couldn't have a normal family life like other dads.

Then in the sixth grade, the morning after her daddy-daughter dance, she caught her mother alone in the kitchen. They exchanged good mornings and talked about the dance as Charlotte poured herself a bowl of Apple Jacks. She'd had so much fun with Dad last night. But in the afterglow of the evening, the question she'd submerged for years burst to the surface.

She settled across the table from her mother and drew a breath of courage. "Mom . . . who's my real dad?"

Her mother's spoon stopped halfway to its destination. She blinked. "Patrick is your father, Charlotte. The only one who matters."

But she was old enough to be curious about where she'd come from. And old enough to wonder why he couldn't be with her. Her class had done a family tree last semester and half of it felt fake. "You know what I mean. Don't I have the right to know who my real father is?"

Just then Dad appeared in the doorway. He stopped short. His eyes turned down at the corners. His lips loosened. He seemed ten years older than he had last night when he was laughing and spinning her around the dance floor.

Heat crawled up Charlotte's neck. Shame bloomed inside, making her feel all squishy and awful.

Mom changed the subject again, but Charlotte couldn't forget the hurt look on Dad's face. Not for weeks. And she didn't know how to make it right. He had never brought it up again, so neither did she.

Things soon returned to normal, and though Charlotte was still curious about her biological father, she would never risk hurting her dad that way again.

Three

The robust aroma of java hit Charlotte as she entered Milly's Mug and Bean. She knew her friend would be working this morning because she'd begged Charlotte to take her nursery class at church for the late service.

Charlotte checked her watch. She only had twenty minutes to enjoy her morning brew. She took her spot in line and minutes later she was at the front.

"Good morning, sunshine," Brianna said.

"Morning."

"Your usual?"

"Yes, please."

Brianna wore her black spiral curls slicked back into a ponytail. Her bronzed skin and sculpted cheekbones weren't compliments of Maybelline and artistry. If she ever got tired of managing the coffee shop, Brianna could definitely model. But she didn't have time for makeup, much less a modeling career.

Brianna finished out the transaction, prompting Charlotte to say, "Oh no you don't. I insist on paying this time."

"Not a chance."

"Why did you give me that gift card for my birthday if you're gonna comp all my drinks?"

"You know, you really shouldn't complain about free lattes."

Brianna had a point. Charlotte's argument died on her tongue. "Thank you."

The bell over the door jangled. Charlotte glanced over her shoulder. She stiffened as Jeff Robinson entered with his son Cooper. The younger man wore his sheriff's uniform this morning.

She hadn't seen either of them since she'd found that manila envelope in Mom's safety-deposit box back in March. It was labeled *Charlotte's family* and contained articles about the Robinson kids, an old blurry photo of her mom with a man, and a war medal of some kind.

Boisterous laughter drew her attention to Cooper. The last time she'd seen him was last year when he pulled her over for speeding. Not her finest moment. Her face warmed at the memory.

Charlotte shot her head straight forward, latching onto Brianna's gaze.

Everything in her longed to turn back and stare, to find something familiar in each of their faces. But she had to play it cool.

Brianna was the queen of cool. "Breathe. You go sit down. I'll bring your drink and take a break."

"Thank you." Charlotte scuttled off before the pair approached and chose the only available two-top in the busy shop. She took the seat that allowed her to observe the father and son.

Jeff Robinson, who appeared to be near sixty, was handsome for his age, tall, and fit-looking. He wore a blue button-down shirt with khakis. He was just the sort of man she'd always envisioned as her father, minus the superhero cape. Except since Charlotte was the youngest sibling, that meant he'd been married to Lisa when he and Charlotte's mom had conceived her. That scandalous detail flew in the face of Charlotte's childhood hopes and Jeff's stellar reputation in the community. But it also explained why he might have abandoned his fatherly duties to Charlotte—and why her mom might not have wanted Charlotte to know about him.

The affair definitely complicated matters, then and now.

The father and son chatted as they waited for their order. They seemed to share an easy relationship. She didn't detect any tension between them.

The bell jingled and Lisa Robinson entered. She looked a bit younger than her husband. Her blonde hair was swept up in a messy bun, revealing kind eyes and a dimple that hollowed as she hugged her son. The three stood talking, Jeff's arm wrapping around his wife's waist as they chatted.

Charlotte watched them, feeling more like an outsider than she'd ever felt in her life. They seemed so at ease together. The perfect family. How could she ever approach Jeff and tell him who she was?

Her heart shrank two sizes at the thought she'd tried to stuff down each time it emerged. He'd never even spoken to her that she remembered. She might've seen him a dozen or so times in her life. She didn't have any reason to go into his hiking supply store, and he'd never had reason to visit the ranch. They didn't attend the same church. Though his children frequented the Trailhead Bar and Grill, she rarely saw him or Lisa there. Or maybe Charlotte just hadn't noticed them. Why would she?

"Get that look off your face." Brianna appeared in the seat across from her and slid her latte across the table. "It's killing me."

"They seem like such a close-knit family."

"He deserves to know he has a child."

"What if he already knows? I mean, how couldn't he? If he and my mom, you know. And she turned up with a pregnant belly a few months later."

"If he's denied you all these years, then he's not the man everyone thinks he is."

"I still can't believe she had an affair with a married man. It was so unlike her."

"People make mistakes, even good people. Besides, that was a long time ago. I'm sure she grew a lot as a person over the years. She probably deeply regretted her actions—but she never would've wished it away since the affair gave her you."

"Maybe I should just try to forget all this. I don't want to cause trouble. That woman might be devastated."

"You didn't do this—he and your mom did. And even if Jeff knows, it's obvious his kids don't. They deserve to know they have a sister, and you deserve to know your family."

Emerson meant the world to her, but their parents' deaths had left a huge void in her life. She was lonely in a way she'd never experienced before. She glanced at Jeff. "He has half my DNA. How can I not be curious about where I came from? And I can't bear to have family out there and not do anything about it. I have to get to know them. I can't help it."

"Have you talked to Gavin at all?"

"Briefly when he came out to check on the footers yesterday." When she'd gawked at him. She closed her eyes at the memory. "He caught me staring at his lips."

Brianna sputtered her cold brew. "Why the heck were you staring at his lips?"

She touched her upper lip. "He has that defined Cupid's bow, like me."

Brianna just shook her head. "Girl."

"I know. But I think it went okay other than that."

"Other than your brother thinking you were ogling him?"

"Well, when you put it like that."

"So how long are you gonna carry on before you tell the guy?"

"I think I should confront Jeff first. He should have the chance to tell his family." Charlotte glanced over as the couple hugged their son goodbye and left the coffee shop. Cooper settled at a vacant table with his coffee and a newspaper. "There should be some kind of guide for this."

"*How to Introduce Yourself to the Birth Family You Never Knew You Had*? Maybe you can write it when this is all said and done."

"If I live through it. My nerves are shot." Between losing her mother, the ranch's uncertain future, and this unexpected discovery, she was up to her ears in stress.

"You're strong. You can do this." Brianna squeezed her hand. "You know, Avery is an amiable person. She's Granny's primary physician. Maybe you should try to get to know her a bit." Brianna's grandma was in the advanced stages of multiple sclerosis.

"And how do you suggest I do that?"

"I don't know. Go see her at the clinic."

"For what?"

Brianna lifted a shoulder. "Fake something."

"I can't afford a real doctor's appointment, much less a fake one."

"Just do it. What could it hurt?"

Charlotte thought a minute. "Well, I am overdue for a tetanus shot."

"There you go. Plus, you'd be killing two birds with one stone."

"I guess that's true. I'll give it some thought."

Brianna sipped her cold brew. "Hey, aren't you interviewing that potential trainer later today?"

"Actually he stopped by yesterday and I hired him already. So that's one thing off my list of things to worry about."

"That was fast."

"He has an incredible résumé. I can't imagine why he'd want to work at our dinky little ranch, but I'm not complaining."

"You sure he isn't a felon or something?"

"His references gave glowing reviews. They all said they'd rehire him in a heartbeat."

"It's only temporary though?"

"Through the end of October. He agreed to get the program up and running and help train the next person. I'll take what I can get at this point. It's not like there's a line of skilled applicants outside my door. Certainly none with his qualifications." Charlotte glanced at Cooper. "Do you think we look alike? No, don't turn around—you turned around!"

"He's too busy reading the paper to notice. I think he might have your nose."

Charlotte touched her nose. "Really?"

"No, not really—he's thirty feet away."

Charlotte scowled at her friend.

"I have to say this makes me really glad I voted for him. I mean, he's doing a good job and everything, but especially since he's your brother."

Heat seeped into Charlotte's cheeks. She took a swig of her latte. Watched as Cooper leaned forward, resting his elbows on the table.

"You didn't vote for him. You didn't vote for your own brother."

Charlotte lowered her voice. "I didn't know he was my brother! And I didn't vote against him either . . . I just didn't vote at all."

"You did not just say that. You gotta vote; it's your civic duty."

"All right, all right, I'll never miss Election Day again."

Cooper sipped his coffee. How did he take it? Was he dairy sensitive like her? There were so many things she'd always wondered about. Her athletic ability, her allergies to penicillin, her cleft chin. Would she find the answers in her dad's side of the family?

Brianna leaned forward. "Um, don't look now, but there's a hottie at two o'clock who keeps checking you out. Black fitted tee and a pair of very nice shoulders. Oh, mama."

Charlotte tore her attention from Cooper to find Gunner staring at her, a knowing glint in his eyes. Because, of course, he'd seen her gawking at Cooper.

He gave a nod.

She pulled her lips into a semblance of a smile, then jerked her gaze back to Brianna. Her internal temperature had risen at least ten degrees. "That's my new horse trainer. And naturally, he just caught me staring at Cooper."

"So?"

"So yesterday he caught me gawking at Gavin."

Brianna shrugged.

"With *binoculars*."

Brianna's features froze. Then she let out that exuberant laugh she was known for.

Charlotte scowled. "It's not that funny."

"Oh, sweetheart. You are the comic relief I so need in my life."

Four

Charlotte squirmed in the waiting room chair. The clinic's antiseptic smell hardly settled her nerves. It only reminded her of those hours in the hospital with her mother. The aneurism had taken her pretty quickly, but she'd been on life support for two full days. The smell ushered her right back to those days—the terrible blend of shock and dread mingling in a poisonous cocktail.

The man next to her was called by a woman in a lab coat. Dr. Lucy Chan, according to her name tag.

Charlotte hadn't realized she might be seen by someone other than Avery. She should've made an appointment. This whole thing could end up being a waste of time and money. Except she really should keep her tetanus shot up-to-date.

She flipped through a copy of *Appalachian Magazine*, the contents not even registering. Gunner had arrived when she'd been feeding the horses. He'd needed little guidance, the work of ranch life obviously familiar and easy for him.

After morning chores were done, she left him with Dominic, a boarded gelding that was rearing up or striking out whenever he got nervous. Once, he'd unseated his owner, a thirtysomething woman who valued her relationship with the horse. Charlotte had tried to help Dominic to no avail. Gunner had some ideas, and she was happy to leave him to it.

"Charlotte Simpson?" a woman called.

Charlotte faltered at the sight of the blue-eyed blonde standing at the mouth of the hallway. She hadn't realized Cooper's wife worked here. Katie would be Charlotte's sister-in-law. Ever since she'd found out about her biological family, it seemed the Robinsons were everywhere she looked.

Offering a smile, Charlotte stood and followed the woman down the short hall and into the exam room.

Katie closed the door behind her. "Is it still hot as blazes out there?"

"At least."

"Have a seat right there and I'll get your vitals."

Charlotte sat by the desk and set her purse in the other chair.

They made small talk about the weather and the Braves while Katie took her blood pressure. The woman seemed warm and extroverted. The sort of person who might encourage Cooper to welcome his new sister into his life? Charlotte could only hope.

She thought the couple had had a baby a while back but couldn't remember if it was a boy or a girl or even how old the child might be. No doubt, he or she would grow up to be quite attractive with Katie and Cooper as parents.

I have a niece or nephew. Two, actually, since Gavin and his wife, Laurel, had recently adopted. Their friends had died in an airplane accident, leaving their little girl orphaned. And Laurel and Gavin stepped right in to care for the girl. It had been all over the paper. Charlotte wanted to be part of their lives. Wanted to be the auntie who kept them overnight and fed them too much sugar.

Katie took down a few details and headed for the door. "The doctor will be in shortly." And she left the room.

Only question was, which doctor would it be?

She should probably figure out what to say in case it was Avery. Her brother and husband were building Charlotte's barn, so that gave her something to lead with.

She was also eager to see the woman up close. To find something familiar in the angles and planes of her face. Would they immediately connect? Would some part of her DNA recognize their bond and vice versa?

Guilt pricked. Did longing for these sibling relationships make her disloyal? When Emerson found out about Charlotte's biological siblings, would she feel she'd been replaced? It was the last thing Charlotte wanted, but she couldn't seem to quell her desire to explore this other

49

half of her family tree. Didn't she have a right to know where she'd come from?

While her mother had never told her the truth, she had left that folder. So she meant for Charlotte to find out eventually. She probably just didn't expect the truth to be revealed so soon. After all, who expected to die in their early fifties? But finding that file had been exhilarating. She'd felt like she discovered a rare gem. She now had the information that satisfied her long-standing curiosity. That would allow her to fill that void in her life. Just knowing that her mom had finally divulged the truth had brought tears of relief to her eyes.

The door opened and Avery entered with a wide smile. "Good morning, I'm Dr. Garrett."

Charlotte shook away the memory. She had to make this visit count. "Hi." Avery was taller than she remembered, with dark-brown hair and wide-set green eyes, the same shade as Charlotte's. She'd always assumed she'd inherited the color from her mother. But maybe Jeff had green eyes also.

Avery shook Charlotte's hand. "I'd say 'nice to meet you,' but I think we went to school together, didn't we?"

"I'm surprised you remember. I was a lowly underclassman when you were a senior."

Avery laughed. "You were a star on the girls' softball team, as I recall. A pitcher, maybe?"

"That's some memory you have. Then again, you were valedictorian of your class."

"I see you have an excellent memory yourself." She took a seat at the desk. "What have you been up to since high school?"

"Running the family horse ranch—and, of course, working at the Trailhead to support my horse habit."

Avery's eyes crinkled. "There are worse habits to have."

There was something about Avery that put Charlotte at ease. "I'm currently expanding the ranch. I'd rather make the horses my full-time livelihood. Your brother and husband are actually helping turn that plan into a reality—they're building my new stable."

"Ah yes, Wes mentioned that. I didn't put it together till now. Well, you couldn't be in better hands. Gavin and Wes are very good at what they do."

"You don't look anything alike." The words were out before Charlotte had a chance to filter them. "I mean, you and Gavin are siblings, right?"

Avery didn't seem put off by the random comment. She just opened the folder and began skimming the contents. "Well, technically we're not related by blood."

Charlotte tried to keep the surprise from her expression. But her heart charged like a bronco from a starting gate. "Oh?"

"Gavin and Cooper's mom married my dad when we were young, so we're only family by marriage."

Charlotte froze. How had she not known that? "I didn't realize." That meant Avery wasn't her sister after all. And it also meant Jeff Robinson was not her biological father. Maybe the picture in the file should've been a clue. But it was blurry and taken from a distance. She'd just assumed . . .

But if Jeff wasn't her father, then who was? Who was Gavin and Cooper's biological father? She couldn't remember ever hearing any of this. But it explained some things. Like why there'd been no information about Avery in the folder. Charlotte had assumed it had just been because the woman hadn't made the news like her brothers, but she should've known better. Opening the town's first clinic was definitely newsworthy.

Of course she'd wondered why there was nothing in the folder about her father, save the photo and medal. But she assumed the file was incomplete because it was unfinished. Had told herself her mom had probably intended to write her a letter later with all the answers to her questions. Like, did her father know about her? And why had Mom kept the information from Charlotte until her passing?

She blinked the thoughts away. She'd missed what Avery was saying.

". . . so we've been together a long time, and they're still family, genetics or no." Avery glanced up with a warm smile that said everything about how she felt about her brothers.

"I get that. I have a sister I feel the same way about."

"That's right. I vaguely remember that. Also, I should say how sorry I was to hear about your mom. She popped into the clinic from time to time. I really liked her."

"Thank you. It was quite sudden." By the time medevac got her to Asheville, it was too late. "I was in a fog for months, but it's getting better."

"I understand. I lost my mom when I was very young. You never really get over that kind of loss, but that doesn't mean you won't be happy again."

"Of course." Charlotte was still reeling over Avery's revelation. Well, she'd wanted information—she'd certainly gotten it.

Not related to Avery or Jeff. Copy that, God.

Now she just had to find out who Gavin and Cooper's biological father was—because he was also hers.

"Now, how can I help you today?"

Five

Gunner led Dominic around the paddock, watching for signs of nerves. He was a seven-year-old chestnut warmblood with a white star on his forehead. He was shaking, his flesh twitching beneath his soft, shiny coat and his ears flicking back and forth.

"Easy there, buddy. I got you."

Dominic snorted.

This was not a horse at ease. Gunner just had to figure out what was disturbing his peace. He continued to lead the gelding as they got better acquainted.

At least Gunner had slept well last night in the one-room cabin he'd rented. It was simple but clean, and the mattress was as soft as a warm embrace. It was convenient, only a stone's throw from the ranch. He'd worked out a short-term lease with the owner, Mr. Dixon, who was a widower and seemed happy to have some company.

Construction noises carried across the valley. A crew of four had shown up at eight to frame the stable.

His first morning on the job was going pretty well. Charlotte had been feeding the horses when he'd arrived, and he jumped right in. She kept a detailed log on the wall of each horse's feed, exercise, and medication schedules. He liked how meticulous she was when it came to the horses' care. It said plenty about her.

Even if she did confuse him in other ways. First he'd caught her gawking at the construction guy, and yesterday she'd been gaping at the sheriff across the coffee shop. She didn't strike him as the kind of woman who'd be desperate for male attention. Much less be attracted to married men. (Because yes, the sheriff also wore a wedding ring.)

But what did he know?

He was better at reading horses than humans. People attempted to hide their feelings. Horses didn't do that. When they were afraid, they twitched, tremored, or reared. When they were happy, they nickered and swung their tails. When they were angry, they pinned their ears back and pawed the ground. Pretty straight-forward.

From inside the barn Cleo nickered. The boarded horse was barn sour. Charlotte had been working with him, but the gelding still resisted leaving the stable.

The sound of rustling grass drew his attention. Gavin headed toward him, Braves ball cap pulled low, shading his face from the sun. "Nice horse you got there."

"This is Dominic. You ride at all?"

"Only horsepower I'm familiar with is the kind in my Sierra Denali."

"It's a nice truck."

"It gets the job done."

Gunner glanced up the hill. "Stable's going up fast. Every time I look up, there's another wall in place."

"Framing is nice that way. Charlotte around this morning? I thought I saw her truck earlier."

"She took off a while ago. Said she'll be back shortly though."

"I'll catch her later then. I thought, if she didn't mind, I might bring my daughter over sometime to see the horses—that's all she's been talking about lately."

"How old is she?"

"Just turned four."

"That's not too young to start riding. We have a gentle pony who'd be just the right size for her."

Gavin gave a sideways grin. "Let's see if I can talk her mom into the idea first. Emma's been trying to ride our golden retriever, but that's not working out too well."

"Don't guess it would."

"Well, I should get back to the job. Try to make some progress before the storm rolls in."

"Take it easy."

Gavin took a few steps, then turned, walking backward. "A few of us guys are heading to

57

the Trailhead tonight at six. Good band. You're welcome to come hang out."

Gunner considered the offer. "Thanks. I might do that."

Gavin nodded and continued up the grassy slope.

Gunner wasn't much for close ties—he enjoyed the whole footloose-and-fancy-free way of life. But he'd be here awhile and it wouldn't hurt to make a few friends. He gave the rope a tug. "Come along, Dominic. How do you feel about saddling up, huh, boy?"

A plume of dust rose in the distance from behind Charlotte's vehicle as she navigated the drive. He waited around the paddock a minute, hoping to have a word with her. Get more background on Dominic. Usually the solutions to problems lay in the past, and he wasn't afraid to dig around a little for those answers. In the long run it would save a lot of time.

But when Charlotte exited her truck, she just waved and headed inside the house.

"Well, I guess that ride can wait." He didn't think the gelding was too eager for a saddle anyway, and forcing the issue would do more harm than good.

"Let's get you back to your stall, huh, boy? I'll bet Cleo would like the company."

A few minutes later Gunner loped up the porch steps and knocked on the front door.

Shortly Charlotte appeared behind the screen door. Her eyes looked a little bloodshot like she might've been crying. Or maybe she had a bad case of allergies.

"Sorry to bother you. This a bad time?"

"No, no. It's fine. Come on in. I have about fifteen minutes. I was just getting some iced tea. Want some?"

"Sure. I was hoping to learn a little more about Dominic's history." He started to take off his boots.

She glanced down. "Don't bother. We're used to a little dust around here. Make yourself at home. I'll be right back."

Charlotte poured the tea and checked her appearance using her phone. It had all kind of hit her on the way home from the clinic. Jeff Robinson was not her biological father. As he was something of a paragon around these parts, the revelation was pretty disappointing.

For two months she'd dreamed of him as her father. Dreamed of him inviting her into his big family. A little unrealistic? Perhaps. But she couldn't seem to help herself. Ever since her parents divorced when she was a teenager, she'd missed that fatherly presence in her life. After the divorce Patrick had seemed much closer to Emmie—because she was biologically his? Things hadn't been the same with the distance between them, and then at the young age of fifty-one, he'd had a massive heart attack in his rig.

Her stomach twisted and tears welled up again. *Stop it.*

So there was all that. Plus the fact that she was now even further from knowing the identity of her biological father—if he was even still alive. After all, she'd never heard a single thing about Cooper and Gavin's birth dad. Of course, he could've just abandoned them at a young age. She wasn't sure which would be worse.

How was she supposed to get any answers without making Gavin and Cooper suspicious? On the other hand, it was now possible her bio dad hadn't been married when he was with her mother. If that was the case, at least Lisa Robinson wouldn't hate her on sight.

Probably.

She wiped beneath her eyes even though there was no makeup to smear. She looked a little teary, but that could be anything, right?

Time to get down to business. She grabbed the tea and walked through the small dining area and into the living room where Gunner was checking out her bookshelves.

He turned and took a glass. "Thanks. You're well-read on horse health."

"As you can probably see, I like a holistic approach. Have a seat and tell me what—" Her eyes caught on the manila folder bearing her name and sitting on the table beside the seat where Gunner was about to sit.

Heart thrumming in her chest, she reached out and snatched it off the table. But she'd grabbed the bottom and apparently hadn't fastened the brad. The articles fluttered to the floor at Gunner's feet and fanned out like a headline heyday.

She reached for them at the same time he did. Their heads bumped.

"Ow," he said. "Sorry."

She barely felt the collision as her gaze locked on the articles. On the photo of Gavin from *The Herald*. A headshot of Cooper in uniform under the headline "Robinson Wins Bid for County Sheriff."

Gunner reached for the latter article.

Charlotte snatched it away, nearly ripping the yellowed copy. She made quick work of the rest. But not so quick that her astute new hire didn't see every last item. What must he be thinking?

Heat flooded her cheeks. "These are just . . ." She had no words to finish the sentence.

Hands shaking, she shoved them back into the folder—those precious articles she'd scoured for every tidbit she could learn about her brothers. She'd gotten sloppy and left the folder lying around since her sister was out of town. *Stupid.*

His eyes focused on her like heat-seeking missiles as she tucked the folder into a drawer.

Did it seem weird that she'd stashed away articles about two attractive, married men—one of whom she'd hired to build her stable?

It's very weird, Charlotte! Very. Weird.

"You okay?" he asked.

No, she wasn't okay! Oh, he was talking about her head. She touched the sore spot at her temple. "I—I'm fine. Are you all right?"

"I have a hard head." He stood, offering a polite smile. "Listen, I think I'll just come back later. At a better time."

He must think she was a complete wackadoodle. And why wouldn't he? It didn't help that Gunner was also good-looking and working for her. A prime candidate for her next stalking victim.

He edged toward the door, no doubt questioning his decision to work here. He'd caught her spying on one of those men through binoculars! And being an observant man, he'd probably noticed the wedding ring too. He'd also caught her staring at Cooper yesterday, and today he discovered she kept a *file* on them.

No wonder he couldn't seem to get to the door fast enough.

"Wait, I should explain about . . ." She waved back toward the living room. "I promise I'm not a—"

He threw a hand up, then reached for the door handle. "None of my business."

She could just feel him slipping away—and she could not lose her new trainer. "No, wait. *Please.*"

He paused on the threshold.

Yep, definitely some guardedness in those eyes. She'd spooked him good. Lost his trust. He must be thinking she was like that nutjob in *Misery* and might lock him in her house and break both his ankles.

"They're my brothers. Gavin and Cooper. I just found out recently they're my biological brothers, but they don't know yet. At least I don't think they do. They've certainly given no indication . . ."

"Whoa. That's why you were . . . ?"

"Spying on him through binoculars, yes. I'm not some psycho stalker, just a curious secret sibling, so please don't say anything to anybody. This is a very small town and news like this . . . I just want to handle it the right way. Soon as I figure out what that is exactly."

His gaze roved over her features as his eyes softened. "Who would I tell? I'm new here, remember? And this really is none of my business."

"Still, you need to know your new employer isn't planning to start a secret file on you. When my mom died, I found a key to a safety-deposit box, and that envelope was inside. I was planning to talk to my biological father first and give him the chance to tell his family. But I just found out this morning that the man who I thought was Gavin and Cooper's dad is really their stepdad. So I'm kinda back to square one."

His eyes narrowed as he took that in.

"Please don't quit on me. I really need you here, like desperately if I'm honest, to make this expansion work. To put this ranch in the black so I don't lose it or have to moonlight as a waitress the rest of my life."

"I didn't realize."

"It'll work—the expansion. I've got horses lined up needing your help, and I've already booked a few trail rides since I hired you. We're on our way, but we can't do it without you."

He took it all in with quiet eyes that seemed to understand much more than she'd said. "I'm not going anywhere. I promised you six months and I'll give it to you. Maybe I'm not one to stick around long term, but I don't take commitment lightly."

His gentle voice rumbled deeply. She was beginning to see why he had such a way with horses. Those silent appraisals and soft words had a certain effect. Those soulful eyes didn't hurt either. "Thank you. I appreciate you." She widened her eyes. "*That.* I mean, I appreciate *that.*"

Her face flooded with heat. And she was ever so grateful when the sound of an approaching vehicle drew their attention to the picture window. A blue GMC pulled a horse trailer toward the house. "That's my eleven o'clock. And your newest challenge—if you're up for it."

His smile kicked her heart into a trot. "Always."

"Whooaa!" Charlotte said as Midnight crashed into the trailer.

Ben Hughes leaped out of the way in the nick of time, barely avoiding being crushed by the gelding.

Gunner grabbed the lead line, speaking gently as the horse quivered and reared. Working with Ben, the two got the horse's halter off. And as soon as it was gone, Midnight wrenched his head away and bolted for the farthest corner of the paddock.

Charlotte closed the gate and the trio settled at the fence, watching the stricken quarter horse.

"Whew, that was a trip. Sure you still want him?" Ben asked drolly. He was a middle-aged man who wore a Tar Heels cap and a gray goatee. It had taken him ten minutes just to halter the horse.

"Are you okay?" she asked him.

"No worse for wear. Thought I knew a thing or two about horses until that one came along."

"How long have you had him?" Gunner asked.

"Bought him 'bout six months ago for my twelve-year-old son. We were at an auction and came across him in the dogger section. He was

65

a fine-looking horse, but I figured there must've been a good reason he'd been passed over. My son took a liking to him and begged me to save him. Couldn't say no—no horse deserves to become pet food. Got him for a bargain price."

She'd just bet he had. He was the most skittish horse she'd ever seen.

"You get any history on him?" Gunner asked.

"Unfortunately, there's none to be had. He was left over on some estate where the owner died. I have no idea if he was neglected or abused or just traumatized some way. I thought we'd be able to work with him a bit, earn his trust. But we've gotten nowhere, and I'm afraid he's gonna hurt my son. Grant's heartbroken about losing him, but I need to find him a horse he can ride. Appreciate you taking him in, Charlotte. I hope you can get somewhere with him."

"If anyone can, it's Gunner. But no matter what happens, he won't end up as pet food, I can promise you that."

"That's the only reason Grant's still talking to me. He knows Midnight'll have a good home here."

They talked awhile about some of the things Ben had tried and how the horse had responded. Ben gave them the feed Midnight was on so they could slowly acclimate him to the new feed. Then they shook hands and said goodbye.

"Well," Charlotte said as she and Gunner

watched Midnight paw the ground in the paddock's corner. "Looks like you've got your work cut out for you."

"Looks like." He cast her a sideways glance. "He'll need to be vetted too. Hope he didn't set you back much."

"He was free to a good home."

Gunner gave a nod. "Sounds about right."

Six

The smell of smoked chicken, grilled burgers, and anticipation hung in the air. It would be a packed house at the Trailhead. The wings were BOGO tonight and the Silver Spurs were playing. Charlotte's tables had been full since five o'clock, and now that it was nearing seven, there wouldn't be much turnover until the band was done playing.

She grabbed some empty glasses off a full table and took them for refills. She could do this job blindfolded, she'd been at it so long. A while back she'd been offered the manager's position when it had become available. But she was already working thirty hours a week, and she could earn just as much serving and have a lot less responsibility.

Besides, taking a leadership position here reeked of failure. This job had always been just a temporary gig until the ranch became self-supporting. She'd been telling herself this for six years. But with her mom's second mortgage hanging over her head, it was now or never. If the pressure felt like an iron yoke, so be it. She would make this happen.

The band was introduced and kicked off the night with a rousing rendition of "Country Girl." Half the place hit the dance floor, and chitchatting with customers became nigh impossible. Fine by her. Now that her guests had finished eating, it was mostly just a matter of keeping their glasses full—and maybe she could finally go to the bathroom.

She dropped off the drinks at a table and high-tailed it to the restroom. She was washing her hands when Brianna entered, the cacophony rising with the opening door.

"Full house tonight," her friend said as she disappeared into a stall.

"Another fun night at the Trailhead. How's the date going?" She was out with a guy named Jeremy, who worked at the local radio station and who'd been coming to the coffee shop, subtly making his interest known. He'd finally asked her out yesterday.

"Not bad. He has good taste in music at least. He can also carry on a conversation, and he actually looks me in the eye when we're talking. And get this: he graduated from Cornell."

"You always did like the smart ones."

"Also, he moved back home to take care of his mother. How sweet is that?"

"Smart *and* sensitive. Sounds like a keeper."

She arched a brow. "We'll see. He might get a second date anyway."

"High praise from you."

"What can I say? I'm picky."

"You should be. You have a lot to offer." She

was glad Brianna was taking a rare night off. She and her mother took turns working and caring for her granny. It didn't leave much time for anything else.

Charlotte finished drying her hands and tossed the paper towel in the trash as Brianna emerged from the stall. If the woman was attractive without makeup, she was stunning with it. Tonight she'd played up her eyes with a smoky look that had an exotic effect.

"You know, it's not fair you got the looks *and* the brains."

Brianna rolled her doe-brown eyes. "Please. You make a messy bun seem like high fashion with that gorgeous red hair of yours. Speaking of genetic traits . . . what will you do about the whole father thing?"

Charlotte had texted back and forth with her friend after her visit to the clinic this morning. "I have no idea. It's not like I can ask anyone such a random question without stirring up curiosity."

"I know you're disappointed. I mean, who wouldn't want Jeff Robinson for a father? He's practically a legend around here. But I'm sure your bio dad is great too—after all, you have half his genes."

"I hope you're right."

"And maybe as you get to know Gavin a little better, the subject will come up."

"Maybe."

"He and Cooper are here tonight, you know. You should stop by their table and chat a little."

Charlotte hadn't noticed them. But then, she'd been pretty busy. "Do you know what the decibel levels are out there?"

"Not ideal for conversing, I agree. But there's an excellent chance of dancing in my forecast." Brianna finished washing her hands and reapplied her nude lip gloss.

Charlotte peered down at her friend's heels. "Good luck in those things."

"They put me at just the right height." She winked.

Charlotte's thoughts returned to her biological father as she tried to smooth the strands that had come loose from her bun. It was a lost cause. "Aren't divorces public record? Maybe I could learn his identity that way."

"That's a great idea. All the records are probably online. There you go."

"I'll see what I can find tomorrow."

"Let me know if I can help in any way." Brianna straightened her skirt. "I should get back to my date."

"And I should get back to work. Have fun."

They exited the restroom and went their separate ways. Charlotte's customers were content, so she bussed an empty table for a newer server who was in the weeds.

As she worked, she scanned the crowd for

Cooper and Gavin and found them at a four-top near the bar, sitting with Wes and— She frowned at the familiar face.

Why was Gunner hanging out with her new brothers? Had Gavin or Wes invited him, or had they just run into Gunner and invited him to share their table? It happened often enough on crowded nights like this.

It was just like the Robinsons to be so neighborly, but did they have to go getting close to the man who kept her most guarded secret? Could she trust Gunner to keep his mouth shut? What did she really know about him anyway? Maybe he was a troublemaker or one of those people who created drama at every turn. She really had no way of knowing.

She wished she'd never divulged her secret. But what choice did she have?

Now she didn't know if she should stop by their table. What if when she walked away, she became the subject of their conversation and Gunner spilled the beans?

Then again, maybe putting in an appearance would keep him honest. Let him know she'd seen him with her brothers and would hold him accountable if the truth came out.

She took the dishes to the kitchen and checked on her tables, brought out some barbecue sauce, and removed bone baskets. Then she made her way to the table near the bar.

"How's it going, fellas?" she fairly yelled over the rollicking tune.

She took pleasure in the slight widening of Gunner's eyes.

Gavin and Wes offered pleasant smiles and greetings. As they introduced her to Cooper, she took in his dark-brown eyes, strong jawline, and crooked grin. And his nose. Because yep, he really did have her nose. *Take that, Brianna.*

"Boys' night out?" She was careful to keep her voice level, even though being near her brothers came with a shot of adrenaline.

"Something like that," Cooper said. "Noise is too loud for the little ones, so the wives opted to stay home."

Wes flicked his dark-blond hair from his eyes. "I don't have any little ones, but my wife's had enough of these clowns."

Obviously he was kidding; Avery had spoken so lovingly of her stepbrothers, and Charlotte could tell the feeling was mutual. Would they eventually feel the same way about her? Longing compressed her chest.

"I didn't realize you worked here." Gunner eyed her in that quiet, knowing way of his.

"It's my part-time gig until the expansion starts paying off. Provided it does." She gave him a warning look. *I've got my eye on you, Gunner Dawson.*

74

His gaze sharpened on her. "You've got nothing to worry about."

"I sure hope not."

"You definitely don't."

They silently locked horns for a long moment.

"Speaking of your expansion," Gavin said, "did you check out the progress on the stable? The framing went smooth as glass today."

"It looks great. I can't believe how much you got done."

"Thankfully the rain held off," Wes added.

Across the way the hostess sat a party of three at Charlotte's empty table. "Hey, it was good seeing you. I gotta get back to work. You guys enjoy your evening."

They said their goodbyes, and Charlotte grabbed three glasses of water and delivered them to the table. The group hadn't had a chance to peruse the menus, so she gave them some time. The band lowered the energy a notch with a slow ballad that had couples pairing up on the dance floor.

Jeremy led Brianna that way and took her in his arms. They made a striking couple, but she doubted Brianna would make room in her life for a man right now. She had her hands full with her grandma and work.

Charlotte headed to the poolroom to help clear away the empties folks often left on the high tables or, worse, the pool rails.

Her gaze caught on Gunner, who grabbed a pool cue before perching on a stool. Ignoring him, she collected empty bottles and glasses on her tray, then stopped to chat with a couple of neighbors. She was about to leave the room when someone touched her shoulder.

Gunner leaned close. "Hey, you really don't have to worry. Your secret's safe with me. Gavin invited me out and I didn't have other plans." He closed with a shrug.

"You don't owe me an explanation."

"You were worried. I just wanted to put your mind at ease."

He'd read her well. Then again, she hadn't exactly been subtle. "This is really important to me. I don't want to mess it up."

"I don't want to mess it up either. You don't know me well, but I'd never betray a confidence." His steady, unflinching gaze backed up his words.

"Fair enough. I appreciate your saying so." His pleasant masculine scent carried to her nose as the moment lengthened. "I, uh, have to get back to work."

"Sure. Have a good evening."

"Enjoy the band. They're the best in the area if you like country music." If her voice sounded a little raspy, it was only from raising her voice so much.

"See you in the morning."

She sent him a parting smile and headed toward the kitchen with the full tray. She was a little rattled. But it was just the close call with her brothers. And the feeling that Gunner might reveal her secret too soon and ruin her relationships with her siblings before they even had a chance to develop.

Seven

"Good boy, Dominic." Gunner worked the gelding on a lunge line around the pen. He'd taken a bit to warm up this morning, but he was cooperating nicely now. "That's it. You've got it."

He glanced toward the barn where Charlotte had disappeared a while ago with her vet. Kyle Lemmings was average height with a medium build. He wore his dirty-blond hair cropped short and drove a brand-new F-450 that proclaimed business was going quite well, thank you very much.

Charlotte had introduced the two right off. The vet's manner with Charlotte was professional enough, but he sneaked glances at her when she wasn't looking and paid extra attention when she was speaking.

Dominic whinnied.

The gelding was growing bored—Gunner wasn't paying attention to his job. He turned the horse and led him around the ring in the opposite direction. "Thatta boy. Keep it going now."

"Hey, Gunner, you got a minute?" Charlotte called from the barn's shade.

"Sure." He stopped Dominic, gave him some attention, then set him loose in the paddock.

When he entered the barn, Charlotte and the vet were chatting over by Midnight's stall.

The horse tossed his head and snorted.

"Midnight checks out fine," Charlotte said as Gunner approached. "As best Kyle could tell anyway. Midnight wasn't very cooperative. Kyle suggested some dietary changes."

They talked about the horse's specific needs.

"I'll write everything on the board," Charlotte said, "but of course we'll have to take it slow as he acclimates to our feed."

"Got it."

Midnight pawed the ground.

"He wouldn't let me check his hooves." The vet glanced at Charlotte. "You're probably gonna need a farrier for that—if Midnight will even cooperate."

"I'm hoping to make some headway with him," Gunner said. "But that'll take time."

"A lot of time is my guess. No telling what the poor guy's been through. Too bad you don't have any background on him."

Charlotte glanced at Gunner. "If anyone can figure him out, it's Gunner. He comes from Four Winds in Louisville, and he has quite a track record."

For the first time Kyle gave him a speculative glance. "That so?"

"I enjoy my work. The more I learn about horses, the more fascinated I am by them."

"I agree." Kyle's eyes drifted around the barn. "Which one is yours?"

"I don't have a horse."

"Really?" His gaze toggled to Charlotte and back. "That's unusual for someone who enjoys them so much."

"I think Gunner likes to keep things simple. He brought all his worldly goods to Riverbend on the back of a motorcycle. He's helping me get this expansion off the ground, but he's only temporary."

Her way of allaying the vet's jealousy? Seemed to work.

"Ah, I see. Well, I hope you enjoy our little town while you're here. You've got a great boss." He sent an affectionate glance Charlotte's way. "She really cares about her horses."

"Well, what's not to love?" she said.

"Your stable's sure going up fast," Kyle said. "When's the open house scheduled for?"

"Open house?" Gunner asked.

Charlotte gave him a pained look. "With everything else we've had to discuss, I guess I forgot to mention it. We're having an open house on the first Saturday in July to celebrate our expansion. Gavin and Wes assure me the stable will be done by then. I hope we can get a good turnout. We need the community's awareness if not its support. With all the tourists coming through, we need to be on their radar for trail rides."

Midnight approached the stall door.

Gunner held out his hand and let the horse sniff it. "Good boy." He tried to reward the horse with a stroke, but the quarter horse jumped away. Two steps forward, one step back. "An open house will help get the word out about your training program too."

"Exactly. We've already got a lot of interest through the website. You're the best trainer for miles around."

"I can help spread the word," Kyle said. "Got any brochures I can hand out?"

"I sure do. Thank you. That'd be a big help."

"You should get some media out here to cover the event," Kyle said. "They're always interested in new businesses."

"I had hoped to, but it doesn't look like our expansion is newsworthy enough."

"What if the mayor turned out for a ribbon-cutting ceremony?" Kyle said.

Charlotte released a droll chuckle. "That's a great idea. I'll just give him a call."

"As it happens, I take care of his son's cattle. I could try that angle if you like. He's a really nice guy. I think he'd be willing if it works with his schedule."

Her eyes brightened. "Seriously? That would be amazing. If he'd come out for the cere-mony, I could surely get *The Herald* out here at least."

Kyle beamed at her. "I'd be happy to ask him for you."

"Thank you. You're the best, Kyle."

They wrapped up the conversation, and Gunner excused himself to the paddock while Charlotte walked the vet to his truck.

Gunner stared after them, noting Kyle's body language, always angled Charlotte's way. When they stopped by the truck, he set his hand on her arm.

Gunner glanced away. Didn't know why he was so averse to the guy. Seemed nice enough, if a few years too old for Charlotte. He had some gray hair at his temples and fine lines at the corners of his eyes, which probably put him around forty.

Oh well. None of his business. He was here to help get this program off the ground, enjoy some time in the mountains, then he'd be off to that job as trainer of a Derby horse at Belle Vista—a bucket-list job for him. He was working his way up in the world of horse training just as he wanted. The job here was an unlikely pick, but getting in on the ground of this expansion was a new experience that could teach him things he wouldn't otherwise learn.

A while later Charlotte showed up at the rails where he was working Dominic on the lunge line again. "He's looking good today."

"He is. This is a good place to stop." He ended the session and gave the horse some praise before he turned him loose in the paddock again. Then he joined Charlotte at the fence. "I was thinking about the open house. Maybe we could do pony rides for the kids. Or I could do a training demonstration."

Charlotte beamed. "I love those ideas. I'm making a schedule for the day. Maybe you could do a Join-Up demonstration. I'll bet I can find a horse for the job."

"People love watching a Join-Up. We did demonstrations at Four Winds." That moment when a horse finally decided to trust and follow his leader was magical. As many times as he experienced it, it was still a humbling thrill to gain a horse's confidence.

"Sounds great."

She seemed excited about the open house, but she had a ranch to run, a part-time job, and a big event to plan. "You've got a lot on your plate."

"It'll be worth it to see this place thrive. And once it does, I'll be able to quit my part-time job. Anyway, my sister helps out some. You haven't met her since she's been in Asheville, but she's coming back today. Oh—speaking of lots to do— we've already got a couple trail rides scheduled for this weekend."

"That's great."

"It is, but it occurs to me you're not familiar with the trail yet. I've been riding it with our work horses to familiarize them with it, but maybe we could do it together later today or tomorrow."

"Sure, whenever you want."

Charlotte checked the time. "How about in twenty minutes? That'll give me a chance to grab some lunch."

"Sounds like a plan."

Eight

Charlotte let out a deep breath when she spied Emerson's Camry in the driveway. She'd only gotten a few short texts from her sister since she left four days ago.

Since then Charlotte had had time to cool off. In fact, it was time to eat a little crow. She did tend to take charge sometimes, especially when it came to the two of them. Emerson had always needed direction, but it was probably time to stop treating her like the baby sister. The fact was, Charlotte had taken the reins of the ranch when their mom died. Someone had to.

She'd definitely made that promise to their mom without consulting Emerson. There wasn't really anything she could do about that now, but she could at least apologize. Maybe that would put them back on solid ground.

She entered the house and found Emerson in the kitchen, slipping Charlotte's leftovers from the Trailhead into the microwave.

My lunch. Charlotte bit her tongue and pasted on a smile. "Hi, how was your trip?"

"It was good. April says hello. Her new apartment is great."

"I saw the pictures. Did you get to use the pool?"

Emerson closed the microwave door and set the timer. "No, it was being serviced."

"What was wrong with her computer?"

"Nothing a reboot wouldn't cure. She's so helpless when it comes to technology. But guess who's on Flutter now? April helped me with my profile and took my photo—she's really good with a camera."

Lots of people used dating apps these days, but Emerson was a little gullible. "Be careful on there. Only meet a guy in a public place and never let him know where you live."

Emerson scowled. "I know that. I'm not an idiot."

"Of course not. I just worry about you."

"Well, you don't have to. I can take care of myself."

Time to defuse the situation. "I've been thinking about what you said before you left, and you were right. I'm sorry about the way I handled things after Mom died. Looking back, I can see I was so set on the expansion that I didn't want to hear what you thought. I should've taken your opinions more seriously. And I shouldn't have made Mom that promise without consulting you."

Her jaw set. "And she shouldn't have asked you to. That wasn't a conversation for just the two of you. She should've included me."

Charlotte winced. She hadn't realized her sister

was also angry with Mom. "You're right. She should've talked to both of us about it."

"But she didn't because she knew I wasn't as invested in the ranch as you are. She wanted the ranch to stay in the family, and you were the only hope of that happening."

"Come on, Em. It just came up while we were working one day, that's all."

"Well, she could've brought it up to me later."

But their mom died less than two weeks later. What was at the bottom of this? "She loved you so much. You know that, right?"

"Of course I know that."

The timer went off and Emerson removed the steaming plate. The tempting smell of beef brisket filled the kitchen.

Emerson headed for the living room. "There's no point in discussing this. What's done is done. I'll help out where I can, but if you need a full-time stable hand, you're gonna have to hire someone else. Now, if you don't mind, I plan to have my lunch and watch *Top Chef* before I head to the bakery." She set her plate on the end table and stooped for the napkin she'd dropped.

Charlotte sighed. That could've gone better. "I'm gonna grab some lunch." She headed for the kitchen already thinking about what was in the fridge—basically next to nothing since she hadn't had time to go to the grocery.

"Where'd this come from?"

Charlotte turned back. And froze in place.

Emerson held the photo of their mom and Charlotte's biological father—the one from that manila envelope. It must've fallen out when she'd spilled the contents of that envelope.

"Who's this riding with Mom? I've never seen him before. They're on Luna." She glanced up at Charlotte. "What? What's that look for?"

The timing wasn't great, but she had to tell Emerson the truth. She'd probably waited too long already. Charlotte ran her sweaty palms down her pant legs. "Listen, Em, let's sit down and talk. There's something I've been meaning to tell you."

"That doesn't sound good." Emerson sat in the chair, lowering the photo, her gaze locked on Charlotte. "Is this about Mom?"

Charlotte sat opposite her. She wasn't even sure where to start. The beginning, she supposed. "Remember when we were cleaning out Mom's stuff in the office a couple months ago, and we found that safety-deposit box key?"

"Yeah . . . Did you find a million bucks in there or something? Because that would be welcome news."

"I wish." Charlotte swallowed hard. "But I did find that photo."

Emerson glanced down at it. "Who is it? Why didn't you show it to me with the other stuff—the legal papers and such?"

"There was a manila envelope in there that had my name on it."

Emerson's chin jutted out. "Don't tell me she wrote you a letter."

"No, no, it wasn't anything like that. There were newspaper articles inside it and that photo and a medal."

Emerson frowned. "I don't get it. What articles? What kind of medal?"

Here goes. She had to tell her sister—there was no escaping it unless Charlotte wanted to drop the whole thing. Never find her birth father. Never tell her biological siblings of her existence. Just let the whole truth die right along with her mother. But it wasn't in her to do that. She wanted to know them.

Sure, she had Emerson, and she loved her dearly. But she also had family out there who shared her DNA. How could she not care about that? Want to know them? Want them to know her?

"Charlotte?" The word held an edgy note.

She focused on her sister, whose arms were crossed, body rigid. But maybe she'd be happy for Charlotte. It wasn't every day you discovered you had a family you didn't know about.

Charlotte cleared her throat. "The articles had been clipped over the years. They were about Gavin and Cooper Robinson. Mom apparently saved them anytime they made the papers—

Gavin during his baseball days and when he opened his business. The articles about Cooper were published when he was running for sheriff. Stuff like that."

Emerson gave her head a shake. "That's weird. Why would she save those? We don't even know them. And what about the medal?"

"It belonged to the man in the photo. You can see he's holding it."

Emerson glanced down at the picture. "So what are you saying, Charlotte? Who is this guy?"

"He's . . . he's my biological father." Charlotte gestured toward the articles. "And those are my siblings."

Their gazes held for a long-drawn-out moment. Charlotte's heart galloped in her chest, possibly looking for a greener pasture. Or maybe just wanting to make an escape.

Emerson's lips tightened. "Wow, that's . . . I don't know what to say. You never really talked about him."

"That's because I didn't know anything about him, other than he'd served in the Gulf War. Mom didn't like talking about him, and I didn't want to make Dad feel bad." Charlotte leaned in. "I know Patrick was my father. He was the one who was *here,* the one who raised me. No one can ever replace him."

Emerson arched a brow. "Not even Jeff Robinson? Isn't he like the epitome of the perfect family man?" Emerson tossed the photo on the table. "Sounds like you have a ready-made family, Char."

"That's not Jeff Robinson in the photo. That's what I assumed at first too. But it turns out Lisa Robinson was married before Jeff came along—to Gavin and Cooper's biological dad."

Emerson seemed to curl in on herself. "They have a sister, too, don't they? That doctor who started the clinic?"

"Avery—but she's Jeff's daughter. So technically she's Gavin and Cooper's stepsister. She's not related to them, or me, by blood."

Emerson's laugh was bitter. "Well, neither am I."

"Emerson." Charlotte's eyes burned with tears. "You have to know you're my sister in every way that counts. I've never thought of you as a stepsister. And I don't believe you think of me that way either."

"That was before you had a real family."

"You *are* my real family. This doesn't change anything between us. You'll always be my sister and I'll always love you."

"This is why you hired Gavin to build that stable."

"He's the only builder in town."

"You wanted to get to know him better."

Charlotte weighed her words. "Of course I'm curious about him. How could I not be? But I

93

also don't want to charge into their lives like a bronco and make a big mess. Or hurt anyone. I need to tell my biological father first and give him a chance to break the news to his kids. But I don't even know who he is, much less where he lives."

Emerson stood and paced over to the bookshelves, shoulders stiff. "Why did you hide this from me? You should've told me as soon as you found that envelope."

"You're right, I should've. But we were grieving Mom, and I didn't even know what I would do with the information, if anything."

"And now you've decided to pursue this?"

Charlotte huffed. "Please try to see it from my perspective. What if you just discovered who your mom was and had a chance to know her?"

"I don't care to know my mom at all."

Charlotte's heart squeezed tight. Emerson's mother had abandoned her shortly after she'd been born. Charlotte stood and approached her sister. "I'm so sorry that happened to you. Trust me when I say it was her loss. She missed out on a lifetime of loving you. I actually feel sorry for her."

"Well, don't. She made that choice and she has no one to blame but herself." Emerson ran a hand over her face. "I know I should be happy for you, but I just feel so betrayed that you hid this from me for two months."

And probably threatened by the revelation since Emerson only had Charlotte. They only had each other.

Until now.

"I thought we were close." Emerson wrapped her arms around her waist.

Charlotte touched her sister's shoulder. "Emmie, we are. I didn't intentionally hide it from you—I just wasn't ready to talk about it yet. Can't you understand that?"

"How do you think this would've made Dad feel? After all he did for you?"

She didn't appreciate the guilt trip. "He'll always be my dad. There's nothing that can change that."

"Then why go looking for your real father?"

Charlotte stiffened. "Dad *was* my real father."

"Then why do you need this other man in your life?"

"Because I'm curious about where I came from. I know your mom leaving was awful, but at least you know who she is. What she was like. Your dad told you stories about her. I know nothing about my biological father. I feel like half of me is a complete mystery." Charlotte raised her voice. "Who am I even?"

"That's ridiculous! You've always known exactly who you are. You were probably the only teenager in the history of the world who never had an identity crisis."

"Well, I'm having one now!"

Nine

A warm breeze blew through the valley, carrying scents of pine, grass, and horseflesh. Gunner finished his sandwich and took a swig of water. He'd found a nice bale of hay on which to enjoy his lunch. A makeshift office was next to the tack room, but the barn was warmer, and no matter how clean you kept the stalls, the odor of manure pervaded.

He was a little tired today. Last night after supper he'd checked in with Mr. Dixon and ended up in a long, challenging game of chess. The elderly man had kept him entertained with stories of his misspent youth and some sneaky chess moves that kept Gunner on his toes. It had been almost midnight by the time he'd turned in.

Daisy, a pregnant chestnut mare, whinnied in the pasture where she was grazing peacefully. Midnight snorted from his stall. Gunner was giving the horse attention in small doses, getting the quarter horse used to him. Earning bits of trust. It would likely be a long process with the high-strung horse, but Gunner was a patient man.

The sound of hammering trickled down the slope from the building site. It seemed they might finish the framework today. He was excited for his boss. She was obviously determined to make a go of this place, and he saw no reason she couldn't succeed. He'd do everything in his power to ramp up this training program before he left.

He finished the chips, put the wrappers in his bag, and tossed it in the office trash can. Since he had a few minutes till he had to meet Charlotte for the trail ride, he stopped by Midnight's stall. He stood at the gate, speaking softly while the horse tossed his head and pawed the ground.

By the time the gelding finally quieted, five minutes had passed. Gunner had better go find Charlotte. "See you later, buddy."

He headed out of the barn and up the gentle slope. His eyes locked on the house, and adrenaline flooded his system at the sight.

Black smoke drifted from one of the windows. The acrid smell, though faint, burned his nostrils. Singed his thoughts. Stirred up memories long dead and buried.

Charlotte.

He was charging toward the house before he'd told his legs to move. His feet ate up the ground in seconds, and he burst through the front door, vaguely aware of Charlotte and someone else.

"Fire! Get out of here!" He flew past them and toward the west end of the house, busted through the door and into the kitchen just as the smoke alarm began blaring.

Smoke rolled from the oven door.

He stopped, his chest heaving with breaths. Thank God. Just something burning. He strode to the oven, turned it off, and opened the door. More smoke rolled out, consuming him in a pungent cloud. He coughed as he rooted through a drawer for an oven mitt.

Charlotte appeared at his side, donning a mitt. She removed the charred remains from the smoky cavern.

What was she doing in here? "I told you to get out!" he yelled over the blaring alarm.

Her eyes sharpened on him. "It's just a loaf of burnt bread."

"Well, you didn't know that, did you?"

"Neither did you, and yet you came charging in here." She removed the oven mitt and pushed the casement window open farther.

Gunner turned on the oven fan, and the loud hum joined the *bleep* of the smoke detector.

"Emerson's shutting off the alarm."

His gaze drifted around the smoky kitchen as the adrenaline faded.

Settle down. Everything's fine. No harm done.

There was no roaring fire about to tear through the house. Or singeing heat that could melt skin from bones. Just a loaf of burnt bread.

And his soaring blood pressure.

No one's hurt. No one died.

Charlotte peered at him like a skittish horse assessing a potential threat—because Gunner had just stormed into his boss's house and *yelled at her.*

He winced as he ran a hand over the scar on his stomach, feeling the rigid network of bumps through his T-shirt. His heart pounded like a jackhammer in his chest. The aftereffects of the adrenaline rush had left him shaky and restless.

The *bleeping* stopped. Silence fell over the room and the space between them bloomed with tension.

The scare had set him off in a way he hadn't felt in years. Had caused him to overreact. And the timing couldn't have been worse. Charlotte had known him for only a matter of days. And he'd just given her reason to question his composure. Unhinged people were useless for horse training. Animals sensed human emotion. And Gunner had just completely lost his cool. It was out of character, but she couldn't know that.

Maybe this job didn't pay so great, but he didn't want to lose it. He wanted to help her take this place to the next level. There was a lot to learn here about ranching, and he could see how much it meant to Charlotte. Plus, this little town in the valley was pretty and peaceful. He'd been looking forward to hiking the trails and doing a little fishing on his days off. But now his job might be on the line.

Even so, smoke still hazing the air, he couldn't seem to keep from asking, "You do have a fire extinguisher on hand, don't you? In case of emergencies?"

She gave a sharp nod. "Of course I do . . . It's in the pantry."

A woman burst into the kitchen waving a hand in front of her face. She was younger than Charlotte, with wavy blonde hair and an athletic build. Must be the sister Charlotte had mentioned.

"Wow, it's awful in here," the woman said.

Charlotte frowned at her. "You forgot you were reheating the bread?"

"Forgive me if I was a little distracted. Someone delivered some unexpected news and I was caught a little off guard."

He'd have to be clueless to miss the tension between them. Now that he thought of it . . . when he'd charged into the house, the strain had already been there. He'd been so intent on keeping Charlotte safe that it hadn't registered.

He extended his hand to the woman. "You must be Emerson. I'm Gunner."

The woman's attention shifted to him, the spark of irritation fizzling from her blue eyes as she sized him up. "You're the new trainer. Yep, I'm Charlotte's sister—and co-owner of the ranch," she added with a hitch of her chin.

That was new information. "I apologize for the abrupt entry." His gaze toggled to Charlotte and back. "I saw smoke rolling out the kitchen window and thought the worst."

"We're not in the habit of starting oven fires around here," Charlotte said.

Emerson rolled her eyes. "It was just a little burnt bread, Charlotte. But thank you for your help, Gunner. Nice to have a take-charge man around the house. Well, listen, it was nice meeting you." Her gaze swung back to her sister. "I'm gonna go eat my lunch in peace now." Then she spun from the room.

The message was clear: she was done with her sister. Just as well since a trail ride was next on the agenda. If his heart ever settled down. The scare had left him shaken. Had resurrected memories from that awful autumn night. Memories best left dead and buried. But now he and Charlotte were alone again, and he owed her an apology. He didn't normally take that tone with any woman—much less his boss.

Charlotte was scraping the charred mess into the garbage.

The smoke had cleared enough that he turned the fan to Low. "Listen, I'm sorry for yelling at you like that." He wanted to add more, but what could he say without dredging up a past he had no interest in talking about? Especially with his boss. "I was out of order."

"You were just concerned."

"I don't normally raise my voice. I don't want you to have questions about my temperament. I know I gave reason for you to think otherwise, but I assure you it's not a problem for me."

When she glanced at him, her expression softened. "You'd be a lousy trainer if it were—and your glowing references tell me that's not the case."

A weight lifted from his shoulders, the feeling so freeing he realized only then how much staying here actually meant. His eyes were still locked on hers when something passed between them, making him forget how to breathe for a few seconds. Was there more to his reasons for wanting to stay? The chemistry was there—had been from day one—but he'd put that on lockdown.

Hadn't he?

He cleared his throat. "Thank you. I appreciate your understanding."

She placed the empty pan in the sink and met his gaze. "Honestly, I could really use that trail ride. Why don't you head back to the barn and saddle up Rogue? I was thinking he might be a nice fit for you."

"He's a beauty and very well-behaved."

"The other horses will follow his lead. I'll be out in a minute to saddle up Stella."

"Sounds good."

Ten

Emerson wolfed down her lunch and left. The tension between her and Charlotte was unbearable. But it was Charlotte's own fault. She shouldn't have kept such an important discovery from her sister.

By the time Charlotte reached the barn, Gunner had both horses saddled. In no time at all they were heading toward the trail behind the new build. Gavin and Wes glanced up from their work and gave a wave, and Charlotte waved back.

As they approached the woods, she slowed Stella. "We'll have to go single file on the trail. Why don't you go first so Rogue gets used to leading the way."

"Sounds good." Gunner urged Rogue on and soon they entered the coolness of the woods.

Charlotte took a few deep breaths, letting her problems melt away as she listened to the sounds of nature. The quiet clopping of the horses' hooves. A breeze rustling the treetops. Something small scuttling through the underbrush. The earthy smell of the forest soothed her too.

Even so, her mind flashed back to the moment Gunner burst into the house. She'd been too caught up in her argument with Emerson to notice the smell of smoke. She'd seen a flash of relief in his eyes upon sight of her, but that hadn't stopped his race to the kitchen. Or hers.

She barely knew him, but she'd never seen him rattled before. His intensity in the moment surprised her. Otherwise, he seemed so laid-back, so calm and controlled.

She hoped she hadn't missed something. She peered at him, sitting tall and effortlessly in the saddle. She didn't think so. The horses had already begun to respond to him, and they weren't fooled. He'd perceived danger and reacted—a little intensely, sure, but hopefully not a red flag.

"Who keeps the trails cut back?" Gunner asked over his shoulder.

"I do. But they shouldn't take much upkeep with horses coming through on the regular. It was originally a deer path my family used for walks in the woods. The trail is a loop and it'll take about an hour by horseback. It leads to Wildflower Falls and Stillwater Creek, then through the pasture and back to the barn. Eventually I'd like to add a lunch option to the trail ride, but we'll put that on hold until I can afford more help."

"Tourists would like that. Especially if it's a barbecue."

"I was thinking the same thing. Eventually I'd like to put in a firepit for guests to gather around."

"Are you a good cook?"

"I'm adequate but I'm no caterer. I'd been

106

thinking it was something Emerson could do, but she's been kind of resistant to the expansion."

He tossed a smile over his shoulder. "Isn't she the one who just charred a loaf of bread?"

Charlotte snorted. "Good point." But truly, her sister was a great cook. She could take a handful of random ingredients and turn them into a meal that would make your mouth water.

Rogue led them up an incline that would eventually take them to a great view of the falls. "I assume you've got some experience matching guests to horses?" she asked.

"I do. I did trail rides at Cedar Creek in Tennessee for almost a year. You've only got two ponies, though, so we're limited where kids are concerned."

"I'll keep that in mind when booking rides. Anyway, with only one trail boss, two kids are probably plenty. So at Cedar Creek, did you do much talking on the trail?"

He shifted in his saddle. "We were encouraged to tell the history of the area and also engage with the guests about where they were from and what they did for a living. I'm comfortable with whatever you'd like me to do."

"I think covering the history of the area would be great. Both the town and the ranch itself. The story's up on the website, so you can use what's there. As for the town, it used to rely on silver mines, and when that came to a close in the seventies, the town began a pretty quick economic decline. Riverbend Gap's town council made a risky decision to switch to tourism. They petitioned to have the Appalachian Trail come right down Main Street. It was apparently a big deal and took a while to get the Trail Conservancy on board, much less the time it took to reroute the trail. But it ended up being beneficial for the hikers, who wouldn't have to hitch rides into the nearest towns to restock supplies."

"I had no idea. The plan obviously worked. Most of the businesses here seem to be geared around the hikers."

"And most people who come through never hear that little tidbit, so it would be great to include it in your spiel. The man primarily responsible for the rerouted trail passed away years ago, but his family—the Robinsons—still live in town. Gavin and Wes, who are building the barn, are part of that family."

"What a great legacy."

"Yeah." She'd thought for a brief moment that it was her legacy, too, Jeff Robinson being the son of the man who'd led the town's revitalization efforts. She pushed aside the thought. "Facts about the Appalachian Trail would be great to include too. Its length, how many months it takes to complete, and how many people set out to do it—only one quarter actually make it."

"I'll do that."

"You could talk about trail names too. Every hiker ends up with a trail name, usually given to them by another hiker. When you meet someone on the trail, that's the name you give. My dad gave me the name Flash when we hiked. You know, my red hair and my apparent need to get places in a hurry. Emerson's name was Sprout because she was no taller than a bean sprout."

"You don't seem to be in a rush these days."

"I've slowed down in my old age."

He tossed a grin over his shoulder. "Yeah, you must be getting up there. What are you, all of twenty-five?"

"Twenty-six—and four months." Had he been fishing for her age? She was curious about his too. "You can't be that much older."

"Thirty-four."

Eight years wasn't that much. Dad had been seven years older than Mom. And why was Charlotte thinking along those lines? She gave her head a hard shake.

Her warmblood went for a snack again, and she pulled the reins and added, "Heeey," when she failed to comply. "Stella likes to snack on the journey. So I saw you've mostly worked around the Midwest. Is that where you're originally from?"

He hesitated before answering. "Yeah, Minnesota."

That surprised her. "What brought you to horse country? A job?"

"No, I . . ."

Stella bent down to feed on the trailside grass, and Charlotte tugged the reins and urged her on. Horses could choke when they ate with a bit in their mouths. Besides, snacking would slow down the trail riders.

Gunner still hadn't answered. Maybe he hadn't heard her.

"When I was a kid," he finally said, "I moved to Frankfort, Kentucky, to live with my grandfather."

"I've heard good things about Frankfort." She wondered what had happened but didn't want to pry. He'd had to pick up his life and start over somewhere else. That couldn't have been easy. There was so much more she wanted to know. Had he liked living with his grandfather? Did he have any siblings?

But they weren't friends. She was his boss, and she'd done enough prying around what might be the sticky parts of his life. It was definitely better to keep things professional.

"How did you end up getting interested in horses?" she asked.

"A friend of my grandpa's had a ranch and needed some help. Also, my grandpa decided I needed something to keep me busy after school and on weekends." The shift in conversation eased his posture. Even his voice sounded less tense.

"Was he right?"

"Oh yeah. Can't say I loved mucking out stalls, but getting paid was nice. And I liked the horses."

"Well, you've clearly worked your way up from stable hand. And I think it's fair to say the horses like you too."

"It's a two-way street," he said.

"That it is."

"I assume you were born to ranching since this place has been in your family three generations."

"You read the website."

"I try to do my homework."

"I guess you should if you're gonna pick up and move three hundred miles."

"When did you know you wanted the ranch life for yourself?"

"I don't ever remember questioning that. My first memory was watching my mom's mare foal when I was three or four. I still remember the wonder of it all. Growing up, I never minded the chores—well, almost never. I found it satisfying, taking care of the horses. Now I'm responsible for maintaining a property that's been passed down through my family."

"Sounds like a lot of pressure."

"Maybe. But I wouldn't trade it for anything. I always felt so blessed to be raised here."

"You were. It's a beautiful property and you own some fine animals."

"I wish Emerson saw it that way."

"She doesn't take to ranch life?"

"She says she'd rather do something else—though she doesn't seem to know what. She's helped a lot since Mom died, but lately her interest has waned."

"How's that work, with you being partners and all?"

"Not very well. I'm hoping she'll come around. This place could be a real moneymaker. I feel it in my bones. I think when we turn it around, when the money starts coming in, she'll see things differently."

Stella snatched at some tall grass as they reached the summit and Charlotte redirected her. "You might warn whoever gets Stella that she likes to snack. They'll need to nudge her along."

"Maybe I can break her of that habit. In the meantime I'll be sure to let riders know. Rogue is handling the trail like a boss."

"He's a natural leader. Did I tell you we're getting another boarder? A mare that needs to be saddle trained. She'll be coming on as soon as the stable's finished. And we have another trail ride scheduled for the weekend. You're gonna have to holler if I give you too much to handle. I'm happy to be trail boss if I'm not working at the Trailhead."

"I'll keep that in mind, but I like staying busy."

"Well, that's good, because busy you're definitely gonna be."

The ground dropped a bit before climbing again. "Other than the grazing, Stella's holding up pretty well back here. She's sure-footed. I think she'll make a fine trail horse."

"You picked good ones. They're built for trails and have even temperaments."

"I'd like to get more eventually so we can handle larger groups, but that'll have to wait."

"Good horses aren't cheap."

"No, they're not. But we already had my horse and Emerson's, so I only had to buy a few. Do you ever think about getting one yourself?"

"Nah. My lifestyle isn't really compatible with horse ownership."

"You'd have to buy a truck and trailer for starters."

"I don't see that happening anytime soon."

Was it the money? He'd surely made a decent salary at Four Winds with his skills and reputation. His old boss would've clearly upped the ante to keep him. But his résumé proved he never stayed in one place for long. "As much as you move around, you must like starting fresh, huh?"

"Guess I do. New challenges keep things interesting. I like to travel, too, and moving around allows me to experience different places."

"Sure. I get that." But he was in his mid-thirties. Didn't he ever want to settle down, start a family? It wasn't a question she should ask—as his boss or as a woman. No way was she getting involved with another man who would only leave her behind.

"My dad was a little like that too," Charlotte continued. "He was a truck driver. His routes were just regional, but he loved driving around that big rig. I'd go with him sometimes."

"How'd you like it?"

"I didn't mind the travel, but mostly I loved talking on his CB radio. What does your grandpa think of this nomadic lifestyle of yours?" she asked with a teasing tone. "Or maybe you got the wander bug from him."

"He actually passed away about ten years ago."

Charlotte winced. Did Gunner have anyone else in his life? He hadn't mentioned anyone. Maybe that's why he was so footloose and fancy-free—no one tethering him to any one place. "I'm sorry for your loss."

"It was almost a mercy really. He'd had Alzheimer's for years."

Now why had he gone and told her that? He'd been careful to share as little as possible. Divulging led to emotions and emotions led to intimacy and, down the road, intimacy led to loss.

"I'm sorry to hear that. One of my friend's

grandmas had it. What a heartbreaking condition. She said it was like losing her twice."

That pretty much summed it up. "Yeah."

He'd cared for his grandpa at home for as long as he could—longer probably than he should have, as Grandpa wandered off one day while Gunner was working. It was then he came to the difficult decision to move him to a memory-care facility, which meant signing the house over. Gunner rented his own place, and Grandpa soon came to the point where he didn't recognize Gunner, making those regular visits painful. He'd lived another four years, and though Gunner grieved his loss, he was relieved for his grandfather's sake. The man was in heaven now, with all his faculties.

He swallowed against the lump in his throat. Not long after Grandpa had passed, Gunner moved on. Nothing to tie him to Frankfort anymore. Nothing to tie him anywhere. And look at him now.

He stopped and gazed at the beautiful sight. The sun burst through the forest, highlighting a waterfall that was about ten feet wide. The two-story drop made a good, loud roar. A fine mist hung over the gorge, catching glimmers of light. If he didn't travel, he'd miss sights like this one.

"Best view you'll get around here. This is Stillwater Creek that eventually flows into the French Broad River and snakes around the outskirts of town. This will definitely be a photo stop for the guests. You might have to take a few pictures."

"No problem. I can check cinches here too."

"Good idea."

He enjoyed the view and the pine-scented air for another minute, then said, "Ready to move on?"

"Whenever you are."

He nudged Rogue forward, across a small summit, then down the sloped trail. The horse was quick to obey and sure-footed on the rocky switchbacks. Toward the bottom of the hill, the trail evened out a bit and finally gave way to a dirt path.

"So let's talk about the other trail horses," Charlotte said. "Like you mentioned, they're all good, solid horses, but as you know they all have their own personalities. Firefly is a little reluctant when she starts out. She'll need a firm hand at first, but once she's on the trail she's fine. Chowder tends to be lazy. Sometimes he wants to stop, but he's responsive to commands to get along. I didn't have any issues with the others."

"I'll pass that information to the riders."

"We already talked about the waivers and paperwork." She slanted a look his way. "I'm guessing you'll make out pretty good on tips."

He came to a stop at the creek bed. "Why's that?"

"Well, I guess it might depend if your guests are male or female."

Their gazes locked as she reined in beside him. "I imagine you'll do pretty well yourself." Why had he said that? Just because she'd flattered him didn't mean he had to return the favor. Heaven knew he thought she was a knockout, but saying so wouldn't keep those boundaries in place.

She sure did have some pretty eyes. They were lighter in the sunlight. And if he wasn't mistaken, that flush on her cheeks had nothing to do with the heat.

He tore his gaze away.

"Sorry," she said a moment later. "I probably shouldn't have stated the obvious, what with being your boss and all. I'm sure you'll wow them with your spiel too."

"No worries." He should apologize for his words, too, but couldn't bring himself to say sorry for paying a woman a compliment. Anyway, she didn't seem offended.

He took a moment to appreciate the view of the water rippling across the pasture, then nudged Rogue forward. The horse navigated the narrow stream with no difficulty, but when he reached the shore he turned.

Stella stopped at the bank and snorted.

Charlotte encouraged her forward, and after a few tries, the horse plodded across the creek.

"She's a little water shy," she said when she reached the other shore.

"That's what this trial run is for. I'll see what I can do about that, but in the meantime, I can help her across if necessary."

They went on through the pasture where the other horses had been turned out. Midnight was standing by himself on the far side of the field. The horse that had been full of anxiety when he'd been brought to the ranch was now grazing peacefully, head lowered, ears turned out to the side.

Gunner had been engaging with Midnight regularly in the stall, slow and steady. He didn't trust people. And he was even a bit of a loner when it came to the herd. He wouldn't stand for being picked on, so Gunner didn't think he was an omega. More likely an alpha.

The horse's ears turned toward them. His head followed and he watched as Gunner and Charlotte passed by the fence. *Hang in there, buddy. It's gonna be all right.*

Eleven

After finding Lisa Robinson's maiden name in a high school yearbook, Charlotte was able to access her public divorce record and discover the name of Charlotte's father: Craig Burton.

Such an ordinary name. If her mom had married him, she would've been Charlotte Burton. She and her father would've shared the same initials.

Enough of that. Dreaming of what could have been was pointless. Besides, she never would have traded Dad and Emerson for the life she could've had. But that didn't mean she wasn't eager to find and get to know her biological father.

After trying a few different searches, she'd located a listing for a property on Rock Branch Road he'd bought years ago with his wife (at the time), Lisa.

But in the two weeks since Charlotte had learned his name and located the listing, she'd learned little else about the man. No pictures were to be found online, at least none she thought might be of her father. Certainly no social media profiles that seemed promising. She'd boldly friended Gavin on Facebook last week. But he rarely posted anything, and Craig Burton wasn't listed as a friend under his profile—or even

Cooper's (whom she'd also cyberstalked but hadn't friended).

She'd located almost twenty Craig Burtons in North Carolina alone, eight of them in the right age range. However, she couldn't just randomly call these men and ask if they were Cooper and Gavin's dad, could she? Anyway, who knew if the man even lived in North Carolina after all these years?

He might not even be alive. Maybe that's why she'd never heard anything about him. The thought of having lost him before she'd had a chance to meet him weighted her stomach. But she hadn't located an obituary online, so she was hopeful.

Pushing aside her fear, she toggled to *The Herald*'s website and put his name in the search engine. A few seconds later three mentions popped up.

The floor creaked above her head as Emerson moved around upstairs. Her sister had been distant since learning about Charlotte's secret family. Charlotte tried to be understanding, but she was losing patience with Emerson's cold-shoulder treatment.

On a happier note, Gunner had settled into his role on the ranch. He'd taken a lot of work off her plate, which allowed her to focus on the grand opening. He'd also worked wonders with the horses. Stella would now cross streams without hesitation and did less grazing on the job.

The trail rides were also going well. Now that they'd earned a few five-star customer reviews online, reservations were building. She'd taken a couple of groups when Gunner was otherwise tied up with training. She enjoyed regaling the guests with the history of her family ranch and the town of Riverbend Gap. Enjoyed showing off their beautiful property and quality horses.

Her gaze homed in on one of the online articles and she clicked on it. She skimmed the account of a break-in at a local gas station. The journalist interviewed the employee who'd been on duty at the time—Craig Burton. The article was only five months old.

The piece gave little away about the employee. But Charlotte's pulse picked up at the few quotes in the article. It was possible this was her father, wasn't it? The shop was located in Weaverville, which was only thirty minutes away. It would make sense that he'd settle nearby.

She did a few quick searches, trying to learn more about this Craig Burton from Weaverville, but came up empty. The man likely still worked at the gas station. She checked the time and the business hours. It would remain open until nine tonight.

What if she just drove over and filled her tank? Checked it out? Maybe he was on duty. And if he was, maybe she'd recognize something of herself—or her brothers—in his face that would confirm he was her father. Maybe he would even recognize her—she bore a fair resemblance to her mother.

That was a lot of maybes. But worth the short drive. She closed her laptop and jumped up from the table, hands trembling at the possibility of meeting her birth father that very night.

Don't get ahead of yourself.

It probably wasn't him, and even if it was, he might not be working tonight. Even so, she couldn't seem to stop herself from taking the chance. She'd talked to Gavin briefly twice more since the conversation at the Trailhead, but at this rate she'd be a senior citizen before she knew him well enough to inquire about his father.

She grabbed her purse and called up the stairs, "Em, I'm going out for a while."

She waited, listening, but there was no response.

"Em, did you hear me? I'm heading out."

"All right," her sister called in a neutral tone.

Charlotte sighed. She slipped outside, where the heat of the day lingered even though the sun had dropped behind the mountains. Being past suppertime, Gunner had already left for the day, but he'd stabled the horses before he went. She'd do a night check when she got home.

As she got into her truck, Midnight's snorting carried from the barn. Gunner said he was making slow progress with the horse, but it would take time. Some horses never recovered from trauma.

After strapping herself into her truck, she headed down the drive and through town, her mind spinning with excitement, her skin tingling with nerves. She'd definitely get gas—she was down to a quarter tank. One of her tires needed air too. But also, she'd have to go inside and purchase something so she could get a good view of the cashier.

That would give her a chance to stock up on M&M's. She'd gone through a month's supply the past couple of weeks, stress eating because of the tension in the house. Thankfully her jobs at the ranch and the Trailhead helped her burn off the excess calories.

Of course, the person at the register could turn out to be a woman or a man too young to be her dad. If that was the case, she would deflate like a week-old party balloon.

But if the man was potentially her father . . .

What? Should she strike up a conversation? Ask about the area or mention she lived in Riverbend and see if he mentioned his sons? Yes, that's what she would do.

A plan in place, she relaxed her grip on the wheel as she drove through town and out the other side, taking the winding road along the river. What would her father look like now? It was hard to tell what he used to look like from that photo in the folder. Charlotte had likely gotten her red hair and green eyes from her mom, but maybe she'd inherited her dad's widow's peak or petite frame.

The man appeared to have Gavin's beautiful dark hair, but did he have Gavin's blue eyes or Cooper's deep-set brown eyes? The man in the photo would've undoubtedly changed a lot in the past twenty-seven years. But surely if she saw her own father, she would recognize him. She refused to believe she could stand in front of the man who'd provided half of her genetics and not even know it.

A while later she passed through the town of Marshall. She was six miles from Weaverville when the loud thumping began, followed by the unmistakable vibration of a flat tire.

Gunner cut across his rental's lawn, bare feet swishing through the long grass. The back of the property ended at the bank of a creek that offered a perfect swimming hole after a hot day's work. He much preferred it to the shower's drizzle of lukewarm water.

He rubbed the small towel over his face, draped it around his neck, then took the small stoop and entered through the front and only door of the cabin. After getting into some dry clothes, he heated a large can of soup on the hot plate. Really needed to get to the grocery.

He was almost finished with supper when his phone vibrated on the table. It was a wonder he even had service out here. He checked the screen. Charlotte.

She'd never called him after work hours. Hopefully something wasn't wrong with one of the horses. He pushed back his bowl and answered the phone, noting his battery life was down to 5 percent even though he'd hardly used it today.

"Hi." The word released on a heavy sigh of relief. "Thank you for picking up. I didn't know who else to call. My sister isn't answering and my best friend can't leave her bed-ridden grandma."

He rose to his feet at the note of panic in her tone. "What is it? You okay?"

"I'm fine, I just—I'm really sorry to bother you like this. I was driving to Weaverville and my tire blew out in the middle of nowhere. It was underinflated and I think I hit a gator back a ways."

"Gator?"

"A piece of rubber in the— Never mind, it's a CB thing. I have a lug wrench, a jack, and a spare, but these blasted lug nuts are on so tight I can't even budge them."

He grabbed his keys and headed out the door toward an old shed that had some building supplies. "Ping me with your exact location. How far away are you?"

"About twenty minutes. I'm really sorry about this, Gunner."

"No worries. Are you safe, off the side of the road?"

"As far off as I could get, and I turned my hazards on."

"Good. Get in the truck and lock the doors. I'll be there soon."

"Thanks."

He ended the call and pulled the string that illuminated the shed's single bulb. He'd been poking around in here last week and seen— yes, there it was. He grabbed the metal pipe and stowed it on his bike before he put on his helmet and took off.

He didn't like the thought of Charlotte sitting alone on the side of the road. Sure, she was a strong, independent woman and this community seemed safe. But idiots were out there, some of them just plain mean—he came across them on the road from time to time.

One guy in Tennessee had slashed Gunner's tires just for making small talk with his girlfriend at a roadhouse. It wasn't like he was hitting on her or something. They were just talking motorcycles.

Gunner drove over the speed limit, frequently checking the map from the phone mount he'd rigged up. Hoped he had enough battery life to get him there. What was in Weaverville anyway, if that's where she'd been heading? A boyfriend? But no, she would've called him to help if that were the case.

It made Gunner a little heady that she'd turned to him. It displayed a certain amount of trust. Of course, it sounded like he'd been a last resort. But she'd also said she hadn't wanted to bother him on his evening off. Charlotte was never a bother.

The thought gave him pause, raised a red flag. But it was true nonetheless. He never wanted her to hesitate to call if she got in a bind, much less in a situation like this one that could end in trouble. He pushed the thoughts aside and, tightening his grip, gave the bike more throttle.

Twelve

Charlotte glanced at her watch. If she wasn't so frustrated, she would've enjoyed the pretty view of the sun setting behind periwinkle clouds tinged with pink.

But the trip had been for naught. The gas station would be closed by the time she had the spare tire on. She wouldn't meet the man who was potentially her father tonight. Plus, she'd likely have to invest in a new tire when funds were already tight.

Also, she was irked with Emerson, who hadn't answered Charlotte's voice mail or responded to her text about being stranded on the side of the road. Gunner was a better option anyway. Emerson only would've been able to offer a ride home. At least this way Charlotte would get her truck home tonight.

But she hated to bother Gunner. He already put in extra hours most days. He had a strong work ethic, and when he was in a groove with a horse, he didn't like to quit. He also insisted on ending each training session on a positive note, and sometimes that took a while.

Although he didn't seem like the sociable type, the trail guests seemed to love him. Since she usually helped untack and groom the horses afterward, she'd witnessed the camaraderie. Some of the guests were a little anxious when they arrived, but they returned relaxed and confident. They often hung around, asking questions or spending time with their horses.

One group had been a family with two teenage girls. It was amusing to watch the girls sneaking admiring looks at Gunner and whispering behind their hands. They were completely smitten. Charlotte couldn't blame them. He was an attractive man who exuded mastery with the horses. He was kind to the girls but seemed oblivious to their furtive glances and quiet giggles.

Lights flashed through the twilight in her rearview mirror. A pickup truck approached. Not the first vehicle to pass, but this one slowed to a stop beside her, engine humming loudly. Charlotte lowered her window.

A grizzled fortysomething man, wearing a Coors ball cap, leaned across his seat and called out the passenger window. "Need some help? I got a jack if you have a spare. If not, I could give you a ride. Headed into Weaverville."

"Thank you, but I have someone coming."

The man scanned the deserted landscape. When he glanced back over, he said, "I'll just pull over and get it started for you then. I could have you back on the road in a few minutes." His truck inched forward.

She bristled but kept her expression friendly.

"That's okay. He should be here any minute. You can be on your way."

"I wouldn't feel right about—"

The sound of a motorcycle drowned out his words. She glanced in her rearview mirror. Her shoulders sagged at the sight of Gunner pulling to a stop behind her.

The pushy man in the truck probably only meant to help. Some men were just clueless about how vulnerable a woman could feel in certain situations.

She dredged up a smile. "That's him now. Thank you for stopping, but we're—"

"Everything all right over here?" Gunner appeared, holding some kind of pipe. He stopped between the two vehicles, his back to Charlotte.

"Everything's fine." She unlocked her door and stepped out. "This man was just offering to help out."

Gunner two-handed the metal pipe. "Thanks, buddy, but I've got it covered."

The man took in Gunner's protective stance. "Jeez, can't a fella help a damsel in distress anymore?" Shaking his head, the guy took off and his tires squealed on the pavement.

Gunner frowned after him, then turned, his gaze raking over her face. "You all right? He didn't hassle you?"

"He was probably harmless, but he was getting

a little pushy about helping. I can't say I'm sorry you pulled up when you did."

He glanced at the flat rear tire. "Well, let's get this spare on before it gets dark."

Charlotte reached into her truck for the lug wrench and handed it over. "If you can't get the lug nuts off, I can just have the truck towed tomorrow." Though it was an added expense she really didn't want to incur.

"They're not rusted, so someone probably just put them on with a pneumatic wrench." He set the lug wrench, threaded it with the long pipe, and stepped onto the extension, using his body weight. The lug gave way.

"You made that look so easy."

"A little leverage goes a long way."

Since he had it under control, she read the directions in the manual for removing the spare tire—more complicated than she'd imagined. But when he was finished with the lug wrench, she used it and some assembly bars to lower the spare tire from beneath the rear of the vehicle.

Gunner got down on the ground and detached it from the assembly.

"What do you do if you get a flat on your bike?"

"I carry a spare tube."

She rolled the tire around to the side while he set up the jack. He worked with the ease of someone who'd done this a few times.

"How do you know so much about changing tires?"

He cranked up the truck. "My dad taught me. And my grandpa went over it with me again when I was sixteen. Wouldn't let me get my license until I could change the oil, a tire, and knew a few mechanical basics."

"If something went wrong with our vehicles, my dad took them to the garage. But we had to learn how to change a flat in driver's ed. It's been a few years, though, and they didn't show us that leverage trick."

Once the rear of the vehicle was lifted, Charlotte removed the loosened lug nuts. When she was finished she moved out of his way. "I'll watch for traffic."

"Good idea."

Did her biological father know how to do this sort of thing? She stared south, down the road that would've taken her to Weaverville. Between the ranch and her schedule at the Trailhead, she wouldn't have a chance to check the man out until Sunday, and the station was closed that day. That meant she wouldn't be able to make another trip until Monday.

Only four days away. She'd been waiting so long to meet him, and the setback hit her like a rogue wave. Why was she in this position to begin with? Why hadn't her mother just told her the truth when Charlotte had asked all those years ago? Even if she couldn't barge into her siblings' lives, she could've gotten to know her biological father. Even with Dad there to fill the spot in her life, a hole had remained in her heart. A knowledge that the man who'd helped create her was out there somewhere, living his life, possibly unaware she even existed.

She blinked back tears.

Gunner stood to roll the flat tire away, but he stopped at her expression. And maybe the tears sparkling in her eyes. "Hey, you all right?"

She nodded, her throat too choked up to speak.

"That guy say something to you?"

She swallowed hard and dashed away a tear. "No, nothing like that. It's stupid, really. I'd hoped to meet my biological father tonight in Weaverville, but . . ." She gestured toward the truck.

"You found him already?"

"No. Well, maybe. I don't know." She told him about discovering his name and about the newspaper article she'd found. "I was headed there tonight, and I was planning to strike up a conversation if he was working."

His eyes softened. "You could still go. I'll go with you if you want."

"That's very kind of you. But the gas station is closed now, and I won't have a chance to go again till Monday. I'm being silly. It's only a few days. I'd just had my hopes up, I guess."

"It's not silly. Let's go Monday night then."

She raised her brows. Why would he want to do that on a night off? "Really?"

"Why not? I'll be your moral support."

"Craig Burton might not even be there." She gave her head a sharp shake. "It might not even be my dad at all."

"Then we'll grab a pizza or something and make the best of it."

Gunner rolled the flat to the back and set it inside the truck. Then he hoisted the spare and pushed it into place on the axle. What was he doing? Where were those boundaries he'd always kept in place?

Of course, he enjoyed female companionship as much as the next man. But he strove to keep things light and uncomplicated. Charlotte was his boss, and getting involved in her personal business was the opposite of uncomplicated.

But the sight of those tears swimming in her eyes had turned his insides to pulp. This whole thing with her biological family had her twisted up in knots, and he couldn't stand to see her going through it alone.

"That's really nice of you," Charlotte said. "I'd like the company if you're sure it's not an imposition."

He couldn't quell the bolt of excitement that seared through him. If that wasn't a warning flag,

135

he didn't know what was. He began turning the lug nut. "No problem at all."

Except he was starting to get a little too involved. Starting to care just a little too much. Even so, he couldn't bring himself to rescind the offer.

Besides, it was just one night. Just one little trip a few towns over. What was the big deal?

Thirteen

Charlotte was mucking out stalls the next morning when the vet entered the barn. She finished fluffing the new straw and leaned on her pitchfork as he approached in his usual uniform of worn jeans and a plaid button-down shirt. Only his Lucchese boots hinted that his veterinary degree had paid off nicely.

"Hey, Kyle. How's it going?"

"Not bad. How you doing, Charlotte?"

"Doing well." Gunner hadn't mentioned a medical issue with any of the horses, but maybe it had slipped his mind. "You're out and about awfully early."

"I just stopped by with some news. I had a chance to chat with Mayor Hinkley last night. I told him about your new stable and expansion and your vision for tourism growth. He agreed to come out for a ribbon cutting at your grand opening."

She beamed. "What? Kyle, you're amazing! I can't believe you talked him into it."

"Aw, I didn't have to coerce him or anything. He said he's always happy to support new and growing businesses. And clearly your ranch is on the verge of big things."

"Oh, I hope so. Now some media will turn up for sure."

"I bet they will. You'll need to call the mayor's office and go over the details with his assistant, Meredith. She'll add it to the mayor's schedule."

"I sure will. That's fantastic news. Thanks for stopping by to let me know and for setting this up. It'll really make a big difference."

"I hope so. You deserve good things, Charlotte."

Cleo nickered from the stall by Kyle, and he reached out to stroke the gelding's nose. "This one still barn sour?"

"Gunner got him all the way to the paddock yesterday, and that's farther than I ever got him."

"Some fresh grass would be good for you, fella. Listen to Charlotte here. She has your best interest at heart."

"He's bonding with Chestnut, so I'm hoping I can turn them out together soon."

"Is Cleo one of your boarders?"

"Yep. The owner doesn't come out much though. Cleo was his dad's, and he passed away last year. I keep thinking the guy will sell the horse, but so far he's happy to just pay for boarding. But I'd sure like this fella to get a little more joy out of life."

"Sounds like he's on his way."

Charlotte rubbed the horse's withers. "We're getting there, aren't we, big guy?" She followed Kyle out of the barn, talking shop as they went.

When they reached his truck, he turned to her.

"Listen, Charlotte. I was wondering if you might like to go out for a bite to eat sometime."

Was he asking her out on a date? Or was this a work-related dinner?

"There's a nice Italian restaurant that just opened over in Marshall, if you like that kind of thing. I've been wanting to try it. Maybe we can do that together."

"Oh." Definitely asking her out. She tried to keep the surprise off her face but wasn't sure if she succeeded. "Um . . ." She'd never thought of Kyle that way. He was like fifteen years older. But he was kind and ran a reputable business that tied him here. And he was easy enough on the eyes. She could think of worse prospects.

He cleared his throat and tugged at his ball cap.

She'd left him hanging too long. "Sorry. I mean, maybe . . . I've got so much on my plate right now, my head's kind of spinning."

He raised his hands palms out. "It doesn't have to be this weekend or anything. You can think about it if you want. I know you've got your hands full right now."

"It's just . . . I'm so nervous about this expansion. Everything's kind of riding on it."

"I understand. Last thing I want to do is stress you out. Why don't we circle back to this a little later?"

A little space was exactly what she needed. "Yes. Thank you. I appreciate your understanding."

He tossed her a crooked grin. "I'm a patient man, Charlotte."

After Kyle left, she put in a call to the mayor's office. The mayor had a busy schedule, but Meredith squeezed him in for an hour on the morning of the grand opening. And just like that it was done.

Charlotte pocketed her phone and headed toward the new stable. In the pen Gunner worked one of their boarders on the lunge line. He was so focused he didn't even notice when she passed by.

As she walked up the grassy slope, she took in her new western barn, pride sweeping over her. Mom would've loved the post-and-beam construction made to look like barns of old. It had been quite the expense, but guests wanted the full experience when they came to ride in the mountains, and Charlotte was determined to give it to them.

In the past two weeks Gavin and Wes had made great progress. They finished the framing and sheeted the roof and exterior walls. The barn doors, already up on both ends, were open to allow a stream of fresh air.

The scent of raw wood teased her nose as she stepped into the coolness of the barn. She waited a moment to let her eyes adjust to the relative darkness. A moment later she spied Gavin and Wes installing windows on the north side of the stable.

"How's it going in here?" she asked.

Gavin lowered his battery-operated screw gun and met her in the middle of the barn. "It's going. We should have the windows installed by the end of the day."

She exchanged greetings with Wes, who kept working.

"It's awesome." She took in the high ceilings and beams running across the open space. She was relieved to have relaxed a bit around Gavin now that they'd had a few conversations. He seemed like a genuinely nice guy. "It's so big. And so much cooler than the other barn."

"There's a nice breeze flowing through." He pointed at the gables. "And we're putting vents up there on both ends for airflow. All twelve windows have ventilation, too, and you can even remove the panes if you want."

"Perfect. The breeze is great and it smells so good in here."

He shot her a sidelong look. "I can't guarantee that'll last."

She laughed. "It definitely won't. It's so beautiful we could use it for events if we wanted to—which we definitely don't."

Gavin gave a wry grin. "Not interested in hosting fancy wedding receptions?"

"Horses are much easier to manage than bridezillas."

He chuckled. "I'll take your word for it. I let my wife handle all the wedding stuff—for both weddings." After their divorce, the child they'd adopted had brought them back together.

"How's your little girl? Emma, right?"

"She's great. She's four now and starting preschool in the fall. I can hardly believe it." His lips tilted in a secret smile. "Also, she'll have a brother or sister by the end of the year."

Charlotte sucked in a breath. Another niece or nephew! She tempered her reaction. "That's wonderful. Congratulations. How's your wife feeling?"

"Laurel's doing great. She had a little morning sickness for a while, but she's past that now."

"I'm happy for you both." He had no idea how happy.

"Thanks. We're pretty excited."

She wanted to ask more questions. Were they planning to find out the baby's gender? Did he want a boy or a girl? Was it bittersweet having a baby on the way after losing their first child? Surely it must be. But these inquiries were too private. To him, she was just another customer.

The reason she'd come up here was to make sure the project was on schedule, because now that the mayor had committed to the grand opening, there was no moving it. She cleared her throat. "So I got some good news this morning.

Mayor Hinkley will be doing a ribbon cutting at the grand opening."

"Hey, that's great. That should garner some attention for your business."

"That's the hope. I've been meaning to tell you, you're welcome to put up a yard sign for Robinson Construction if you'd like. Down at the road and up here by the barn too. I don't know how many people we'll have coming through for our grand opening, but it couldn't hurt."

"Thanks. That's a great idea. We finally had some signs made a few months ago. And don't worry, we'll make sure this place is ready to go by July first. We're ahead of schedule. You should have your stalls up by the end of next week. But the painting crew is backed up. They haven't given me an answer yet on when they can get out here. Have you picked out your colors?"

She laughed. "Months ago. I have the color swatches up at the house."

"Text me or Wes the numbers, and we'll grab the paint and have it ready in case there's a break in their schedule."

"Will do."

"Oh, I almost forgot. As you probably know, my mom runs Trail Days, and I was telling her about your expansion. She wondered if you might want to promote your business at the event. No pressure, just wanted to mention it in case you'd be interested. Booths are pretty cheap since Mom wants as many businesses as possible to participate."

"I hadn't thought that far ahead. Trail Days is in October, isn't it?"

"October twenty-second this year. It gathers a pretty big crowd."

"I'd love to participate." Gunner would still be here. Maybe he'd help with it. She didn't even attend last year because she was still deep in grief.

"I'll text you my mom's number then."

"That'd be wonderful. Thanks."

He whipped out his phone and a few seconds later Lisa's contact information appeared on her screen.

"Got it. Thanks." She was loath to end their conversation. He was so easy to talk to. But she'd held him up long enough. "I should let you get back to work."

"Let me know if you have any questions, okay?"

"Will do." Sadly, she couldn't verbalize the only question she really wanted to ask.

But come Monday maybe she'd finally have her answer.

She didn't have a chance to call Lisa until that evening. Emerson had apparently spent the afternoon making chicken cordon bleu, homemade mashed potatoes, and a cauliflower and broccoli salad. Although her sister had already left for work, she'd left a Post-it saying leftovers were in the fridge. Charlotte would have to thank her for the delicious meal. Sometimes she took her sister for granted.

After the dishes were loaded in the dishwasher and leftovers returned to the fridge, Charlotte called Lisa and identified herself when the woman answered.

"Well, hello!" Lisa said. "Gavin told me all about your expansion—the trail rides and the new trainer and everything. How exciting."

"We're pretty stoked about it. Gavin and Wes are doing an amazing job on the new stable. It's gonna be beautiful."

"Those boys do excellent work. Your ranch is such a staple in the community. I don't even remember a time it wasn't there."

"It's been in my family awhile. My sister and I are third-generation owners."

"In this day and age, that's saying something. What a wonderful legacy."

"I'm very blessed," Charlotte said, though that word *legacy* made her think of her recently discovered biological family. "So Gavin mentioned the possibility of getting some exposure at Trail Days. What would that entail exactly?"

"Well, I have a few options for you. Some businesses rent booths, some just place ads in the program, and others perform demonstrations or exhibitions. Some do all three. I'm open to ideas—and I'll warn you, I'm liable to throw out a few of my own. If you're interested, why don't we get together and chat, put our heads together, and come up with something that just knocks your socks off."

Charlotte smiled. She liked this woman. "That would be great. What's your schedule like?"

"I have some time Sunday afternoon, say around three? We could meet at the coffee shop or you could just come over to the house. I'm getting to be such a homebody in my old age!"

Lisa couldn't possibly be much past fifty—and a very pretty woman at that. But the thought of checking out the home where her brothers grew up was irresistible. "That sounds perfect."

"I'll shoot you the address. And I'm so glad you're interested in participating, Charlotte. We're gonna hit this out of the park for you."

Fourteen

Gunner wasn't having much luck with Midnight. The horse was nowhere near ready for the lunge line, but they were slowly building trust. Gunner had implemented a regular routine of feeding, mucking, turnout, and bonding time. Predictability was an easy, natural way to reduce Midnight's anxiety. Horses, much like people, preferred to know what was coming next. And this particular horse seemed to have reason to fear the unknown.

The ultimate goal with any horse was to establish leadership, and since the gelding's previous leader had likely abused his role, that would take time and patience. Fortunately, Gunner had plenty of both.

He always spent a few minutes with the horse in the morning and evening, talking gently and offering a treat. This nonstructured time served no purpose other than to give each of them an opportunity to learn about the other. So far Gunner had learned Midnight was a loner, didn't like being groomed, and listened intently when Gunner talked softly. Hopefully Midnight was learning that Gunner was a human being he could trust.

He approached the outside of the fence.

Midnight stood just inside the pen, snorting and pawing the ground. Gunner leaned on the rail. "It's all right, buddy. I'm not gonna hurt you."

The horse's ears swiveled forward. "That's right. We're buddies now, you and I. You can count on me."

The horse lowered his head and took a step closer to the fence.

"What was it, huh? What happened to you? Must've been pretty bad to mess you up like this." Gunner held out his hand, hoping the horse would approach and smell it.

But Midnight stopped and stood his ground.

"That's all right. We'll just take this easy. I won't give up on you if you don't give up on me."

"Hey there," Gavin called from the far side of the pen.

Midnight startled and dashed away from both men, then slowed once he reached the barn.

"Sorry 'bout that. Didn't mean to spook him."

"He's a little skittish. Got my work cut out for me with that one." Gunner glanced up the hillside. "The new barn's coming along great. Checked it out this morning before you all got here."

"We're running on time and on budget—that's about the most I can hope for."

"Charlotte's real happy with your work. That barn's built to last."

"I'm glad she's happy with it. She's really easy to work with."

"She's a nice person." And Gavin seemed like a nice guy. Gunner hoped when he and Cooper found out Charlotte was their sister, they'd be kind and accepting of her. It wouldn't necessarily be happy news for guys who already had a big, loving family. In fact, news like that could hit hard, and Charlotte might end up taking the brunt of it.

He didn't like that notion at all.

"Hey," Gavin said. "I was wondering if I could bring my wife and little girl out sometime Saturday to show her the horses. On your schedule, of course."

"Don't see why not. I have a trail ride at noon, but earlier in the morning would work. We have a nice, gentle pony we could saddle if she'd be up for that."

"I'll bet she would." Gavin chuckled. "Don't know about my wife though."

"No rush. We can ease into it."

"Sounds good. Thanks. We'll be over about nine if that works. Laurel likes to make a big breakfast on Saturdays."

"Must be nice. Most of my mornings start with a can of beans and string cheese."

"That's a sad meal there, buddy. Not much of a cook?"

"I like to keep things simple."

"Still, that has to get old. You should join my family for our cookout Sunday. My stepdad throws some burgers on the grill and everyone brings a side dish—go ahead and leave the canned beans at home though."

Gunner slipped him a grin. A home-cooked meal sounded pretty darn good right now. "Sure I wouldn't be imposing?"

"There's always plenty of food. And we usually invite a guest or two, sometimes a friend, sometimes a random hiker off the trail. We like to keep things interesting."

"All right then. I won't turn down a grilled burger. What time?"

"Five o'clock. And bring your cornhole game. You any good?"

"Well, I don't like to brag, but I was the undisputed champion at Four Winds."

Gavin pointed at him. "You're on my team."

Charlotte's nerves began to fray as Gavin's truck rolled up her driveway on Saturday morning. She tucked in her shirt and slipped into the barn to retrieve Firefly.

Gunner joined her as she pulled the pony from the stall. "I hope I wasn't out of line telling Gavin he could bring his daughter over."

" 'Course not. I just get so nervous every time I'm with one of the Robinsons."

"Nerves are perfectly understandable. This is

good, though, right? You're getting to know them just like you wanted."

"I've been wanting to meet my niece and nephew. Cooper has a baby boy I've never met. I've never had nieces and nephews, and now I have two with another one on the way."

"Relax. You're great with kids. I've seen you on the trail rides, remember?"

She walked Firefly out to the yard just as the Denali came to a stop outside the barn. As soon as the door opened, Emma's excited chatter carried across the yard.

"Look at the horsey, Mom! Can I pet them? Can I ride them?"

"We'll see, angel."

When Gavin and Laurel approached, the adults greeted one another, and Gavin introduced his wife and daughter.

Charlotte shook Laurel's hand. "It's nice to meet you. I've heard good things about your orchard. I'm a big fan of apples—especially when they're baked into pies."

"I knew I'd like you. You'll have to come over this fall and pick a bag." Her gaze swept over the property. "What a great ranch. How many horses do you have?"

"Just six but we also board several, and we've kind of adopted that guy." She pointed to Midnight, now turned out and grazing by himself. Charlotte knelt to Emma's level. The girl had beautiful blonde curls and light-green eyes. "You're being very patient, Emma. Would you like to come meet Firefly?"

"Can I pet her?"

"Of course."

Gavin swooped the girl into his arms, and Charlotte led them over to the chestnut mare. "Put your hand out like this and let her smell you. That's how horses say hello."

Emma did as she asked, then jerked her hand away, laughing. "Her nose is wet." She extended her hand again.

"That's right. It's wet and soft."

"She's breathing on me."

"She likes you," Gavin said.

Charlotte stroked the horse's muzzle. "She does. See how her ears are turned toward you so she can hear you better? Horses can turn their ears all around just like you."

Emma scrunched up her face. "I can't turn my ears around!"

"You can't?" Charlotte smiled. "Oh, okay, I guess it's just horses who do that."

"She's probably smelling bacon on your fingers," Laurel said.

"Or syrup," Emma added. "She's wagging her tail just like Sunny!"

Charlotte chuckled. "It does look like she's wagging her tail. But she's actually just swatting at that fly. Don't you use your tail to swat at flies?"

"I don't have a tail! I'm a little girl."

"Oh, gosh, I'm getting it all confused."

"You're silly." Emma touched Firefly's muzzle. "She likes it when I pet her."

"She likes *you*," Charlotte said. "And no wonder. You're being so nice to her."

"Can I sit on her like a cowgirl?"

Her mom shifted. "I don't know about that, angel. Maybe we should take it slow."

"We have helmets in the barn," Gunner said, "if that would make you feel better. And you could walk alongside her. Firefly's real gentle and used to people riding her."

"But no pressure," Charlotte added. "Whatever you're comfortable with."

Gavin turned to his wife. "Come on, babe. I'll walk with her. It'll be okay."

Laurel gave Firefly a once-over. "If you're sure."

They fixed Emma up with a helmct, then Gunner and Charlotte tacked up Firefly. When the horse was ready, Gavin set Emma on the saddle.

"Look, Mom! I'm riding the horsey."

"You're so brave, sweetie."

Charlotte adjusted the stirrups and slipped the girl's shoes inside. "There you go. You all comfortable now?"

"Can you make the horse go?"

"Well, that's your job." Charlotte handed Emma the reins. "Hold these loosely in your hands.

You can hold on to this too—it's called the horn. When you want her to go, just tap her sides with your feet like this." She took Emma's foot and demonstrated. "Now do that with both feet at the same time."

Emma did it but the horse didn't budge. "That was really good," Charlotte said. "But Firefly is so much bigger than you that she thought you were just tickling her."

Emma giggled.

"So do it again but harder this time. Don't worry, you won't hurt her."

Emma gave it another try and Firefly set into motion.

Emma giggled. "I made her go."

"You sure did. Tell her 'good girl' when she listens to you."

"Good girl, Firefly."

"When you want her to stop, just pull back on the reins."

Gavin followed her around the ring, encouraging her.

Gunner headed into the barn, and Charlotte meandered over to the fence where Laurel was snapping pictures with her phone.

"She's really doing it. She looks so little on that horse."

"She's not too young. I was so little when my mom put me on a horse, I don't even remember learning to ride."

"No wonder you're such a natural. Thank you for doing this. She'll be talking about it for weeks."

"You can bring her back anytime. She's a sweet girl, and if she has a fancy for horses, I can definitely help her out."

"Do you give lessons?"

"Not formally. I'd like to offer them eventually, but we're currently a little short-staffed. I'm hoping this expansion can fund additional help."

Gavin showed Emma how to pull the reins, and once Firefly stopped, she kicked the horse into gear again.

"Good job, Emma," Charlotte called, then turned to Laurel again. "I hear congratulations are in order. I hope it's okay that Gavin told me your good news."

"Oh, the cat's way out of the bag. Gavin's mom guessed just about the same second we confirmed it with a test."

"Oh no."

"It's okay. The family managed to keep it under their hats for the first trimester—a real miracle. I thought Lisa would burst."

Charlotte chuckled. "I don't know her very well, but she seems like a terrific woman. I'm meeting her tomorrow to go over some things for Trail Days."

Laurel offered a smile. "She roped you into that, did she?"

"Let's just say she thought it might be a good opportunity to get the word out about my expansion."

"She'll have all kinds of ideas on that. And the event does draw a big crowd. It's definitely worth your time."

"Look, Mom, I'm riding good!" Emma called.

Laurel snapped another photo. "You're a real pro, honey."

"I'm a real pro, Dad."

Gavin seemed like such a good father. Charlotte was proud to have such a stand-up guy for a brother. Proud of the way he'd stepped up for Emma when her birth parents died. The way he'd embraced the child as his own. Did that mean he'd embrace Charlotte, too, once he found out they were siblings? Just the thought of being rejected by him stung.

She pushed away the negative thoughts. "You should take a peek at the barn your husband's been building. It's amazing. I don't know how they're constructing it so fast."

"He has a lot of help and you caught them at a good time. They were between house builds. Come July, they'll be busy again."

"I'm glad I caught them when I did then."

"It's his first barn—he's pretty proud of it."

"He should be. It'll still be standing long after I'm gone."

When the trio completed the full circle, Emma

drew Firefly to a halt. She'd added the word "whoa," apparently on Gavin's instruction. When the horse obeyed, Emma patted her side. "Good girl, Firefly."

Gavin lifted her from the horse.

"She's a natural." Charlotte meant every word. "You should bring her back sometime."

"Can I, Daddy? Can I come back and ride Firefly?"

"We'll see. We don't want to be a nuisance."

Emma's brows furrowed. "What's a nuisance?"

Charlotte laughed. "Something you could never be. Seriously, Gavin, just give me a call whenever you want to bring her over. And as I told Laurel, we don't really offer lessons, but I'd be happy to work with her a bit."

"That's awfully kind of you."

"She clearly loves horses, and I like to encourage that in the little ones."

"Well, we'll give it some thought." He glanced up at the new stable. "Mind if I take my family up to see the barn?"

"Of course not. I was just telling Laurel she should check it out. Take your time. I have some work to do up at the house."

"Thank you again for letting us visit. It was nice to meet you." Laurel took Emma's hand. "Say thank you, angel."

"Thank you!"

"You're welcome, Emma. Great job today. Come back and see Firefly soon, okay?"

"Okay!"

The family traipsed hand in hand around the pen and up the grassy slope that led to the barn. What a nice young family. What a blessing it would be to have them in her life.

Fifteen

Lisa Robinson swept Charlotte into a hug as if she were a long-lost friend. "Come in, come in. I'm so excited to talk about your business and how we can help you get some good exposure." With her short blonde ponytail and simple makeup, Lisa didn't look old enough to have a son Gavin's age. That she was a grandma two times over seemed impossible.

Charlotte wanted to forget Lisa was Gavin and Cooper's mom, but her nerves wouldn't let her. There was something so warm about her. Charlotte wanted the woman to like her.

A dimple punctuated Lisa's left cheek as she ushered Charlotte into her homey living room. She gestured toward a plate on the coffee table. "I hope you like chocolate chip cookies."

"Does anyone *not* like chocolate chip cookies?"

Lisa gave her a sideways hug. "I knew I was gonna like you. Have a seat and help yourself. I can't wait to get started. Gavin has such nice things to say about you and your ranch. I think he's really enjoying working out there on your property."

"He's doing an amazing job. I couldn't be happier with the new stable. Everybody told me what a hassle building would be, but he and Wes have made it a breeze."

"Doesn't surprise me a bit."

Charlotte bit into a cookie. "Mmm. Still warm. These are heaven."

"I'd like to say it's an old family recipe, but I found it online and now my kids ask for it all the time."

"I can see why. Maybe you could send me the recipe if you don't mind sharing."

"Of course! Do you like to bake?"

"Actually, I was planning to pass it on to my sister so she could bake them for me. I've got my hands pretty full with the ranch right now."

"I guess you do. Tell me about your expansion."

Charlotte explained about hiring Gunner and all she hoped to accomplish with the training program. She talked about the trail rides for tourists and how that part of the growth was already underway.

"And you work at the Trailhead too? How do you keep up with it all?"

"I'm really hoping the expansion will allow me to focus solely on the ranch. But I need some exposure to make that happen."

"And exposure is exactly what we're gonna get you. I've thought of a few options beyond just the booth. How about offering pony rides for the kids? I'll bet that would be popular. You could hand out brochures to the parents. Or you could offer a training demonstration of some kind." Lisa chuckled. "I have no idea what that would look like as I have zero experience with horses, but maybe you have some thoughts."

Charlotte found herself relaxing as the two of them tossed ideas around. Periodically she glanced around the room, spotting photos of Gavin and Cooper at various ages. There was one of Gavin and the family on the day he graduated high school. A young Laurel was smiling at his side in that photo. A picture on the mantel featured a shirtless Cooper in his early teenage years, holding a big fish. Avery photobombed him with a cheesy grin and crossed eyes.

What would it have been like growing up in this family? Charlotte's dad had been gone so much. And even when he was home, things were never great between Mom and him. If her mother had told the truth years ago, would Lisa and Jeff have welcomed her into their fold?

Guilt pricked hard. Charlotte had had great parents and a sister she adored. How could she wish for anything more?

Giving her head a hard shake, she turned her attention back to Lisa, and after a while they settled on a plan. Charlotte would have a booth—hopefully operated by her sister. And she and Gunner would run an exhibition twice a day, much like the one they'd do for the grand opening. Because it was an actual event that would draw a crowd, Lisa insisted the exhibition wouldn't cost anything. Charlotte decided to save the pony rides for when they actually offered lessons.

She was finishing the paperwork when Jeff Robinson peeked into the room. "Honey, just letting you know I'm firing up the grill."

"Is it that time already? Sweetheart, come meet Charlotte. Gavin and Wes are building a barn on her ranch."

"The Stables at Wildflower Falls. I've heard all about it."

"Right." Charlotte stood and shook the man's hand when he neared. He appeared to have had blond hair once upon a time, but it had grayed and receded a bit. He had wide-set green eyes like his daughter, Avery. "It's nice to meet you."

"Emma couldn't stop talking about riding your horse yesterday."

"She did really well. Wasn't one bit scared."

"Fear isn't part of her vocabulary," Lisa said. "She's an adventurous one."

"Nothing wrong with that."

When Jeff slipped from the room, Charlotte grabbed her purse. She couldn't believe it was almost five. Where had the time gone? "Well, I should be going. Lisa, thank you so much for brainstorming with me. I think Trail Days will be a good fit for my ranch."

Lisa set a hand on her arm. "Oh, don't go just

yet. Stay for a burger. It won't take long to cook them, and you can meet the rest of the family."

Charlotte's pulse raced. The rest of the family was coming for supper? How could she turn down the opportunity to have dinner with the whole Robinson clan?

Sixteen

Charlotte regarded Lisa's genuine smile. "I think I've already met the whole family."

"That settles it then. You'll stay. But don't let them pull you into their cornhole rivalry. Those kids are so competitive."

"I've never even played cornhole."

"They'll probably drag you into it anyway. I'll show you the way. I have a salad to toss."

"Let me help you. I'm not much of a cook, but I can definitely slice a tomato."

"Well, that's an offer I can't refuse."

The "kids" arrived almost on top of each other. Cooper and Katie came first and they barely had a chance to introduce their one-year-old son, Quinn, to Charlotte before Gavin and Laurel showed up with Emma and—surprise—Gunner.

Charlotte gave a helpless shrug as their gazes met over the kitchen island.

The party trickled into the backyard just as Avery and Wes arrived. Suddenly the yard was filled with laughter and teasing, and the smell of grilling burgers wafted in the air, making Charlotte's stomach rumble.

She helped Lisa and Katie set up the meal on the patio. When they finished, Emma was pushing Quinn in the baby swing and a game of cornhole was breaking out. Charlotte was invited to partner with Avery, and they took on Gavin and Gunner.

There was so much banter throughout the game that Charlotte could hardly keep track of the score. But Avery and Gavin had that well in hand. The other three were practically professional—if there was such a thing. Charlotte's final turn gave Avery and her one last chance to win, but she failed to score the three points necessary.

"Sorry, Avery. I'm nowhere near your guys' league."

"It was fun anyway. And I hope the two of them take down Cooper and Wes. They've been on a winning streak lately, and frankly they need to come down a notch or two."

"Come and get it!" Jeff called a few minutes later, and the group gathered around the two picnic tables.

Charlotte found herself seated between Lisa and Avery and across from Gunner and Cooper. Lisa offered up grace, then the family dug in like they hadn't eaten in a week. Conversation flowed freely like water over a fall. Charlotte must've looked like the proverbial dog watching a tennis match. She could hardly keep up with the stories and zingers.

Lisa kindly explained some of the backstory to Charlotte and Gunner when conversation allowed, but mostly it just pinged back and forth. At one point she met Gunner's gaze across the table and they shared a secret smile.

The food was delicious and Charlotte felt a little guilty for leaving Emerson on her own once again. But her sister was still distant, and Charlotte was tired of the tension. This was a much more enjoyable way to spend the evening.

Guilt jabbed her again. She loved Emerson so much. Another family could never replace what she had with her sister. But the Robinsons were warm and fun, and Charlotte could use a little of that in her life. Especially with Emerson being gone so much.

As the meal wound down, Cooper's words cut through the conversation. "You look kind of familiar." He tilted his head as he studied Charlotte. "I mean, I know we ran into you at the Trailhead a few weeks ago, but it seems like we'd actually met before that."

Charlotte's cheeks flooded with heat at the memory. "You, um, pulled me over a couple years ago down on Mill Creek Road."

Cooper rubbed the back of his neck. "Oh. That must be it."

"Way to go, honey. That's not uncomfortable at all." Katie chuckled, then glanced at Charlotte. "Please tell me he didn't give you a ticket."

She decided to go all in. "No—it might've been the tears that did the trick."

Katie swatted her husband. "Honey. You made her cry?"

He winced. "Whoops."

"It wasn't his fault. I was just having a terrible day. Vince, my boyfriend of two years, decided to move out of state with no warning whatsoever. Then lucky me, I got pulled over on the way home and spilled my guts to the poor guy in uniform."

"Yeesh," Cooper said. "It's all coming back now. Sorry to have added to your bad day."

"To be fair, I was going fourteen miles over. I deserved a ticket and you were very kind about my blubbering."

"You poor thing," Lisa said. "What an awful thing for your boyfriend to do."

Charlotte had wanted to kill him. No, that was too harsh. Maybe just an itchy rash. With pus and scabbing.

"If a guy can't see what he's got in you," Avery said, "and Riverbend for that matter, he doesn't deserve either of you."

"Hear, hear." Wes slipped an arm around Avery. "I tried leaving but I just couldn't do it. I know a good thing when I see it."

"Aw . . . thanks, honey." Avery gave him a peck on the lips.

All of them seemed to have such great relationships. It made her long for that kind of connection with someone.

She glanced at Gunner and found him staring back. Their gazes caught and clung. Tension vibrated between them like a live wire. She was so attracted to him. Because, well, he was attractive. But she also admired his gentle way with the horses. His patience with their guests. He had a quiet confidence that appealed to her. So different from Vince.

She recalled the way he'd come to her rescue this week and his protective stance upon finding that man who'd stopped to "help." There was much to admire in him.

But even as she had the thought, she remembered the man she'd been discussing less than a minute ago. She'd thought Vince was great too. And he'd left her high and dry for an opportunity elsewhere. Gunner would do the same. He'd been perfectly clear about his temporary presence.

"I rode a horsey, Uncle Cooper. Didn't I, Mom?"

"You sure did." Laurel addressed the family at large. "Charlotte was kind enough to let Emma take one of her horses for a spin around the pen."

"Hossey!" Quinn said.

Cooper ruffled his son's brown hair. "I think we're gonna wait awhile on that, buddy."

"He's welcome to come over sometime. Our ponies are really good with the little ones."

"Oh, we don't want to impose," Katie said. "You're a busy woman."

"It wouldn't be any trouble at all. He could even come with Emma if he wanted to. I'm pretty sure she won't be able to stay away."

Gavin chuckled. "I'm afraid you might be right about that. It's all she can talk about."

"Or at the very least you should bring Quinn for our grand opening. We'll have pony rides in the afternoon. But even if you don't want him to ride, I'm sure he'd love seeing them."

"We'll definitely come out for that," Katie said. "He would love seeing the horses, and we want to support your business."

Charlotte's heart melted. "Thank you. That's very kind."

"The mayor's even coming out for a ribbon cutting," Gunner said.

"How exciting." Jeff beamed. "Sounds like you're gonna have a good crowd. Lisa and I will definitely be there."

"Us too, of course," Gavin added.

Laurel nudged his side. "He wants to take credit for your beautiful barn."

"As well he should." Charlotte tried to keep her voice level, though her emotions nearly choked off her words. Was this what it was like to have a big, loving family? The whole clan was coming to support her and they barely knew her.

But that was changing fast. In record time she'd met the entire family, and they were welcoming her into their lives.

This was getting a little out of hand. She'd only meant to get to know Gavin a bit—to see if he might make room in his life for her. But she was becoming pretty wrapped up in their whole family. When they discovered her secret, would it seem as if she'd wormed her way in?

Once Lisa learned who Charlotte was, she was bound to have some reservations just because Craig Burton had cheated on her with Charlotte's mom. Charlotte was the unwelcome result of that affair.

Jeff also might resent her—a surprise offspring from Lisa's first husband. Sure, he'd come to accept Gavin and Cooper, but they'd been children and part of the package deal.

And her biological siblings . . . they'd probably think she'd manipulated them into relationships with her. And it was somewhat true—she had hired Robinson Construction partly as a way to get acquainted with Gavin. Maybe she'd gone about this all wrong. Maybe she really was an awful person.

Gunner's gaze sharpened on Charlotte's face. One minute she'd been smiling and chatting, and the next her expression wilted, her eyes darted around, and her cheeks flushed.

He wasn't sure what had happened, but her demeanor reminded him of a horse backed into a corner. She seemed in need of escape.

He set his napkin on his empty plate. "Hey, Charlotte, would you mind giving me a lift to your place? I wanted to check on Midnight one more time before it gets too late."

Her gaze fastened on him. "Um, no, that's fine. Let me help clear the table, then we can be on our way."

"Nonsense, you're a guest." Lisa winked. "But next time I'll put you to work."

"She actually means that," Gavin said.

Charlotte's smile didn't reach her eyes. "Are you sure? I don't mind helping."

"Of course. I'll be in touch to finalize the details for Trail Days. But I won't bother you about that till after your grand opening. You've got plenty on your plate for now."

Charlotte and Gunner thanked the family, said their goodbyes, and made their way around the house toward Charlotte's vehicle.

"You okay?" Gunner asked once they were belted in. "You seemed a little overwhelmed back there."

She huffed. "It's a curse. I can't have a thought without broadcasting it on my face."

"Not at all. I don't think they noticed anything was amiss. I thought the meal went great. They really like you."

Charlotte made a three-point turn and headed down the long gravel drive. "What if that changes when they find out who I am? I don't want to hurt

172

anybody. Maybe I should just keep this skeleton in the closet."

"Is that what you want?"

"I don't know anymore."

"If that were an option for you, I think you would've already gone that route. Something in you needs to know the truth."

"But I do know the truth."

"Is just knowing enough?"

"No," she blurted. Her hands tightened on the steering wheel. "But maybe it should be. This could cause Lisa considerable grief. She probably doesn't know her ex-husband was unfaithful. And that kind of discovery might be a real bomb-shell for Gavin and Cooper too. It could ruin their relationship with their father."

"If they even have one with him."

"Well, that news certainly won't help."

Charlotte turned onto the road and accelerated. He gave her a minute to absorb everything they'd said. "The Robinsons seem well adjusted. Like the kind of people who could learn something unsettling and be strong enough to come to grips with it."

"Maybe."

"And you can't overlook your own needs. You have a right to know who your biological father is. In the end even your mother agreed with that—she wouldn't have left you the information otherwise."

Charlotte was quiet for a minute as she navigated through town and drove out the other side. "What if they think I tried to connive my way into their family? All I was trying to do was feel out Gavin, see if he'd be the kind of person who'd want to know he had a secret sister. But now it seems like I've become tangled up with the whole family!"

"You've gotten tangled up because they're very welcoming people. And if they give you half a chance, they'll get to know you and see that your motives were pure."

She blinked rapidly in response.

Gunner turned to stare out the window at the passing scenery, giving her a little privacy. If the Robinsons reacted negatively to Charlotte's secret, he wouldn't sit by and let them make her feel bad.

A few minutes later she turned into the ranch and proceeded up the drive. Twilight draped over the rolling pasture, and the moon hung over the silhouetted mountaintop. She'd been awfully quiet the past few minutes.

When she pulled up to the barn, she shut off the engine.

"Sorry if I spoke out of turn. I don't normally jump into other people's business like that."

She slid him a sideways glance. "Let's face it, I invited you into my business. And to be honest, it's nice to talk about it with someone.

174

My sister—she doesn't understand. And my best friend, Brianna, has a lot going on right now with her grandma. I don't want to burden her with this."

"Well, it's no burden to me. I don't mind being a sounding board." He removed his buckle. "Or keeping you company if you still want to head down to Weaverville tomorrow night."

She gave a long sigh and stared out the windshield as if she might find answers out there somewhere. "I still want to see if it's him. I still want to find him. Does that make me selfish?" She turned to find him in the dimness of the cab.

"You couldn't be selfish if you tried, Charlie."

Her lips lifted in a grin that went wider as their gazes held.

"What? What's that look for?"

"No one's ever called me Charlie before."

He hadn't realized he'd done that. But now that she mentioned it . . . he had been thinking of her by that name sometimes. When he thought of her. And that happened more often than he cared to admit.

He opened his mouth to apologize for the informality.

"I kinda like it," she said. Then without another word she exited the vehicle.

Seventeen

Charlotte twisted the seat belt's shoulder strap. Her palms grew sweatier with each mile. Was she about to meet her biological father? What would he think of her? Maybe she should've worn something nicer than a scoop-neck tee and jeans. She'd been thinking *comfort*—and heaven knew she could use that about now—but maybe she should've been thinking about making a good impression.

"Doing all right over there?" Gunner asked from behind the wheel. When he'd noticed how nervous she was, he offered to drive.

"I feel sick to my stomach."

"Should I pull over?"

"No. I've been anticipating this for days, and I just want to get it over with. It probably won't even be Craig working the register."

"Is that what you're hoping for?"

She gave him a wobbly smile. "I have no idea." She'd been praying about this ever since she'd seen his name in the newspaper. *I could really use Your help. Copy that, God?*

"I noticed you got a new tire," he said as they passed the spot where she'd broken down.

"It didn't set me back too much." Still, it was an expense she hadn't counted on. She really needed business to pick up, but she was doing all she could to get the word out about the grand opening. "How's it going with Midnight?"

"He's coming around a bit. But he's still a loner where the other horses are concerned."

"Maybe they just need to earn his trust. It'll take some time."

"He may have been rejected by his last herd—or maybe he just prefers being alone."

"Everybody needs somebody."

"Not necessarily."

At the odd note in his voice, she glanced his way. But his expression gave nothing away.

"As long as he can trust a human enough to be his leader, he'll make a good workhorse. That might be as much of a bond as he'll ever make."

Charlotte frowned. "That sounds like a sad way to live."

"Maybe he prefers it that way."

She wasn't sure if they were talking about him or Midnight. But Gunner had made it clear he preferred a nomadic lifestyle. Was that just the way he was built, or did something happen to make him that way? And how did a person go through this life all alone? She couldn't even imagine. Didn't he get lonely? Were shallow friendships enough for him?

She gave her head a shake. What did Gunner's lifestyle matter to her? He was temporary. A stop-gap. Her only concern should be how she would find another trainer with his skills when he left.

They entered the town of Weaverville, and Charlotte's pulse quickened even as Gunner slowed the truck. There just ahead was the gas station from the article. She squeezed the shoulder strap.

He pulled into the gas station. "Ready for this?"

"I'm not sure."

"Want me to stay in the truck while you go inside?"

"Um . . ." What did she want? And what was she gonna say again? She couldn't seem to string two thoughts together.

"I can go with you. Or I can turn the truck around and we can head back to Riverbend. Whatever you want."

"No, let's do this. Come in with me." He might have to catch her if her legs melted beneath her.

"Sure thing." He parked, then came around to her side and opened her door.

Her legs felt like stilts as they walked the short distance to the old-fashioned gas station and garage.

Gunner held open the door and a bell tinkled as she entered. She located the counter but couldn't see who managed the register for all the items on display around it.

Gunner took her arm and steered her deeper into the store toward the candy aisle.

"Hi there," a male voice called.

"Hello," Gunner said.

Then Charlotte caught sight of the man behind the point-of-purchase display. The heavily bearded guy couldn't have been a day over thirty-five. Her insides wilted like a desert-worn plant.

Gunner stopped in the middle of the candy aisle.

Charlotte couldn't think beyond the horrible sinking sensation. She didn't see anything, hear anything. But the weight of Gunner's hand at the small of her back grounded her. Offered comfort.

And that small, stupid thing made her eyes sting. She pulled in a shallow breath. "I want to go."

"All right. I'm gonna grab a couple things. Will you be okay?"

"Yes."

"I'll meet you in the truck."

"Okay." Charlotte made a beeline for the door and reached the outside before the tears spilled over.

Gunner made a couple of selections and headed toward the counter. His heart broke for Charlotte. Her disappointment had been evident in the slump of her shoulders, in the downward tilt to her eyes. He couldn't even imagine what she was going through. But he wanted to help her through it.

He set the items on the counter.

"This it?" the cashier asked.

"Yep."

The cashier scanned the items. "Six forty-two."

Gunner slipped his card into the machine. "Is Craig working tonight by any chance?"

"He only works during garage hours, nine to five."

"Okay, thanks." Gunner pulled his card.

"Need a bag?"

"No thanks. Have a good evening."

"You too."

Gunner exited the store and headed around the truck.

Behind the passenger window Charlotte swiped at her face.

His gut clenched. She was a wonderful person. Had such a sweet spirit about her. He hated that she was hurting. He would help her find her father if it was the last thing he did. She deserved to have people in her life who loved her. And heaven help the man if he did anything to hurt her.

Gunner got inside the vehicle and started it. He handed her the bag of M&M's. "I know you like them. It's not a cure-all, but it's the closest thing they had."

She breathed out a laugh. "Sharing size. Thanks."

He pulled from the station and headed back toward Riverbend. "Sorry it didn't work out the way you wanted it to."

"I'm being silly. I don't know why it hit me so hard. This isn't even a setback really."

"You're allowed to be disappointed. This is big stuff, Charlie. Your biological parents are a huge part of who you are—even if you've never met one of them."

"It's true, but you know what? I don't have the time or the emotional reserves to deal with all this right now. I think I'll just put it on hold until after the grand opening. Maybe a little longer. Until the expansion is up and running well. Until I have the headspace to deal with it."

"Okay . . . So if I happened to mention your dad's name to the clerk, would you want to know what he said?"

She whipped her head around. "What did you say? What did he say?"

"I asked if Craig was working. He said he works garage hours, nine to five."

"He's a mechanic then?"

"That was my assumption."

Charlotte stared out the window. "Huh. Kind of funny that I had a vehicle malfunction on the way to meet him the first time—if he even is my father."

"Also funny that you're pretty mechanically inclined yourself."

She tilted a smile his way, staring at him with a faraway look in her eyes. "Yeah. Kinda funny." She turned back to the landscape rolling past. A few minutes later she spoke again. "I still think I'm gonna put this on hold a bit. But thank you for coming with me tonight. I feel a little better now."

That one little sentence was all it took to buoy his spirits. "Good enough to share a pizza with me?"

"Do I get to pick the place?"

He would've agreed to a plate of straw right now if that would've made her happy. "Be my guest."

Eighteen

The restaurant Charlotte chose was outside of Riverbend and somewhat of a dive. But their deep-dish pizza could make a girl forget her troubles. The delicious aroma of yeast and garlic was enough to soothe her soul.

The place was pretty empty being a Monday night, but the workers in the kitchen bustled about, probably preparing to-go and delivery orders. The sounds of eighties music filled the space. Faux-wood tables, topped with jars of parmesan cheese and red pepper flakes, dotted the open room.

Charlotte and Gunner had settled into one of the cracked red leather booths lining the far wall. A short distance away, an open doorway led to a poolroom. They'd ordered their pizza a while ago and talked about everything from the horses to the grand opening to all the locations where Gunner had lived.

When the cute twentysomething server stopped by to refill their drinks, her gaze lingered on Gunner. But he didn't seem to notice her appraisal.

"Where's the one place you've always wanted to live?" Charlotte asked once the server left.

"I don't know if there is any one place. I'm

enjoying the mountains for now. Those curvy roads are a lot of fun on my bike."

Charlotte shook her head. "You and that bike."

"Have you ridden before?"

"I prefer the four-legged kind, thank you very much."

"That's only because you haven't experienced my bike. I'll take you out sometime and you'll see what you're missing."

The idea of wrapping her arms around him on that bike was all too appealing. Her face heated and she ducked her head under the guise of sipping from her straw.

Fortunately the server delivered their pizza just then. "Is there anything else I can get you?" she asked Gunner after she'd set down the steaming-hot pie.

"I think we're all set." He eyed the thick layer of cheese and golden-brown crust as the server sauntered away. "This looks delicious."

"I promise it won't disappoint. I don't make it over here very often, but when I do, all thoughts of calories fly right out the window."

Quiet reigned while they went to work on the pizza.

Fifteen minutes later Charlotte tossed her greasy napkin on her plate and leaned back in the booth with a satiated sigh.

"You're not giving up, are you? There's one more slice."

"It's all yours. I'm stuffed."

"I didn't realize how hungry I was."

"Same here." It was hard to believe that less than an hour ago, she'd been sad and disappointed. The good conversation and food had turned her mood around. But who was she kidding? It wasn't the pizza—as yummy as it had been.

Gunner just had that effect on her. With Emerson, Charlotte always felt she had to be the big sister. And Brianna was going through so much these days, she was often the sounding board and encourager. She didn't mind either role. But sometimes it was nice to just relax and not have a designated job in the relationship.

A strange thought since she was actually Gunner's boss. But he was so self-sufficient on the job it was easy to forget that. She almost never had to give him direction; he just saw what needed to be done and did it.

"I feel so much better," she said.

"Well, I hate to put an end to your good mood, but I'm afraid it's time for me to beat you in a game of pool."

She raised an eyebrow. "Oh, really?"

"It was bound to happen eventually. Might as well just get it over with. Have you played before?"

"A few times. But maybe you could give me some pointers before you clean the floor with me."

"I'm a fair guy. Happy to level the playing field a bit."

She rolled her eyes but followed him into the poolroom, which was as empty as the restaurant. She'd never seen this playful, cocky side of him. She didn't even mind as she sensed he only wanted to cheer her up.

She grabbed a random pool cue from the rack on the wall.

"Hang on now," he said. "Let's make sure it's not warped. Roll it across the table like this. It should roll nice and smooth."

Charlotte did so with her cue and ended up putting it back. The second one was better.

He winked as he racked up the balls. "Wouldn't want an unfair advantage."

"That would just be wrong."

"Would you rather I broke?"

"I'll give it a try." Once he removed the triangle she bent over the table, braced her hand on the green felt, and blinked up at him innocently. "Like this?"

"Wait a minute." Gunner moved toward her, then got close. "Move this hand forward. Spread your fingers like this. That's it. Now take the cue and hold it—yeah, like that. Now, what you want is a nice, steady glide, like this." He edged up behind her, leading her through the motion. "Aim for the center ball. You'll have to give it a nice, confident whack if you want a good break."

Charlotte hardly followed a word he said. She was too distracted by the heat against her back, the feel of his hand over hers, and the tickle of his breath at her temple. The sensations crowded out every rational thought. A scent she'd come to associate with him—just a hint of leather and spice—wove around her like a spell, making her dizzy. She turned her head to breathe him in again.

And there he was. So close. His breath stirred the hair at her temple, and his gaze locked on hers as they froze.

One heartbeat.

Two.

Amber flecks glinted in his green eyes. Mesmerizing. How had she not noticed them before? Or that little bump on the left side of his nose? Or the way his shadow of a mustache followed the ridge of his upper lip so precisely?

And then she was leaning closer to those lovely lips. Closer to that tempting scent. Her eyes fell closed. Their breath mingled, warm and sultry. She could almost taste him.

A rush of cold air made her eyes snap open.

He cleared his throat.

Charlotte leaned over her pool cue like that's what she'd meant to do all along. Because yes. She was breaking the balls. Of course.

Not trying to kiss *her employee.* She squeezed her eyes shut.

Then she sucked in a breath and blew it out.

Leveled up the stick, brought her arm back, and swung it forward with plenty of force. Despite her distraction the cue ball struck its target. Balls scattered in all directions, and two stripes sank into the corner and side pockets.

Gunner absently rubbed his stomach. What was he doing? He'd been a breath away from *kissing his boss.* She'd been so tempting, those heavy-lidded eyes taking him in like that. Staring at his mouth, for crying out loud. He knew a green light when he saw one.

And he'd wanted to take her up on it. Nearly had. By sheer luck he'd remembered just in the nick of time exactly who he was about to kiss. Every nerve cell in his body suffered a massive letdown.

So close. Yet so far. He must be getting lonely. It happened from time to time. But usually the acquaintances he made along the way scratched that itch. But since arriving in Riverbend, he hadn't met any interesting women. Other than Charlotte, that was.

Speaking of Charlotte . . . She was carrying on as if nothing had happened, and the silence had grown awkward. He definitely should say . . . something.

He stepped toward the table. "Hey, listen. I'm sorry. I shouldn't have done that. You're my boss—that's never a good idea."

She assessed the table. "You're absolutely right."

"Besides that, you've had a rough night and I shouldn't have—"

"Excuse me."

He backed away as Charlotte took his spot, leaned over the rail.

He'd somehow missed her break—a good one, it seemed like. She'd sunk . . . two balls, both stripes. Quite the lucky break.

A solid *whack* sent the cue ball across the table. It kissed a stripe and the ball sank in the side pocket.

Or maybe not so lucky.

She took her time chalking up her cue, then blew off the extra dust before she slid him an amused look, those green eyes twinkling at him.

Nineteen

From the shadowed window of the barn, Charlotte watched Gunner lead Falcon around the pen on the lunge line. The gelding would be boarding with them once the new stable was complete, and the owner asked Gunner to work with him.

Charlotte's routine had been the same the past few weeks, but a new invisible boundary arose between Gunner and her. When they talked it was cordial and they stuck to business. He obviously felt a closer relationship was ill-advised—as was another game of pool with her. She'd beaten him that night, despite her lack of focus.

But every second they spent feeding the horses and mucking out the stalls, she was aware of his presence. Aware of the way his shoulders contracted under the weight of hay bales. Aware of the snug fit of his jeans over his thick thigh muscles. The trickle of sweat sliding down the back of his neck.

He couldn't come near without her pulse racing and her heart leaping in her chest. And no amount of warning herself of the consequences seemed to help. She was flat-out attracted to him.

Yet she couldn't have him. Both of those things were true, and the sooner Charlotte accepted that the better. For the umpteenth time she mulled over her options. Two of them, as far as she could tell: continuing on as she was, driving herself crazy with wanting more, or firing the man.

The first option was becoming difficult and the second was unfair. Gunner was doing a great job, managing both the training position and the increasing reservations of trail groups with ease.

Besides, she'd never find another trainer on such short notice. And with the grand opening just around the corner, she couldn't afford to be short-staffed. Plus, it would be bad management—and possibly illegal—to fire a perfectly good trainer just because she couldn't control herself. He'd become so invaluable on the ranch that she feared she'd be unable to replace him even when the time came, certainly not for the meager pay she offered.

But that worry was for another day.

For now she had to figure out how she would get over her little crush on Gunner. Because yes, that's what she'd decided to call it. These couldn't be real feelings as she'd known him less than two months. They hadn't even shared a meaningful touch.

So, yes, definitely just a crush.

"Hey, Charlotte."

She jumped away from the window, clutching at her chest.

Kyle Lemmings chuckled as he strode into the barn. "Sorry, I didn't mean to startle you."

"I guess I was lost in thought. Thanks for coming out. I didn't realize Rogue hadn't had his rabies vaccine until I was going over his records the other day."

"No worries. I always enjoy stopping out here." He greeted Rogue, then set his bag down outside the stall. "Almost ready for your grand opening?"

"As ready as we can be. The new stable looks amazing. We'll be ready to move our horses over in a few days. That's why I was going over their vaccination records."

"Good move. I'll double-check and make sure they're all up-to-date."

"Thanks."

He prepared the vaccine and entered the stall. Rogue warmed up to him quickly. It was obvious Kyle cared about the animals he treated. He took a few minutes after the shot to give the gelding some attention.

She didn't know Kyle well outside of their professional relationship, but he seemed like a good man. He had a dependable job he excelled at, and like her, he was born and raised here in Riverbend. He was rooted here and he was attractive for an older man.

Plus, he'd already asked her on a date.

"Everything okay?" Kyle asked.

He'd caught her staring. Her face warmed.

"Um, yes, of course. I was just . . ." *Just go for it, Charlotte.* "I was wondering if you'd still be up for that meal. The one you mentioned before. Italian. Or it doesn't have to be Italian, I just meant . . ." She rubbed her forehead. What had she meant?

Kyle's dark-brown eyes sparkled. "I'd love that. If you're sure you've got the time."

She had the time to ogle her trainer, so . . . "No. I mean yes, I have the time. A bit of fun right now would actually hit the spot."

"All right then." Kyle beamed, revealing brackets at the corners of his mouth. She'd never noticed what a nice smile he had.

"Is tomorrow night too soon?"

"Tomorrow night is perfect. Pick you up at six?"

"Sounds good."

"All right. I'll see you then, Charlotte." He touched the brim of his cap.

"See you." She watched him stride from the barn. *See, Charlotte? You just have to give the guy a chance.*

Twenty

He was going to get through to this horse if it was the last thing he did. Gunner mixed some oats and honey and walked it over to Midnight's stall.

His chores were done for the night. He'd put in a full day and the horses were stabled. Midnight stared at him from across the stall and tossed his head.

Though the horse had plenty of company on the ranch, he felt alone. He'd lost his home, his companions, and any faith in a hopeful future. Gunner hoped to change that.

"I know how you feel, buddy." He kept his voice soft and his tone low. "But I brought something you like." He'd learned over the past few weeks that while Midnight liked carrots, he *loved* oats and honey. Gunner held the pail over the stall door. "It's your favorite. But if you want it, you have to come all the way over here."

Midnight snorted.

"I've got all the time in the world, big guy. You do realize your friends would be all over this, right? But hey, take your time. I'm not going anywhere."

The black gelding stared at Gunner as if appraising his trustworthiness.

"I've been here every morning and every night,

haven't I? I've kept you fed and taken care of all your needs—we don't need to talk about that incident with the farrier. Granted, that was a mistake. But we've come a long way since then, haven't we?" He lifted the pail. "What do you say? Come have a treat. You know I won't hurt you."

Holding Gunner's gaze, Midnight took a step forward.

"That's it. Good boy."

The horse took another step. And another, within reach of the pail now.

"Good boy, Midnight," he crooned. "Good boy."

Midnight stuck his nose in the bucket and went to work on the oats, snuffling his way through the mixture.

"Isn't it good?" Gunner maintained pressure on the bucket until Midnight pulled his nose out and licked his chops. He set the empty pail at his feet and leaned on the stall door. "See, that wasn't so bad, was it? You got your treat and nothing bad happened. When will you figure out you can trust me, huh?"

Midnight turned in the stall, giving Gunner his backside.

He chuckled. "You're a stubborn one, I'll give you that. But guess what, fella? You've just met your match."

The sound of an engine carried into the barn.

Kyle Lemmings's truck passed the barn and headed for the house. Had Charlotte called the vet with a problem? Gunner wasn't aware of anything that needed the man's attention. He went two stalls down to check on Rogue, who'd been vaccinated yesterday.

The horse neighed and moseyed over to the stall door to greet him.

"How you feeling, Rogue?"

Gunner checked the vaccination site. No swelling. The horse was alert, and there were no signs of fever like sweating or shivering. In short, he seemed his usual curious self.

Gunner gave him a few good strokes. "You're doing all right, buddy." He gave the horse a final pat and headed toward the barn door. Maybe Kyle just came to check up on Rogue.

But when Gunner neared the barn door he stopped short. Kyle escorted Charlotte down the porch steps. Her hair fell in golden-red waves around her shoulders, and a grass-green dress fluttered about her legs.

Gunner pulled back into the barn. Charlotte was going on a date with the vet? How long had this been going on?

Sure, he'd known Kyle carried a torch for Charlotte—a blind bat could've seen that. But he hadn't realized the feelings were mutual. Only a few weeks ago Charlotte had been leaning toward him, those delectable lips just centimeters away.

But it seemed Kyle might be the one getting a good-night kiss tonight.

Gunner pushed the thought away. Since that night in the poolroom, he and Charlotte had maintained an appropriate distance. He'd even congratulated himself on the excellent comeback. Though, yes, he'd had moments when he couldn't help but notice the sunlight glinting off her hair or stop staring at those tempting freckles dotting her shoulders. But overall, he'd been pleased with his restraint.

Kyle's truck revved to life, and Gunner pulled back into the shadows of the barn as the vehicle passed. A cloud of smoke bloomed behind the man's truck as it headed back down the drive.

Charlotte and Kyle.

Gunner pressed his lips together. This was for the best. He couldn't offer her a future, and she deserved that with someone else. She was the settling down kind of woman. The picket fence and family kind of girl.

He believed that with all his heart. But if that was so, why had his stomach sunk somewhere in the vicinity of his bootheels? And why did the promise of a free Friday evening only make him feel lonely?

Fifteen minutes later Gunner pulled into the driveway he shared with Mr. Dixon. The grass was still long and his landlord had said he would mow today. But it had been hot and maybe he'd decided to put it off.

Gunner spied the riding mower in the side yard. The back half of the property had been mowed. The man had seemingly stopped right in the middle of the task. Maybe the mower had broken down. It was probably nothing, but maybe Gunner should check on the man.

He pulled back to the main house, turned off his bike, and took the porch steps as he removed his helmet. The screen door thumped in the frame as Gunner knocked.

"Mr. Dixon," he called when the man didn't answer after two knocks. "It's Gunner. Everything all right?"

He listened for a response but none came. The man's rusty old GMC sat in the drive. He had to be around here somewhere. He tried the screen door and found it unlocked.

"Mr. Dixon?" The house was quiet except for the ticking of a clock. No lights were on. He wandered into the living room. A balding head showed over the back of the man's favorite recliner.

Maybe he was just a sound sleeper. Gunner strode forward. "Mr. Dixon?"

The man groaned.

Gunner knelt beside the chair. "What's going on? Are you hurt?"

Without opening his eyes he pointed a

trembling finger at a glass of spilled orange juice on the table beside him.

"You need something to drink?" Gunner grabbed the glass and took it to the kitchen. A half-empty jug of orange juice sat on the counter. It was still cold to the touch, so the man hadn't been out of commission too long. He poured a glass and returned to the living room, where he helped Mr. Dixon drink the juice.

After a few sips he roused a bit. His eyes fluttered open.

"I think we'd better get you over to the clinic, Mr. Dixon. Where are the keys to your truck?"

He gestured toward the entry table.

Gunner had passed the town clinic a couple of times, but it was a Friday evening and he wasn't sure what the clinic's hours were. He withdrew his phone, relieved he had a bit of battery left, and pulled up the number. He frowned when the recording kicked on. But the message gave an emergency number for after-hours calls. Gunner hung up and tapped out the number.

Mr. Dixon tried to lean forward, and Gunner stopped him with a hand on his arm. "You just rest a minute."

A woman answered the call. "This is Dr. Robinson. How can I help you?"

Robinson? He vaguely remembered hearing some medical talk at the Robinson cookout. "Is this Avery?"

"Yes . . ."

"This is Gunner Dawson. We met at a cookout at your parents' house a few weekends ago. I'm with my neighbor, Mr. Dixon. I just came home and found him barely responsive in his living room. Looked like he was mowing and stopped and came inside. I'm not sure what the trouble is. I gave him some orange juice, and he's coming around a bit."

"Is he a diabetic?"

"I don't know—Mr. Dixon, are you a diabetic?"

The man nodded.

"Yes, he is."

"Okay, Gunner. Why don't you bring him over to the clinic. I'll meet you there in fifteen minutes."

Twenty-One

Charlotte smiled her thanks as she stepped up into Kyle's truck's passenger side and allowed him to close the door. Relaxed and pleasantly full, she watched him round the front of the truck. The restaurant served authentic Italian food. They'd enjoyed the meal and conversation so much, they'd hung around for tiramisu.

Now it was almost dark and Charlotte was glad she'd taken a chance on Kyle. She hadn't thought of Gunner one time in the past two and a half hours. Okay, she'd thought of him once when Kyle had leaned forward and the candlelight brightened his dark-brown eyes. The memory of those mesmerizing flecks of amber in Gunner's eyes might have flashed in her mind for the briefest moment. But she shoved the memory away and focused on their conversation.

On the way home Kyle told her about the birthing of twin foals the spring before. He could spin a good yarn and kept her spellbound all the way to the ranch. It wasn't till they pulled up to the house that she started to worry. Would he try to kiss her good night? She wasn't ready for that, and hopefully he could tell. There had been no meaningful touches, moony gazes, or romantic hand-holding between them. Just friendly conversation.

Besides, he'd said earlier he was a patient man. She supposed she'd find out if that was true.

"You must be getting excited about your grand opening," he said as he walked her to the door.

Charlotte was glad Emerson's car was in the drive. She'd been going out late a lot. And also, having her here made things less awkward with Kyle. "Hard to believe it's just a week from tomorrow."

"I'm sure you've got it all in hand."

"The schedule's firmed up. *The Herald* is doing a write-up in Thursday's paper, and as long as Saturday's a slower news day, they'll be here to cover the event. When the ABC affiliate learned the mayor was coming, they said the same thing."

"Let's pray for a slow news day then."

"Amen." They reached her door. "Would you like to come in for coffee?"

Kyle turned toward her. "Thank you, but I have an early morning—and I don't want to wear out my welcome."

"You could never do such a thing. I had a good time, Kyle. Thank you for supper."

"It was my pleasure. I'd like to do it again sometime if you're agreeable."

"I'd like that."

He leaned in for a hug.

Charlotte returned the quick squeeze. "Maybe I'll see you around this week."

"If not, I'll definitely see you at your open house."

They said their goodbyes and Charlotte slipped inside.

From her favorite end of the sofa, Emerson glanced up from her novel. She looked comfortable in a pair of leggings and a teal tee. She'd thawed out a little in the past couple of weeks. Had even lent a hand around the ranch. Probably because Charlotte hadn't mentioned her biological family anymore. Emerson likely thought she'd decided to let it go permanently, and Charlotte wasn't willing to risk the truce by broaching the topic again.

"I thought you might have a date tonight." Charlotte plopped onto the recliner.

"I have to be at the bakery at five."

"How are things going there?"

"Vivian's been teaching me how to decorate cakes. It's a lot more fun than waiting on customers."

"That sounds right up your alley."

"I want to learn more about making the pastries too."

"Feel free to experiment at home."

"I always do." Emerson slid her feet to the floor. "I saw the schedule for the grand opening.

I can help with the kids' rides in the morning if you need extra help."

She was glad Em seemed to be coming around where the ranch was concerned. "What about the food?" Emerson was serving up burgers, baked beans, and chips for lunch.

"I'll have all that prepped. As long as I'm free by eleven, I'll be good." Emerson had roped a couple of friends into helping her.

"That would be great. Gunner will have his hands full with the pony rides, and I want to be on hand to chat with media and potential customers."

"Better you than me. So how was your date with the vet? I was ready to move upstairs and give you some privacy, but he didn't stick around long."

"I asked him in but he has an early morning too. The date was fun. Kyle's nice to talk to."

"How old is he anyway?"

"I don't know. I didn't ask."

"He's gotta be nearly forty. But he's kinda cute for an old guy. And the two of you have a lot in common."

"I'll say. We talked about animals most of the night."

Emerson gave a wry grin. "How romantic."

"There's nothing wrong with starting out as friends. Rushing into a relationship can be a mistake."

Emerson set her book aside, her gaze homing in on Charlotte's face. "Vince was a real jerk for leaving town like that. You deserved better."

Maybe she had, but there'd been red flags along the way. He had never loved Riverbend the way she did. He even mentioned wanting to escape small-town life. Charlotte just ignored those warnings. "Well, lesson learned the hard way. It's slow and cautious for me these days."

"Honestly, I'm surprised you went out with Kyle at all."

"He's not that old."

Emerson tilted her head and a little smirk emerged. "I'm talking about all that chemistry between you and Gunner."

Charlotte's cheeks heated. *"What?"*

Emerson rolled her eyes. "Please. You could put on a Fourth of July show with all the fireworks between you two."

She'd thought she'd been so discreet. "We're not—there's not—he's only here temporarily."

"So you keep saying. And yet . . ." Emerson fanned her face, smiling wickedly.

Charlotte started to protest, but Emerson slid Charlotte a teasing look as she stood. "I'm gonna go read in bed and save you from having to lie."

Charlotte opened her mouth.

"You know what they say about protesting too much. Good niiight," her sister called as she sauntered up the stairs.

Charlotte huffed. She had nothing. Her sister was right and they both knew it. "Good night," Charlotte said finally.

But her sister was already long gone.

Twenty-Two

The hike had hardly begun and beads of sweat already popped out on Gunner's arms. Humidity was a real thing in the South. He took a swig from his water bottle. A warm wind rustled through the treetops, and the French Broad River flowed beside the trail leading out of town. A group of tubers floated by on the current, whooping and hollering.

Wes had invited him along on the hike since his wife was tied up at the clinic today. Gunner had been eager to hit the trails for a while, but he'd been too busy with work and Mr. Dixon to find the time. And he had a feeling after the open house next weekend, he might be working six days a week.

"Enjoy this easy part," Wes said. "Once the switchbacks start, it's a considerable elevation gain to Lover's Leap."

"I'm glad we started early. You've got some hot summers here."

"It's just getting started. I'll admit it's taken some getting used to, but at least the winters are shorter and milder."

"Where are you from originally?" Gunner asked.

"You know, people think I'm prevaricating

when I say the Midwest, but I'm not. My dad and I moved around so much, there's no one place I call home. So I guess we have the vagabond lifestyle in common."

Gunner grinned. "You make that sound like a bad thing."

"When you never start and finish a school year in the same place, it can be a little hard to make friends or settle in."

"Maybe not the ideal lifestyle when you have a child in tow."

"Unfortunately my dad didn't consider that. But you like moving around a lot?"

"It's kind of my thing. I love to travel and I like the challenge new jobs offer."

"More power to you, man. I'm enjoying the settled life myself."

"What brought you to town—the job?" Robinson Construction seemed like a pretty good gig. The business was apparently thriving and Gavin appeared to be a good boss.

"Nah. I was hiking southbound on the Appalachian Trail and got sick. Avery found me on her clinic's porch basically passed out."

"That's how you met your future wife?"

"So much for a good first impression. I was sweating up a fever and stank to high heaven."

"I guess it didn't bother her any. What kept you around?"

"Have you seen my wife?" Wes slid him a droll

look. "Don't answer that—I'm a jealous man," he added lightly. "No, I offered to help her with some remodeling to pay off my medical bills, and I guess you could say the rest is history. I had other plans after that hike . . . but those flew right out the window when I fell for Avery."

"And now you're working for her brother."

"Technically we're partners now, but yeah."

"And your wife works with your sister-in-law?"

"It's a close-knit family."

"I guess so. I was actually at the clinic last night with my neighbor, Mr. Dixon. He had some kind of diabetic episode from rationing his insulin. Your wife was kind enough to help him out."

"I hear that stuff's expensive. He have any family around here?"

"His wife passed a few years ago and they never had any kids. I was worried about leaving him this morning. He said he wouldn't skimp on his meds anymore, but I don't think he can afford what he needs. If I hadn't found him yesterday, he could've died."

"Maybe there's some way to help him financially."

"I tried to pay for his insulin. He wouldn't let me, stubborn old coot. I wonder if there's some kind of fund he'd be eligible for. Or government assistance of some kind. It doesn't seem right he can't afford something he needs to live."

"Avery says there are a lot of people around

here in similar circumstances. They end up in emergency situations because of it. Especially the elderly on fixed incomes. Medicare doesn't cover everything."

Gunner wouldn't be here forever, and he hated the thought of Mr. Dixon being left to his own devices. The man reminded him of his grandfather. But his grandfather hadn't been poor and he'd had Gunner to care for him. Mr. Dixon seemed to have no one. "Maybe I could do a fundraiser or something. I wouldn't have a clue where to start though."

"You should talk to Lisa. She runs all kinds of events. If nothing else, she'd have some good ideas for you."

"That's a great idea. Thanks." Gunner wasn't one to get overly involved, but someone should look out for Mr. Dixon. And Lisa had seemed friendly enough, though she must have her hands full with Trail Days. He'd heard them talking about it at their cookout. Maybe she wouldn't mind if he picked her brain.

The path left the river and turned back to climb up the mountain. He welcomed the smell of pine and the forest's shade. A ground squirrel scampered through the dense undergrowth, and a robin tweeted from the canopy of an oak tree. He loved being out in the mountains. The trail rides took him into the forest, of course, but he had to keep his monologue going while also being mindful of his guests' safety. It didn't leave much time for enjoying nature.

"How do you like working at the ranch so far?" Wes asked a few minutes later. "Charlotte seems happy with your work."

"She's easy to work for." The image of her and Kyle popped into his mind. She'd looked so beautiful last night in that green dress, hair flowing around her shoulders. He wanted to be the one sweeping her off to some fancy restaurant. The one putting his arms around her on the dance floor. The one gazing into her eyes on her front porch just before he . . .

"Is my radar way off, or do I sense a little something going on between you two?"

Gunner cleared his throat. "With Charlotte? Nah. She actually went out with the vet last night." Had Kyle gazed into her eyes over a candlelit dinner? Had he been the one to give her that good-night kiss at her front door? Gunner clenched his jaw.

"You don't sound too happy about that."

"She's my boss. Never a good idea to mix business with pleasure. Besides, I won't be here long, and Charlotte's the kind of woman who wants to settle down."

"You don't?"

"I'm free as a bird and I like it that way." The familiar words rolled off his tongue, but they didn't feel as true as they once had.

"Yeah, well, take it from someone who knows. This town has a way of growing on you." He tossed Gunner a knowing grin. "If you're not careful, it'll suck you right in."

Twenty-Three

Please, oh, please don't let it rain. Why had she picked July, the second rainiest month of the year, for her open house?

Charlotte finished curling her hair and put in some small hoop earrings. She'd chosen a sundress since she'd probably be on the news and would certainly be in the ribbon-cutting photo. Even though last night's forecast predicted a sunny morning, the weather app now showed a 50 percent chance of thunderstorms.

She and Gunner had already fed and turned out most of the horses. They kept the ponies in for the free rides and also the two horses—on loan from a local ranch—that he'd do demonstrations with.

She glanced at the time. Mayor Hinkley and—fingers crossed—the media entourage would arrive soon. She dashed from her room and knocked on her sister's door. "Emerson? You ready? It's almost starting time and we both need to be in those photos. Emerson?"

Her sister opened the door. "Jeez, take it down a notch. We have plenty of time."

She scanned Emerson's outfit: a pair of jeans and a casual top. "You sure you don't want to dress up a bit?"

"I'm on pony-riding detail after the ribbon cutting, remember? You're the one giving the interviews. And you look great, by the way."

"Thanks. Sorry, I'm just a little on edge. Did you see the weather forecast?"

"It'll be fine. That's why we rented a tent, remember?"

She just didn't want anything to keep people away or to ruin their fun. Who'd want to watch a demonstration or have their kids ride ponies in the rain?

Thirty minutes later the mayor paused, scissors poised midcut, between Charlotte and Emerson. They smiled for the cameras belonging to two television stations, *The Herald*, and *Horse and Trail Magazine*. A crowd of about forty people, including the Robinsons, gathered around the new barn, waiting for the cutting. The mayor and Charlotte had each spoken briefly about the new expansion, and now it was time for the photo op.

Once Mayor Hinkley had given the photographers adequate time to capture the moment, he snipped the red ribbon and it fluttered to the ground.

The crowd cheered and the mayor turned to clasp Charlotte's hand in a firm grip. "Congratulations, young lady. It's a beautiful stable and I have no doubt I'll be sending some business your way."

"Thank you, Mayor. I appreciate your support more than you know."

While the mayor congratulated Emerson, Charlotte addressed the crowd. "Thank you all so much for coming out today. Be sure to head over to the round pen where our trainer, Gunner, is getting ready to do a Join-Up demonstration. You won't want to miss it. Afterward, stick around for the pony rides, and then lunch will be served from noon till two. We hope you enjoy your day here at the Stables at Wildflower Falls."

One at a time the reporters stopped by to interview her about the expansion. She credited Robinson Construction with the beautiful new stable and explained the new services the ranch would offer.

She spent about twenty minutes with the *Horse and Trail* reporter, a woman from Marshall who'd been raised around horses. She promised Charlotte a feature in September's edition. Charlotte wished it were being published earlier in the season, but she'd take what she could get.

When she finished the interviews, she glanced around the property in renewed wonder. Talking about the ranch had made her appreciate all over again how blessed she was to live and work where her ancestors had. What a wonderful inheritance. This was where she belonged. And *(please, God)* where she would always belong.

Kyle, who'd waited around for her, approached,

beaming. "Congratulations. Your grand opening is going very well. You're getting great coverage—and I loved your speech."

"Thanks. I'm just glad the weather's holding out." The sun had even peeked through the clouds. "That last reporter I talked to was from *Horse and Trail Magazine*. I've sent them several emails, but I didn't know they were coming."

"Perfect. That's your demographic."

"Isn't it great?" They headed toward the round pen where Gunner's demonstration was well underway. The fence around the pen was surrounded by people. "He's got a good crowd."

They stopped and watched as he continued his demonstration.

Gunner had Nutmeg trotting around the pen, spinning the rope behind her to keep her moving. "Nutmeg's doing pretty well," he said loudly. "She's following my direction." He moved to the horse's front and began spinning the rope. The filly turned and trotted the other way.

"Good girl," he said, then addressed the crowd again. "Some people think it's mean for humans to assert dominance. But horses are pack animals. Almost all of them want a leader, and a good leader has to be trustworthy. I've been building trust with Nutmeg for about"—he glanced at his watch—"thirty-five minutes now. And as you can see, she's coming around. See how her head and ears are turned my way? She's listening for my direction. That's a good sign she's on board with me."

He encouraged the horse as she trotted around the circle. "So what I'm gonna do now is give her an opportunity to show me how she feels about me. I'll stop what I'm doing and walk away from her. Let's find out how she responds."

A hush fell over the group as Gunner coiled his rope, turned away from the horse, and walked a few steps before he stopped.

Nutmeg slowed her trot, watching him.

The crowd murmured as she walked slowly toward Gunner. When she reached him, she nuzzled his neck with her nose.

The children exclaimed and the crowd applauded.

Beside Charlotte, Kyle joined the cheering. "That never fails to amaze me."

Smiling, Gunner turned to Nutmeg and stroked her face, murmuring softly to her.

Charlotte was so proud of Gunner that she beamed. The connection he'd made with the horse in such a short time was a credit to his skills. He had such a way with the horses. The audience obviously adored him too. He'd probably made half their guests want to go out and buy horses of their own.

Gunner spied her in the crowd, and their gazes clung for a moment. She hoped he could see how proud she was to have him on staff. He'd added so much to the ranch. So much to her life.

He gave her an almost imperceptible nod. Then looked away.

That's when she remembered to breathe. "It's truly magical."

Charlotte brushed down Ginger in the new stable. The scent of raw wood still hung in the air, now mixed with the smells of horseflesh and hay. The late-afternoon sun cut through the open doorway, flooding the open space with natural light.

"You did good today with the kiddos," she said to Ginger.

The dun mare's ears swiveled her way.

"You liked all the attention, didn't you? Yeah, I know you did."

The demonstrations were finished, the meal had been served, and the last riders had left the property. The grand opening had officially come to an end. Charlotte was still running on adrenaline.

She thought of the Robinsons' participation today, and her heart glowed warm. They'd stayed for all the events, and her niece and nephew had seemed to enjoy their pony rides. Charlotte had felt like she had a real family today, and it meant the world to her—even if they didn't know about their genetic connection to her.

Yes, today had been a great success, and with

the articles still to come, she was reasonably reassured that new business would follow. And *(listening, God?)* she could finally quit her job at the Trailhead and become a full-time rancher.

The clopping of hooves alerted her to Firefly's—and Gunner's—presence. He tossed Charlotte a grin as he began untacking the pony. "It was a good day."

"It *was* a good day." She chuckled. "It was such a whirlwind. And those Join-Ups were nothing short of enchanting. The spectators were in awe of you."

"You picked good horses. They don't always go that quickly or that smoothly."

"Tell me about it."

"Those kids really enjoyed their rides too. A lot of parents asked me about riding lessons."

Charlotte winced. "Quite a few asked me too. I'm starting to think I missed an opportunity."

He pulled the saddle from Firefly. "It's not too late to change your mind."

"But we missed the chance for sign-ups."

When he returned from the tack room, Gunner reached into his back pocket and handed her a slip of paper.

She unfolded it to find a list of names and numbers scrawled in pencil.

"I started a list just in case."

She blinked at him as something warm and wonderful unfurled in her chest. It was such a thoughtful gesture. "Thank you. There are at least fifteen names here."

"Imagine what you could do if you advertised it."

She pushed through the unexpected mushy feelings and forced herself to think practically. She loved the idea of another income stream. But time was the critical factor. Gunner was already swamped with his current workload, and Emerson wasn't interested in putting in more hours. "When will I find time to give lessons?"

He removed the last of the tack and began brushing down Firefly. "What if you gave up your other job? That would free up a lot of hours."

"Oh, I wish. Not that I dislike working at the Trailhead, but it was supposed to be a temporary gig, just until the ranch could be self-supporting. But it's dragged on like this for six years now."

He glanced at her over Firefly's back. "Maybe that time has finally come."

Could that be true? Her pulse raced at the thought. She'd need to run the numbers. Make sure she could make it work. At that point it would be an act of faith. She could trust God with this, couldn't she?

"Maybe you're right." Perhaps it was finally time to take off the training wheels and see if she could ride this bike.

Twenty-Four

The first Saturday of August sweltered with heat and humidity. Charlotte walked from the barn to the house thinking about the full day ahead. So much had happened in the five weeks since the grand opening. But most importantly, the news coverage and articles had done their jobs.

The names on that list Gunner made for riding lessons had panned out. And after working the numbers she finally bit the bullet: she gave her two-week notice at the Trailhead. On her final day Lonnie wished her luck and assured her the job would always be there if she needed to return. Fingers crossed, she wouldn't.

Charlotte had signed up eight kids for two different riding classes and three additional students for individual lessons. Gunner had taken on three additional clients, and Emerson agreed to help out with the trail rides on Saturdays, their busiest day of the week. In short, even with Charlotte working the ranch full-time, they would need an extra hand if business picked up much more. She hoped that person would be her sister.

When she entered the house, she was glad to hear Emerson moving about since her sister had a trail ride scheduled for nine. The aroma of something delicious wafted in the air as she walked into the kitchen.

Emerson was loading the dishwasher.

"Good morning and *yum*. What is that amazing smell?"

"I made Belgian waffles with brown-sugar butter. Help yourself."

"Don't mind if I do." She opened the oven, forked a plate-sized waffle, and heaped on the whipped butter that sat on the counter. She didn't even wait until she was seated before she took her first bite. "Wow. This is really delicious."

"Thanks. I got the recipe from Vivian at the bakery. You should taste her orange crescent rolls. They're so flaky and they practically melt in your mouth. I haven't talked her into giving me the recipe yet, but I'm working on it. Did you know she trained in France? She's really a genius in the kitchen."

"She's not the only one." Charlotte helped herself to another bite. "I'd probably starve if it wasn't for you."

Emerson tossed her a grin. "Nah. You'd just be eating frozen pizzas and PB&J sandwiches."

"True enough." Charlotte noticed her sister's overnight bag by the door, and her stomach dropped a few inches. "Are you going some-where?"

Emerson glanced at the bag. "Yeah, I'm heading to Asheville to visit April."

"Um, you didn't forget about those two trail rides today, did you?"

"Of course not." Her voice took on that familiar defensive tone. "They're at nine and eleven. I'm going afterward."

At least she wasn't shirking her duties. "That's good. But I was hoping you could stick around and help me with my first group lessons. They're back-to-back at two and three this afternoon. I'm a little nervous about handling four kids plus the horses on my own. I think I'll be okay, but I wouldn't mind an extra set of hands just in case."

"Sorry, can't do it today. I'm meeting April for lunch at one. Ask Gunner. That's what you're paying him for, isn't it?"

As if Gunner didn't work more than his share of hours. "What *we're* paying him for. And he's got his hands full with the horses he's training."

"I'm sure you'll be fine. You're good with kids and horses."

Charlotte bit back a retort. She was glad Emerson had stepped up to help on Saturday mornings, but it wasn't enough. Charlotte would need more help if they continued to grow. But she hadn't really vocalized that to her sister. Maybe it was time she did so.

Emerson loaded the last dish and started the dishwasher.

"You know, the expansion has been going very well. We're in the black even with me quitting my second job. And with these extra lessons and Gunner's new clients, there'll be enough money to pay another ranch hand a modest salary."

"That's great." Emerson grabbed the dishrag and began cleaning up the mess she'd made.

Her sister wasn't taking the bait. "I was kind of hoping you might like to fill that position. You wouldn't have to work at the bakery anymore. No more getting up at five in the morning . . ." She chuckled nervously.

"Thanks, but I like my job. I'm learning a lot and Vivian's pretty flexible with my hours."

"We could be flexible too. I'm pretty sure we could afford to pay you more than she is."

Emerson tossed the rag in the sink. "I don't want to work the ranch, Charlotte. I've tried to tell you that about a million times. I don't know how to make it any clearer than that."

Charlotte blinked. "I did hear you. But Mom left this place to both of us, not just me. And I thought once the ranch was turning a profit—once it was a success—you'd want to be part of it."

"That's because you're not listening. I don't care if it makes the Fortune 500 list, I'm not interested in working here."

Charlotte winced. Her jab felt so personal, as if she was rejecting Charlotte *and* the ranch in one fell swoop. Em had been raised here just like Charlotte, and she was great with horses. Why didn't she want to do this together—make it a real family business?

Emerson's expression softened. "I know you love the ranch. It's obviously in your blood—but it's not in mine."

Understanding dawned. "Is that what's going on here? Because the ranch was passed down from Mom's family? Have I made you feel you're not a part of it? Because that was never my intention. I know I kind of pressured you into the expansion, but that was the only way this place would ever make it. It's been going for three generations. I can't be the one to run this place into the ground. Em, you're my sister in every way that counts. And you were Mom's daughter too. She wanted us to share this place."

Emerson shook her head. "That's not it. Mom, Dad, and you have always been my real family." She gave Charlotte a pointed look. "*I'm* not the one searching somewhere else for that."

Charlotte sucked in a breath. And there it was. The topic that had been pushed to the back burner all these weeks was suddenly moved to the front and set to boil. "That's not fair."

"Maybe not, but the whole subject leaves a bad taste in my mouth. I saw your laptop the other day—you're still searching for him." Emerson straightened and headed for the door. "And I saw the Robinsons here in full force for your grand opening. I can't compete with that."

"You don't have to—Emerson, please don't go. We need to talk about this."

"I have to tack up the horses. Good luck with your lessons." And just like that she was gone.

As it happened, Gunner ended up helping Charlotte with the classes. And she was grateful since one of the kids had trouble listening and waiting his turn. Gunner was great with the little guy, giving him one-on-one guidance while Charlotte adjusted the stirrups for the two students on the ponies.

After class he waved as the last car pulled down the drive. "It was smart scheduling the classes back-to-back."

The August sun beat down mercilessly, making Charlotte wish for some shade trees. "No reason to tack and untack twice. I'm glad it worked out for everyone's schedule. That didn't go too badly, did it? If the second lesson goes that well, I think I'll be able to manage on my own going forward."

"You did great and the kids had a good time."

"That's important. It'll keep 'em coming back. And they each learned the safety rules and got some saddle time. That little Audrey is a natural. Did you see the way she praised Ginger?"

"She seemed comfortable in the saddle. They all did pretty well though. Even Ethan, once he settled in." Gunner leaned against the fence, propping one leg up. His arm muscles bunched as he took a swig from his water bottle.

He was a sight in those rugged jeans and faded green shirt. The moms had noticed, that was for sure, even the married ones. They'd be disappointed next week when the eye candy wasn't around.

Charlotte stroked Firefly's muzzle and the horse released a soft sigh. "How are the new clients doing? What are their issues?" Gunner was so competent that she'd completely handed the training program over to him.

"They're coming along. The paint doesn't like the saddle, and the bay has been biting her stall mate. I think the owner of the paint was just too impatient in his training. I should be able to turn him around pretty quickly. I'm not sure yet why the mare is biting, but hopefully I'll figure it out."

"I have no doubt you will." She thought of Midnight, their resident loner. She'd noticed a special connection between Gunner and the gelding that seemed to extend beyond the training pen. He spent a lot of bonding time with the horse. "And Midnight? How's he doing?"

"He's a stubborn one, but I think I've found the key to his heart."

"Love and affection?"

"Oats and honey."

She laughed. "Sounds about right."

They shared a smile that lingered. His skin had

bronzed under the summer sun, making his eyes appear even greener. And his dark hair had grown out a bit since his arrival, giving him a roguish appearance.

"You going out with Kyle tonight?" he asked softly.

Where had that come from? She blinked and tore her gaze away. She'd been out with Kyle several times in the past month. But Gunner had never mentioned him before. She hadn't even realized he was aware they were dating. "Not tonight. Why?"

He lifted a shoulder. "Just wondering."

She got the feeling there was more to his question than that. "Because . . ." Why was she pressing for an answer? Deep down she knew the answer: She was hoping he'd invite her someplace. That he wanted to spend time with her outside work.

You're an idiot, Charlotte. Because even if she and Kyle weren't exclusive, Gunner was the last person she should spend time with.

"You'd mentioned before about putting your search for your father on hold till things settled down. I didn't know if you were ready to pursue that again."

A small part of her felt let down at the reason for his inquiry. But it warmed her that he was still willing to help. She just wasn't sure she was ready for that.

"No pressure," he said. "Ball's in your court, of course. I just wanted you to know I'm here if you decide to go forward with it."

There was that warmth blooming in her chest again. Sometimes the depth of his sensitivity took her by surprise in such a wonderful way.

"Or maybe you'd rather have Kyle along."

"It's not that." She hadn't even told Kyle about her biological family. Gunner wouldn't even know about them if he hadn't happened upon the evidence. She'd planned to pay that gas station another visit when things settled down. But after Emerson's bitter words this morning . . . should she carry on with that plan? "I need to think about it. Can I let you know?"

"Of course. No rush."

A car rumbled up the drive, the first of their four students, no doubt. "Ready for another lesson?"

Gunner pushed off the fence. "Let's do it."

Twenty-Five

It was well after eleven and Charlotte couldn't stop tossing and turning. The house was too quiet with Emerson gone. Her sister's soft snoring sometimes annoyed her, but at least it made her feel less alone.

She thought back over the day. The lessons had gone well. The kids and parents seemed pleased. Gavin had brought Emma to the second class, and he hung around afterward to chat. They talked about Emma's participation in the lessons, and he asked how her expansion was going. He told her about the home he and Wes were currently building up in the mountains for a couple from Asheville.

He also mentioned that Gunner had initiated a fundraiser to benefit his elderly landlord and other residents in town who were underinsured. Apparently he'd somehow pulled Lisa and Avery into his efforts.

Gunner had mentioned Mr. Dixon to Charlotte—he and his neighbor sometimes passed the evenings with a game of chess. And he'd told her about the diabetic episode. But she'd heard nothing about this fundraiser. It was touching that he cared enough to help the man.

She rolled to her back and stared up at the

darkened ceiling, remembering the question Gunner had asked earlier. Was she ready to find her father?

With Emma in her riding classes and the Robinsons now orbiting her world so closely, she needed to make a decision, and soon. The more entwined her life became with theirs, the harder it would be—and the worse it would look—when the news finally came out.

She needed to expedite this process. Meet her father and give him the opportunity to tell his sons about her.

Emerson was the only thing holding her back. Charlotte understood why her sister felt threatened. But Emerson was paving her own path these days, and Charlotte wasn't sure where that would lead her. Currently it had led her to Asheville. Emerson hadn't even said when she was coming home. Surely before her trail rides next Saturday.

Charlotte should definitely go forward with her plans. Emerson would simply have to adjust. Maybe if the Robinsons accepted her, they'd accept Emerson too. They seemed like inclusive people. She could just imagine attending their family cookouts with Emerson. Playing cornhole and chatting at the picnic table over grilled burgers.

She and Emerson could even have the family out to the ranch. Her sister could cook up a feast and they could eat out back under the big oak tree. The image she'd conjured up was so lovely and inviting, Charlotte's heart gave a tight squeeze. That was what she wanted. It was probably wishful thinking, but she couldn't stop herself from hoping.

A wave of relief washed over her now that she'd settled the issue. She just needed to let Gunner know. Because this wasn't something she wanted to do alone, and he'd somehow become her confidant.

She envisioned him propped against the fence as he had been earlier. He was so attractive. So capable. Sometimes she just watched in wonder as he worked a horse in the ring.

In her experience men weren't the most patient of creatures. Her dad, as good a man as he'd been, had little patience. And Vince could fly off the handle at the smallest things—an annoying rattle in the car, a crying baby in a restaurant.

But Gunner could work for hours with difficult horses and never lose his patience. He had a calming presence. When she was with him, she didn't worry about her business or anything else. She frowned at the thought. Spending time with Gunner hadn't factored into the decision to track down her father.

Had it?

No, she hadn't even thought of Gunner when making her decision. And even if she had, maybe it was just that calming presence she craved. Meeting her biological father was a big deal and a scary prospect—a prime opportunity for rejection. Besides, she spent time with Gunner every day, caring for the horses. She was just being paranoid. Overly cautious because of her attraction.

She was dating Kyle now, wasn't she? And they were having fun. He'd kissed her good night on their third date. It was pleasant. Sweet. He was careful not to push her, and she appreciated that. Their last date had also ended in a good-night kiss. It was a little better than the first. Not that the first had been bad. If it was a little awkward and maybe teeth were involved, well . . . practice made perfect.

She pushed away thoughts of Kyle and returned them to her search for her biological father. Tomorrow was Sunday, so the garage would be closed. Maybe Gunner would be free sometime Monday. He'd have to quit work early as the garage closed at five o'clock. But after all, she could arrange for that to happen.

Now that she'd made up her mind, she was eager to get the ball rolling. She grabbed her phone off the nightstand and opened her texting app.

Once she'd located her thread with Gunner, she began writing. *I've been thinking about what you said earlier. I'm ready to find and meet my father. Would you be available sometime*

Monday to go with me to the gas station again?

She sent the text and settled back in bed. When he didn't respond right away, she glanced at the time. She shouldn't have texted him this late. It was probably unprofessional—never mind that she'd already invited him into a very private area of her life. But tomorrow was his day off and she didn't want to spring this on him Monday.

They texted pretty regularly, of course. She scrolled up and began reading their thread.

Did you pick up some more Probios? he'd asked.

It's in the clear tub by the glucosamine.

Thanks. You might want to put a stable sheet on Dominic tonight. He was a mess this morning.

Will do.

He'd sent a photo of Rogue and Daisy nuzzling in the pasture. *Check out these two.*

True love.

Except for that last correspondence, their messages had been business only and sent during work hours. She'd just texted him at almost midnight on a Saturday night about an entirely personal matter. Where were her boundaries? Oh well, his phone was probably dead anyway. He had an older model that hardly had the battery life to make it through an entire day.

She poised her fingers with an apology for texting him so late. But just as she began to type out the message, three little dots appeared in the text box.

Twenty-Six

Gunner had just been ready to fall into bed when the text came in. He'd had a fun night at the Trailhead with Wes and Gavin, who'd brought their families this time. Laurel had begged to set him up with Bridgett, the pretty brunette bartender with a direct gaze and an edgy look. He laughed off Laurel's attempts and promised he was all good in that department.

But the fact was, he couldn't seem to get a certain auburn-haired rancher off his mind. And another woman, no matter how pretty or interested, wouldn't change that.

He grabbed his phone off the nightstand where it was charging. Charlotte. She was up awfully late. But then again, so was he. Her message about wanting to locate her father buoyed his spirits. He did want to help her in this quest. But also he craved time alone with her.

Idiot.

He must be a glutton for punishment. He thumbed out a response. *Sure, we can go anytime Monday. I'll work my schedule around it.*

He sent the message, then saw she'd sent it almost ten minutes ago. Maybe she'd fallen asleep. He was just settling in bed when another message dinged in.

Thank you. And sorry I texted so late. Hope I didn't wake you.

No worries. I was just getting in from the Trailhead.

Wild Saturday night?

He grinned. *In a manner of speaking. There was a four-year-old involved.*

???

Wes and Gavin invited me out with their families. Emma was a hoot.

A pause followed after he sent the message. Did it bother her that he was hanging out with one of her brothers? Was she still worried he might divulge her secret? *You know I'd never say anything about your connection with Gavin and Cooper, right?*

She answered almost right away. *I'm not worried about that. Maybe just a little jealous.* ☺

Now he felt bad for bringing it up. *I saw Gavin chatting with you after class today. I can tell he likes you. I can even see a family resemblance.*

I hope he still likes me when he finds out who I am.

How could he help but like Charlotte? She was so kind and thoughtful. *I'm sure he will.*

What was the fundraiser he was telling me about? Something to do with your landlord?

Just something Lisa Robinson and I worked out. They donate 10 percent of Trail Days' profits

242

to some cause. *This year it'll go to townsfolk who need financial help with medical care.*

According to Gavin this was your doing.

I just brought up the subject to Lisa, and she took it from there. Avery will oversee the non-profit and disbursements as she's in a position to know where the needs are.

I think you're being modest. But I'm sure Mr. Dixon and all the others on fixed incomes will appreciate your efforts. I'll be sure to tell Brianna. Her grandmother could use the help.

She actually came up in the meeting.

I'm glad to hear that. Thank you for doing this.

He was no knight in shining armor. He'd figured that out long ago. *I didn't do much.*

There was another pause. This one probably just because the topic had petered out. But he was loath to end the conversation. *Have you thought about what you might say at the gas station?*

How 'bout, "Can I get an oil change?"

He smiled. *Funny. Are you even due one?*

No. 😂

Well, maybe you'll recognize his facial features and know it's him on sight.

I thought I might say I'm from Riverbend and see how he reacts. Maybe he'll mention his sons live there.

Good idea.

I hope I'm not too nervous to think. I froze up last time and he wasn't even there.

I'll be there too. I can keep the conversation rolling.

Whether he wants it to or not? 😂

Anything for you. He stared at the comment he'd just typed out. He meant every word. But it wasn't something he should tell his boss. He deleted the words. He was honored that she trusted him enough to include him in such a personal matter, but he didn't want to overstep.

A text came in. *Did you fall asleep on me? Am I that boring?*

If only she knew he lay awake some nights just thinking of her. His thought life had gotten a little out of control. But it wasn't as if he was acting on it. *Just zoned out for a minute. How sure are you that this guy is your father?*

Not sure at all, really. But he's the only Craig Burton who lives within a hundred-mile radius of Riverbend. Have Gavin or Cooper mentioned their dad to you at all?

Before he could respond, another text came in. *Sorry. Shouldn't have asked you to divulge something a friend said in confidence.*

I would've told you if they'd mentioned him. You deserve to know who your dad is.

You really think so?

You have a right to know where you came from.

Emerson doesn't seem to think so.

She probably just feels threatened by the idea of you having other family.

244

I'm sure that's part of it. Sometimes I feel guilty for wanting a relationship with them.

It's perfectly normal to want to know your family.

Says the man so filled with wanderlust he has no connections at all. 😂

Wanderlust?? There's a word you don't hear every day.

If the shoe fits.

You're not wrong. He didn't want to think about his lifestyle right now. He'd rather help her strategize. After a moment he typed out another message. *If you're gonna get an oil change, maybe you should make an appointment for the end of the day. Then you could leave your vehicle and we'd have to return to pick it up.*

That would give me two opportunities to talk to him.

But you'd have to be brave enough to ride on my bike with me.

Bring it on, buddy.

He smiled. As long as she was game. He wouldn't complain about having her arms wrapped around him on the ride. Kyle probably wouldn't love the idea, but they couldn't be that serious. Besides, that wasn't Gunner's problem. And it wasn't as if his relationship with Charlotte could go anywhere.

He glanced at his phone. Never mind that it was after midnight and they were texting each other.

He sent her another message. *I should probably let you get to bed. Tomorrow's my day off, not yours.*

Those darn horses are so needy.

The nerve.

Would it kill them to go a day without food?

He sent a laughing emoji.

Good night, Gunner.

Good night. He set his phone back on the charger and settled in bed. But it was a long time before he drifted off.

Twenty-Seven

Surely her heart was going to explode. Charlotte shut off the engine and set her palm against her chest as she glanced around the gas station's exterior. The garage door was pulled shut, but there was movement inside. Her father? In mere minutes she might find out.

Was she ready for this? What if he wasn't anything like what she'd hoped? What if he was gruff or rude or weird? What if he wasn't her father at all? Her mind had spun off in all directions on the long drive over. She wished Gunner had been in the truck with her. He would've served as a nice distraction.

The sound of Gunner's bike roared closer as he pulled alongside her. He removed his helmet, then his gaze flitted toward the building and homed in on the garage.

She stepped from the truck, her legs wobbling like a three-legged table.

He came around his bike. "There's an entry door to the garage. Still want me to come with you, or would you rather do this alone?"

"Oh, you're coming with me."

The corner of his lips quirked up. "It's gonna be fine. You'll see. If you get stuck, I'll fill in the gaps."

As they moved toward the building, he set his hand on the small of her back. The gentle pressure comforted her. At least she wasn't in this alone. Before she knew it they were at the door.

Gunner held it open for her and she entered, pulse racing, mind spinning.

Could really use Your help here, God. Give me the words. Maybe don't let him reject me? Okay. This is it. Over and out.

The smells of motor oil and rubber assaulted her nose as her gaze scanned the interior, stopping on a man bent over a car's open hood. He wore a mechanic's jumpsuit, but only his lower half was visible.

"Be right with you." The metallic sounds of his work echoed throughout the open room.

She and Gunner stopped in the shop's corner by an old metal desk and two plastic chairs that served as the office space. Despite the large glass garage door and the sun beating in, the place was adequately air-conditioned. Nonetheless, heat prickled beneath her arms.

"Breathe," Gunner whispered.

She did seem to be holding her breath. She drew in a steady lungful of oxygen and released it, rehearsing what she might say. That's when she remembered.

"I forgot to remove the sticker!" she whispered.

"What sticker?"

"The one that says I'm not due for an oil change for another two thousand miles."

He placed his hand on her back again. "We'll get it on the way out."

Right. No big deal. Why did her heart seem to be stuttering in her chest? Her mouth was as dry as the Sahara, and no wonder since all the liquid in her body seemed to have pooled in her palms. She wiped them down the sides of her jeans.

A clatter of tools snagged her attention. The mechanic came out from under the hood. He was as tall as Gunner and stocky in the gray mechanic's jumpsuit. He looked to be in his midfifties with swarthy skin. He had short gray hair and a slightly crooked nose, but it was his deep-set eyes that nearly made her gasp. They were Cooper's, right down to the chocolate-brown hue and prominent brows.

It was definitely him. It was her father. Did Gunner see the resemblance? She couldn't tear her gaze from the mechanic long enough to gauge his reaction.

"Help you?" The man neared, rubbing his hands on a dirty cloth. He wasn't wearing a wedding band.

That was good. She wouldn't have to take a wife's feelings into account, so that would make her sudden appearance less complicated. If he even wanted anything to do with her.

The man lifted his brows.

"I have an appointment," she blurted. "Um, for an oil change."

He riffled through a paper schedule on the desk. Then peered up at her. "Simpson?"

She tried to read into his expression. He didn't seem to recognize her surname, but it wasn't an uncommon one. "Yes. It's the beige Tahoe."

He went through some basic questions about her preferences regarding oil and services, jotting down her answers. "Should have it finished by noon tomorrow. Keys?"

She handed them over, then remembered her lines. "I, uh, usually get it serviced by Brooks over in Riverbend Gap. That's where I live."

His smile didn't quite reach his eyes. "We appreciate your business."

Her spirits plummeted and her mind went blank. She glanced at Gunner.

"We found you online. Your customer service ratings are good."

The man perked up. "I'll do a nice job for you. I've only been here about a year, but I've been working on cars all my life."

"What got you interested?" Charlotte asked. "In cars, I mean."

He shrugged. "Always liked tinkering around, seeing how things work. Turns out you can make a living at it." He turned toward Gunner. "That your Harley Roadster outside?"

"It is."

"Used to have a lowrider. Had a kid, though, and we needed a family vehicle. Always regretted selling her."

The opportunity had practically fallen into her lap. She jumped on it. "How many kids do you have?"

"Two boys—they're grown now though." He glanced at Gunner. "You need that bike serviced, you should bring it here. I can take one of those apart and put it back together blindfolded."

"Will do. We'll let you get back to work." Gunner squeezed her elbow.

Yes, they'd gotten enough information for now. Enough to assure her they'd found the right man. They'd be back tomorrow.

The man nodded and headed back to his current project.

Gunner opened the door for her, and they slipped out into the sultry afternoon. She couldn't believe they'd located him so easily!

"That's him," Gunner said once they were a safe distance from the building.

"It's definitely him."

When they approached her vehicle, Gunner opened the driver's-side door and removed the oil-change sticker. Then he joined her by his bike.

"I completely forgot about that."

"You have a few things on your mind."

"Can you believe how much he resembles Cooper? Those eyes."

"Cooper? He has your cleft chin and that little furrow between the brows."

"Really? You think so?"

"I saw it right away."

She stared at Gunner. "I can't believe it's him. I can't believe we found him."

"If his appearance wasn't enough, he mentioned having two sons."

"Can you believe the way he just offered that piece of information? I've sweated tears over how to casually extract information from him, and he just threw it right out there."

"It was a gift, for sure. But once I saw him, I knew. That's your father."

Her smile widened until she was beaming at him. "That's my father." Now came the real question: What would she do about it?

Gunner was riding as high as Charlotte. He was so happy for her and glad to have had a small part in her discovery. He was proud of her, too, for facing her fears and going forward with this. It had to be scary. She didn't know Craig Burton. He could've been a real jerk. Even so, he could refuse to accept that Charlotte was his daughter or admit she might be and want nothing to do with her. Maybe he already knew she existed and hadn't cared enough to look her up.

It took a brave woman to step into the unknown like that. These were the thoughts he tried to focus on all the way back to Riverbend Gap. But it wasn't easy when she was wrapped around him, pressed against his back—a mere formality when riding on the back of a bike.

But still.

It was distracting. And yes, it was nice. So nice he felt a little guilty wishing the ride were just a little longer. She leaned into the curves with him, their hips and torsos shifting together. She was a natural. He'd taken the drive cautiously at first. But on their first couple of curves she'd laughed in delight, which encouraged him to speed up. That lusty laugh of hers just drove him wild.

They took a downhill curve and she squealed, making him smile. He liked that she was adventurous. The last woman he'd gone out with had refused to ride with him at all. They'd gone on dates in a yellow Volkswagen that forced him to sit with his knees in the dashboard.

What did that have to do with anything? He gave his head a shake. He was not dating Charlotte. She was his boss. His temporary boss. Why did he have to keep reminding himself?

And why did she have to feel so good pressed up against him?

They reached the ranch too quickly. Charlotte hopped off the bike and removed the helmet. "That was so fun. I can see what all the hype's about."

He dismounted the bike. "I knew you'd like

it. Mind if I check on Midnight before I go?"

" 'Course not. I'll come with you. Daisy seemed a little off when we stabled her earlier." They headed toward the barn.

"What was wrong with her?"

"I'm sure she's fine. She just seemed a little down."

"She's not due to foal for a few weeks, is she?"

"Kyle says about another month."

Kyle. Gunner hated the thought of the two of them together, but he should be grateful for the extra barrier the man presented. "How's that going, you and Kyle?" He couldn't seem to stop himself from asking.

"Oh, it's fine. It's good. He's a nice man."

Fine. Good. Nice. Not exactly the words a woman typically used to describe a man she was falling in love with. But that was none of his business. He shoved those thoughts aside as Charlotte went to see about Daisy.

"Hey, fella." Gunner approached Midnight.

The horse stared at him from the other side of the stall, lowering his head, ears turning toward him. He remained relaxed despite Gunner's appearance—a positive sign.

"How's it going tonight? Why don't you come over here and see me." The horse stared back. "You know you want to." On another night Gunner might've gone straight for the oats and honey. But tonight he wanted the horse to seek him out simply for the pleasure of his company. Whether it would work or not was another matter.

But a few seconds later Midnight gradually approached the gate.

"Thatta boy." Gunner reached out slowly and stroked the horse's face. "See, I'm not gonna hurt you. You know that already, don't you?"

The gelding held steady eye contact with Gunner. His eyes were more warm and inviting than wide and wary, as they'd been in the beginning. Another good sign of progress.

"I know you've been through some bad things, but you can trust me, buddy. You're starting to figure that out. I think you could use a friend. What do you think?"

"He's letting you touch him."

Midnight darted toward the back of the stall.

"Sorry. Didn't mean to spook him."

"Doesn't take much. That was only the second time he let me touch him, and the first time with no treat involved. He's coming along. How's Daisy doing?"

"She seems fine now. Maybe she was just in a mood before."

He followed her to Daisy's stall. The mare whinnied at their approach. Gunner stroked her face and the horse nudged him. "How you feeling, girl? Taking good care of your foal?"

Charlotte propped her foot on the gate. "Kyle

suggested we cut back on her grains. She's getting a little too big."

"I saw that on the board."

"Otherwise she's coming along great. Aren't you, girl?" Charlotte leaned in to give the horse some affection, bringing her closer to Gunner.

He caught a pleasant whiff of her shampoo, something light and fresh. Addictive. Their arms touched on the stall door. He really should move away.

"I admire your patience with Midnight," she said softly.

"He's obviously been through a lot. He deserves a little patience." Gunner felt a strong connection with the horse. As if they understood each other somehow.

"Do you think he's ready for more?" Her gaze burned a hole in the side of his head.

For some reason, his pulse raced. "Nah, he's still pretty nervous."

After a moment she straightened, ending their brief contact. "You're probably right."

When she headed out of the barn, Gunner followed her.

"Thanks again for going with me tonight," she said. "I don't think I would've had the courage to do it alone."

"Sure you would've. But I'm glad it turned out so well."

She gave a wry grin. "Now I just have to figure out what to do about it."

"What time do you want to head over there tomorrow?"

"End of the day again? Why don't we aim to be there just before closing time."

"Sounds good."

She shook her head as they reached his bike. "I still can't believe we found him so easily. But there are still so many unknowns. Does he have a relationship with Gavin and Cooper? Did my mom tell him about me? I mean, she was pregnant with me when they lived in the same town, so he has to know, right?"

"You would think."

"So maybe he just didn't want anything to do with me. Maybe he isn't interested in knowing his long-lost daughter."

"You can't assume that. Who knows what was happening at the time your mom got pregnant with you. He was married to someone else, remember? There are a lot of unknowns here."

"I guess there's only one way to fill in the missing gaps." Her gaze connected with his and held on tight. Fear flickered in those green depths.

"He'd be the one to ask."

"Yeah, but I might not like the answers."

He softened at her vulnerability. He couldn't even imagine being in her place. Not knowing if she'd been wanted by her biological father. Not knowing if he'd accept her appearance in his life now. "Whatever you find out about him and his decisions, it's no reflection on you. You're a wonderful person, Charlie, and you can handle this. You're strong. Don't forget that."

Her gaze softened a moment before she reached out for a hug. Her arms wound around his neck.

She was small and pliable. Warm and welcoming. He held her to him, drew in the soft fragrance of her hair and the scent of sunshine on her skin. Despite their difference in size, she fit him perfectly. Tucked in below his chin just right.

"Thank you," she whispered against his chest.

"You're welcome." Could she hear the way his heart thundered at the contact? He couldn't bring himself to care.

When she let him go, it felt as if she took a piece of him with her.

Stupid.

He stuffed his hands in his pockets as they said good night, then watched her walk toward the house. Somehow, despite all his self-admonishments, despite his best intentions, he was falling for his boss.

Twenty-Eight

She was going to do it. Charlotte leaned to the left, holding tight to Gunner as he took a curve on the bike. She'd been going back and forth in her mind all day, weighing all the possibilities—the scariest of which was that Craig Burton knew all about her and hadn't cared enough to even meet her.

But every time that scenario came to mind, she heard Gunner's soft, adamant voice. *"You can handle this, Charlie. You're strong. Don't forget that."*

The bottom line was, if she didn't ask, she'd never know. Maybe Craig couldn't care less about the daughter he'd produced. But maybe he wasn't aware. And if that was the case, he had as much right to know about her as she had to know about him.

At least that's what she told herself as they drove the familiar route toward Weaverville.

She leaned into Gunner's back, resting her helmet against his shoulder, drawing from his strength. He hadn't pressed her about what she would say to Craig when she picked up her truck. She was grateful for that. The ticking clock was pressure enough.

By the time they reached the gas station, fear

259

coursed through her veins, tightening her chest, restricting air flow. She stepped off the bike onto legs that didn't feel capable of supporting her weight.

Gunner took her arm. "You okay?"

"I'm fine." She removed her helmet and tried to fluff her hair. She'd curled it this afternoon, which was stupid. It wasn't as if it mattered what she looked like. Would Craig see their likeness? He was more likely to see her resemblance to her mother.

"You look great," Gunner said. "Beautiful."

She soaked in his kind words. Maybe he was only trying to bolster her courage, but she appreciated it nonetheless. "I'm gonna tell him who I am."

He gave a nod. "All right. How can I help?"

"Just go in there with me." She let out a mirthless laugh as she glanced at the building. "I might need you to prop me up if my legs give way."

"You've got this, Charlie."

She drew two steadying breaths and stared at the garage. "That poor man has no idea what's about to hit him."

"He's a lucky guy. If he's any kind of man, he'll feel like he just hit the lottery."

Her heart softened as she met his gaze again. He said the sweetest things. "All right. I think I'm ready."

When she headed toward the door, Gunner

followed. *Please, God. Please, God.* It was as far as her thoughts would go. The only plea she could articulate at the moment with her head spinning and the pressure in her chest crowding out oxygen.

She stepped into the cool space to find Craig standing behind the desk, talking on the phone. He acknowledged them with a nod as he spoke to someone about pistons and internal combustion engines.

While Craig was too distracted to notice, she let her gaze rove over his face. This time she passed over his eyes. Gunner had been right. She had gotten her cleft chin from him. He wasn't frowning at the moment, so she didn't see those familiar furrows between his brows. His hairline had receded a bit, but he still had plenty of hair. She didn't see much of Gavin in him, but she knew from the photo her mom had left that he'd had thick black hair once upon a time.

Craig glanced over and caught her staring.

Face heating, she turned and walked toward a bulletin board by the entry that boasted business cards and flyers. Gunner stepped up behind her. She was grateful for his steady presence. No matter how Craig Burton received her, Gunner was here to help her with the fallout.

"Sorry 'bout that," Craig said a moment later. "Sometimes it gets crazy around here since there's just one of me."

Charlotte's smile wobbled as she approached the desk. "No problem."

"Everything checks out with your Tahoe. The filter was still in pretty good shape so I didn't replace it." He rattled off the total.

Charlotte fumbled through her wallet for her credit card. Finally she had it in hand. She rubbed her lips together as he rang up the purchase.

"Go ahead and insert your card."

Charlotte did as he requested and selected *Okay* for the amount. She signed with the stylus. Her gaze bounced off Gunner's as Craig stapled the receipt to the work order. His expression said, *You got this.*

"Here you go. Keys are in the vehicle. There's a 10 percent coupon right there. I hope you'll come back for your next service."

"Thank you." Charlotte took the papers. "Um, do you actually have a few minutes to talk?"

Craig glanced at his watch. "Sure. You got another vehicle I can help with?"

"Not exactly. I, uh, I'm not sure how to say this . . ."

Craig's gaze grew wary as it toggled between Gunner and her. "What's this about?"

"Do you remember a Connie Simpson? She used to live in Riverbend Gap."

His eyes widened with surprise. Or maybe a flicker of recognition. "Yeah. Sure. Oh . . . Simpson. You must be a relative. How's Connie doing these days? I haven't seen her in years."

"She's, uh . . . I'm afraid she passed last year."

His smile fell. He rubbed the back of his neck. "I'm real sorry to hear that. She was a nice lady. She owned a ranch outside of town, right?"

"Right." Charlotte swallowed hard. *Just say it.* "She was—she was my mother."

"Now that you mention it, I see the resemblance. I'm sorry for your—" He stilled. Something shifted in his expression. His eyes grew intense as he scanned her face. All the blood seemed to drain from his face as the moment drew out unbearably long. "You didn't come here for an oil change."

It was now or never. Unfortunately, his response so far gave no indication of whether he would welcome her news.

Gunner set his hand on the small of her back.

The gentle weight of it bolstered her courage. "I guess there's no easy way to say this, and maybe you already know, but . . . I have reason to believe you're my biological father."

He blinked. Otherwise his features seemed set in stone.

Charlotte fumbled through her purse for the photo. "My mom never told me about you. Whenever I'd ask about my biological father, she'd change the subject. But after she passed I found an envelope in a safety-deposit box marked with my name. It contained newspaper articles about Gavin and Cooper Robinson—they're your sons?"

He nodded, then sank onto the desk chair as if his legs would no longer support him.

"I also found this with the clippings." She handed over the old photo of Craig and her mom.

His hand shook as he focused on the image. He stared at it for a long time.

But she couldn't read his expression. Did he have fond memories of her mom? Had he loved her? It was impossible to tell by his reaction. He was obviously shocked. "You didn't know about me then?"

His eyes were still locked on that image. "No . . ."

His reaction seemed genuine, but it was hard to believe. "Riverbend's a pretty small town. I figured you must've known."

He returned the photo. Rubbed a hand over his face.

The phone rang, loud and shrill in the quiet.

Craig glanced at the clock, then stood and headed toward the door. He flipped over the Closed sign. Voice mail must've kicked on as the phone stopped ringing. He turned to face her. Ran his hands down the pants of his jumpsuit. "Listen, maybe we could go somewhere else and talk. There's a coffee shop—no, they're closed now. There's a diner. Or maybe the park. It's just up the street."

He wanted to continue the conversation. That was good, wasn't it? She didn't want to talk at a crowded diner where they could be overheard. "The park by the river?"

"Yeah, that's the one. There's a picnic table by the bridge. I can meet you there in a few minutes?"

"All right. That sounds good."

Craig let them out and locked up behind them. Charlotte headed toward her vehicle feeling numb. She wasn't sure how that had gone, but at least the hard part was over.

"You did great." Gunner ushered her toward the truck. "I'm really proud of you."

"Everything about this feels so surreal. He didn't exactly seem overjoyed, though, did he?"

"It's a pretty shocking thing to tell a man."

"So you think he was telling the truth—that he didn't know about me?"

"I do. He seemed blindsided. He might need a minute to catch up."

Her shoulders sagged with relief. She'd been hoping he never knew about her. Otherwise, he'd rejected her from the beginning, and who wanted to believe that of their biological parent? "He didn't deny I could be his. I was afraid he might." Or mention a paternity test, which would be understandable. She wouldn't mind taking one with him, for both their sakes.

"He wanted to talk some more, so I'd take that as a good sign."

265

Something terrible occurred to her. Her head snapped toward Gunner. "Unless he just said that to ditch me. What if he doesn't even show up?"

Gunner squeezed her shoulder. "He'd be crazy to miss out on knowing you."

The picnic table sat in the shade of a towering pine tree. The river rippled past and birds tweeted overhead. A squirrel scampered through the pine needles nearby. If this wasn't the most stressful meeting of her life, she might appreciate the peaceful surroundings.

Gunner shifted on the seat beside her. He'd offered to let her handle this alone, but his presence gave her strength. And she needed all the fortitude she could get.

She glanced at her watch. It had been seventeen minutes since they'd left the garage. If he didn't show, she didn't know what she'd do. Probably cry. The burning behind her eyes verified the thought. Talk about the ultimate rejection.

"He had to close up the shop," Gunner said. "I'm sure he's coming."

"That makes one of us." Her breath felt stuffed in her lungs.

"What do you need? What can I do?"

His thigh pressed against hers beneath the table, a solid presence. "You're already doing it. I'm so glad you're here."

"I didn't even say a word back there. You did it all on your own."

That was true, but it was still nice knowing he had her back.

"Look, there he is," Gunner said.

Charlotte followed his gaze to the man walking up the same pathway they'd taken. A breath escaped her. Her father hadn't ditched her after all. He'd exchanged his jumper for a pair of jeans and a white button-down shirt. The street clothes made him seem younger somehow. More approachable.

When he glanced their direction she gave a little wave.

Gunner nudged her. "See, what did I tell you?"

"I'm so relieved I don't even mind the not-so-subtle 'I told you so.' "

"I was counting on that."

A moment later Craig took a seat across the table. "Sorry it took so long. I had to close up."

"No worries." She gestured toward Gunner. "I should've introduced you at the garage. This is my friend Gunner."

The men shook hands and exchanged pleasantries.

Then Craig clasped his hands on the weathered tabletop and met her gaze. "I'm sorry, I didn't even catch your first name."

"It's Charlotte."

He nodded, his lips lifting a little. "I also want to apologize to you. I didn't handle that very well back at the station."

"I understand. It must've come as a big shock."

"It was, but . . . there's more to it than that. Hearing your mom's name, seeing her face, brought back some memories for me. Unpleasant ones."

Charlotte frowned. She'd assumed they'd been in love or something close to it. But maybe it had ended badly. "Oh. I didn't realize."

"It's not what you're thinking. Your mom was great. She was a sweetheart. The unpleasantries are all on me. I wasn't . . . I wasn't a good person back then."

What did that mean exactly? Was he referring to his affair? "Okay . . ."

He leaned forward. "I don't know what you already know about me, but I was married to Cooper and Gavin's mother when I met your mom."

"I'm aware of that."

"I have a lot of regrets about how I've lived most of my life. The affair was unfair to your mom and to my wife. But it was just one of the many ways I let people down." His brows furrowed. "I owe you the truth, Charlotte—I'm an alcoholic and have been for many years. Since I came back from the Gulf War."

It was Charlotte's turn to reel. This was a far

cry from her childhood fantasies. But she was an adult now. Her father was only human, and people made mistakes.

He shifted on the bench. "That's probably why your mom never told me about you. I was in no shape to be any kind of father."

It all made sense now. Her mom had wanted a good life for her, and that didn't include an alcoholic father. She was trying to protect Charlotte. The realization went a long way toward assuaging the anger and frustration she'd felt over the situation.

"That's why I never noticed your existence. I had my head so far down in the bottle I couldn't see daylight."

Gunner raised an eyebrow. "Had?"

Craig pulled a green chip from his shirt pocket and held it up. "Been sober for nine months now."

"Congratulations," Gunner said. "That's quite an achievement."

"Hasn't been easy, that's for sure. But it's been worth it." Craig's attention swung to Charlotte. "I'm sure you were hoping for a better man when you set out to find me. But I'm determined to remain sober and make better decisions for myself."

Her heart softened at his raw honesty. "You seem like an earnest, hardworking man."

"Thanks for saying that." He blinked back

some tears and his gaze roved over her features. "You're a beautiful girl. You look like Connie. Those eyes, that hair. But I see a little of me too. You actually remind me a bit of my mother in her younger days."

"Are your parents still alive?"

"My dad died when I was little, and my mom passed from cancer a few years ago. She never got to see me sober up."

"She'd be proud of you now though."

"What do you do, Charlotte? Are you married? Kids? You're living in Riverbend, you said?"

"Yes. I'm single, no kids. And I run the ranch my mom left my sister and me."

"Took after your ma, did you? She always loved those horses so much. You have a sister?"

"When I was young Mom married my dad." She winced at the word. "He adopted me."

"It's okay. I'm glad you had a father figure in your life. A whole family. I'm real glad to know that. Do they know you've found me?"

"Emerson knows I've been searching. We lost our dad a few years ago. Do you see Gavin and Cooper very often?"

He glanced down at the table. " 'Fraid not. I wasn't much of a dad to them. I'm sure I was more of an embarrassment than anything."

His regret was obvious, but it sounded as if he'd all but abandoned his sons. Her mother's decision to keep her pregnancy under wraps had been for the best. After all, he probably would've abandoned her too.

"Do you know them very well?" Craig asked. "Cooper's county sheriff now, and Gavin has his own construction business."

Despite Craig's regrets he was clearly proud of his sons' accomplishments. "They recently came into my life. They're good people."

Craig's expression fell. "They don't know about . . . ?"

"No. I didn't feel it was my place to tell them."

"It's not that I don't want them to know about you. But they don't know I cheated on their mom. I already have so many strikes against me. I'd like a relationship with them, but I wanted a year of sobriety under my belt before I contact them again. I want them to know I'm serious about changing my life. I've been working hard toward that goal. Some days the hope of a relationship with them is the only thing that keeps me going. I have two grandchildren I've never even met. I need to make amends with them if they'll let me."

That wasn't what she'd hoped to hear. Craig was still three months from that goal. And with the Robinsons circling the perimeter of her life, sooner was better than later. "The thing is . . . Gavin and Cooper are kind of in my life now as friends. I feel as if I'm keeping this deep, dark secret from them."

He held her gaze for a beat, then defeat flickered in his eyes. "I understand if you feel you should tell them. This is my problem, not yours."

But it would set Craig back another step in gaining his sons' forgiveness and earning back their trust. He had so much to lose.

He gave her a kind smile as he patted her hand. "It's okay, honey. You do what you have to do. I'll be fine one way or another."

Twenty-Nine

Three weeks later Charlotte was still reeling at the idea. She was sitting across from her biological father. Ordering supper as if it were just another day. After a lifetime of thinking she'd never know his identity, he was here. And he wanted to know her. It was a dream come true. Maybe he wasn't exactly as she'd hoped he'd be, but he seemed kind and humble. And he seemed eager to spend time with her.

She slid the paper across the booth's table. The diner near Marshall smelled of grilled burgers. Her stomach rumbled as she watched her birth father closely.

They'd gotten together a week after their first meeting for a mouth swab, and it had taken two weeks to receive the test results. She'd checked the results online right away, palms sweating, heart racing. She'd known deep down he was her father. But a niggle of fear had washed over her as she clicked open the results.

Craig frowned at the paper. "What am I looking at?"

"It's our paternity test. I received the results today."

He offered her a wobbly smile and patted her hand. "Oh, honey, I didn't even need this.

I knew the second you told me who you were."

She placed her finger on the last line where the results showed that the probability of Craig being her father was over 99 percent. "Well, now we have the test to back it up."

"That cleft and your expressive eyes were all it took to convince me. So much like your grandma. I wish you could've met her."

"I wish that too. But meeting you has been everything I'd hoped."

He leaned forward, his gaze focusing on her. "Honey, you are without a doubt the happiest surprise I've ever gotten."

Charlotte's mind spun with everything that had happened this summer. As the blazing heat of August melted into September, providing cooler nighttime temperatures, she marveled at the changes.

With the growth of the training program, she'd become worried about finding a suitable replacement for Gunner. Finding a ranch hand was one thing. A good trainer was harder to come by. Gunner had put her mind at ease a couple of weeks ago. "It'll save money if you do the training yourself. You've got good instincts and you're a fast learner. You can always hire a ranch hand to care for the horses." So they made time in the schedule for training lessons.

She was also getting to know her father better.

They'd met up twice in the past month and discovered they shared some similar interests. They both liked watching true-crime shows, shooting pool, and listening to country music. They both hated algebra in school and agreed that kale in any form was inedible. Their outings had become less awkward as they'd become better acquainted.

Charlotte had told Emerson about him soon after she'd met him that first time, but her sister's reaction had been anticlimactic. She hadn't gotten upset, but she didn't warm to the subject either. And when Charlotte had suggested she meet Craig, her response was clear.

"What for? He's not my dad."

Emerson had thrown herself into her job at the bakery this month. But she'd also met her obligations on the ranch. Charlotte hated the distance between them, but what could she do? She hoped Emerson would come around eventually. That she'd come to see that Charlotte having Craig in her life didn't mean she loved her sister or their dad any less.

Despite Craig's assurances that Charlotte could tell Gavin and Cooper who she was, she refrained from doing so. He'd even offered to tell them himself, but she could see what it would cost him. It wasn't asking too much to wait a bit, was it?

Even so, she felt a prickle of guilt each time

Gavin showed up for Emma's lessons or Cooper brought Quinn by to see the hossies. But she shoved the guilt aside. Craig had a lot more at stake than she did.

Besides, for men who hadn't had much of a father, Cooper and Gavin had turned out amazingly well. They were great dads and loyal, loving husbands. It was probably true that Jeff Robinson had more to do with that than Craig did. But how much of a grudge could they carry when everything had turned out so well for them?

On the first Saturday in September, she entered Milly's Mug and Bean and smiled at Brianna, who worked the front counter. She was working so many hours these days to help pay for her grandma's care that Charlotte had begun to come in and chat on her breaks.

Once Charlotte ordered her drink, Brianna brought it over and flopped into the seat across from her. She looked as beautiful as usual, even if a little tired around the eyes. "You came at a great time. We've had a line out the door all morning."

"I have good timing like that. How's your granny doing?"

"About the same, I guess. Some days are better than others." Brianna didn't like talking about her grandma much lately. It was a depressing subject.

Charlotte sipped her latte. "Mmm. Just the way I like it."

"I take care of my girl. Even if I rarely see her these days." Brianna's eyes teased.

"Don't blame it on me. You're the one with the eighty-hour workweek." And a grandma to care for, but Charlotte didn't want to bring that up again.

"I'm not the one with a thriving ranch and a boyfriend to keep up with."

"Kyle's not my boyfriend. We're just . . . talking."

"For over two months? Girl. Glaciers have been known to move faster."

Charlotte chuckled. "He's just being respectful. He's a very nice man. We have a good time when we go out."

"*Respectful* I can get on board with. *Nice? Good?* Those aren't words that thrill me, and I'm guessing they don't thrill you either."

"We have a lot in common, don't we? That's important in a relationship."

"Please tell me you don't talk about horses all night."

Charlotte waved her off, even if it was a little true. "Stop it. He's a steady, responsible man who runs his own business. And most importantly—he's not going anywhere."

Brianna's face softened as her lips lifted in a gentle smile. "He really did a number on you, didn't he?"

She felt like a fool every time she thought of

277

Vince. "I should've known better. It wasn't like Vince didn't talk about living someplace 'more exciting.'" She enclosed the words in air quotes. "I just believed what I wanted to believe, and I paid dearly for it."

"You're being too hard on yourself. I never thought he'd leave either. It seemed like he was digging his job at the bank. He even got promoted. Do you ever hear from him?"

"Here and there. Nothing major, just asking how I'm doing. How the ranch is. A random meme, that sort of thing."

Brianna pursed her lips. "You should block his number, that's what you should do."

"I don't want to be like that. He's no threat to my well-being anymore."

"Now that you have the exciting Kyle in your life?"

Charlotte tilted her a wry look.

"Is that little thing between you and your trainer holding back your relationship with Kyle?"

Brianna had stopped to borrow a pair of Charlotte's boots this week and arrived when Gunner was giving Charlotte a training lesson. She had been so caught up, she hadn't even heard Brianna's car pull up the drive.

"What little thing?"

Brianna arched a knowing brow.

This wasn't the sort of thing that escaped her friend's notice. Or the sort of thing she'd back down from. "All right. Fine. So there's chemistry, I admit it."

"Finally."

"But it can't go anywhere. You and I both know he's just passing through, and the last thing I need is another heartbreak."

"And yet you took him with you to meet your biological father. That's kind of big, don't you think?"

"A moment of weakness." She'd had a lot of those actually.

"I get it. He's temporary and you don't want to get attached. Kyle provides a nice buffer."

Charlotte winced. *Buffer?* "That's a little harsh, don't you think?"

"But true?"

Charlotte hoped that wasn't what she was doing. At least, not entirely. She was giving Kyle a real chance.

Wasn't she?

Brianna put her hand over Charlotte's. "I'm sorry if I'm prying. You know I'm no good at beating around the bush. I want you to be happy. I just don't see any excitement from you where Kyle's concerned. The beginning should be the fun part of the relationship. The exciting part. If it's lacking that now . . ."

"Point taken. But maybe every relationship doesn't have to be the exciting kind. Maybe it can just be . . . comfortable."

"Only you know what you feel. I just don't want you to settle. You deserve so much more than that."

"Look who's talking. You went on two dates with Jeremy and called it quits. He seemed like a really great guy."

Brianna waved her hand. "I don't have time to date. I've got my hands full with Granny and my job for now."

"And giving me dating advice."

Her brown eyes sparkled. "What are friends for?"

"Well, that goes both ways. I think you should give Jeremy a real shot. You seemed to hit it off very nicely, and if I'm not wrong, there was a spark or two."

"Or three . . . ," Brianna muttered.

"What was that?"

"I said 'I agree.' But there'll be time for dating later."

She let her friend get away with that, but only because Charlotte had no room to talk.

Thirty

"You didn't have to come over on your day off." Charlotte felt bad about that. Gunner already worked long hours. She led Maxwell, a bay quarter horse, from the stall. "We could've done this one day this week."

"I didn't have anything better to do at home," Gunner said. "Just had to mow the property, and I got that done this afternoon."

"Isn't that the landlord's job?"

"I don't mind giving Mr. Dixon a hand."

What he wasn't saying was that he worried about his landlord. She focused on his handsome features. For a guy who avoided close connections, he sure was looking out for his elderly friend. Gunner had a softer heart than he wanted to admit.

But he didn't seem to have any family or close friends with whom he kept in contact. Didn't he get lonely? Didn't he ever long for a kind word, a soft touch, a meaningful connection?

His gaze met hers and clung. A familiar expression came over his eyes—sadness or longing? She couldn't be sure which.

Her fingers twitched with the desire to reach out and touch his face. To let him know someone cared. How could he be satisfied with a transient lifestyle and temporary relationships? It must all feel so empty and meaningless. She knew what it was like to have a void, and she wanted to fill that empty space for him. He was so deserving.

Maxwell nickered as Gunner came to a stop beside her.

She pulled her gaze from him. Stroked the gelding's muzzle. Why was she having these thoughts? Even if Gunner had a void, she wasn't the person to fill it. He wasn't staying here.

And, oh yeah, there was Kyle.

She cleared her throat. "So, uh, what do you think's going on with Maxwell here?"

"That'll be your puzzle to solve. His owner says he's always been an easygoing guy, a good companion. But they recently moved to a new property, and now he gets antsy whenever she rides him."

"Any change to his feed?"

"Nope."

"How recently did they move? Maybe he's just settling in."

"It's been six months. He's fine in the stable and pasture. It's only when she's riding him that he becomes agitated."

When a horse exhibited a problem, their human was sometimes the root cause. "Maybe the owner's conveying nervous energy for some reason."

"All right. That's a reasonable conclusion. What should we do next?"

"Saddle him up."

Gunner gave a nod. "Let's do it."

She led Maxwell to the tack room and together they saddled the horse. The gelding exhibited no signs of distress. Instead, his ears perked up and his nostrils flared—signs of curiosity.

Once he was tacked up, she led him out to the ring and mounted. "So far so good." She pulled the reins to get his attention, then squeezed with her legs and made a clicking sound.

Maxwell began walking.

"Good boy." After walking a minute, she urged him into a trot.

Gunner took the center of the ring, watching their progress.

When she changed directions the horse responded perfectly to her instruction. She urged him into a trot again and maintained the pace a minute. The horse had effortless transitions and a nice, smooth gait.

She pulled back on the reins. "Whoa."

When he slowed to a stop, she stroked his neck. "Good boy. Well, so far he seems fine."

"I agree. So what should we do next?"

"Ride him around the pasture?"

He gave a nod. "Hang on a minute." He disappeared into the barn and returned with Rogue, all saddled up. After Gunner mounted they left the ring and headed toward the pasture at a leisurely walk.

Maxwell was responding beautifully. Charlotte was ready to lay his problem at the owner's feet. "Has the owner recently been thrown?" Gunner would've talked extensively with her before taking on the horse. "Or have another reason to be nervous about riding?"

"Nope."

"Hmm. Should we ride for a bit and see if any problems crop up?"

"You're the detective on this case."

She nodded. "All right. We keep riding then."

They kicked it up into a trot, then transitioned to a canter, then a gallop. They flew over the rolling hills and then, after a short while, eased back to a walk.

"I don't get it." Her pulse was still racing from the exhilarating ride. "He's a solid horse. No signs of anxiety at all." If Gunner had a clue what was going on, he didn't voice it.

The sun hung low in the sky, the heat offset by a gentle breeze that cooled the back of her neck. She glanced at Gunner. She'd loved working closely with him over the past month. He wasn't just a good trainer; he was a solid teacher. And now, with their horses clomping in tandem, she had a vision of the two of them working together for years to come, side by side. Partnering with him on this ranch would be a dream. The thought of it made something warm and wonderful bloom inside.

That was just a fantasy. He was leaving in less than two months. The thought of his departure made her heart bottom out. "I need to find another hand. I'll definitely need someone before you leave."

"What about Emerson?"

Charlotte shook her head. "She's made it clear she's not interested in being more involved with the business."

"For a partner, she sure isn't very involved."

"It's my fault. I kind of forced her into this expansion. She wanted to sell and I wouldn't listen to her."

"She wanted to sell a property that's been in your family three generations?"

"She never took to the ranch life like I did. Right now she seems more interested in exploring her culinary skills." She'd been baking quite often, in fact. It seemed to put her sister in a better frame of mind. The wall between them had even dropped a bit. Things were almost back to normal. Of course, that might be because Charlotte had stopped pressing Emerson to do more around the ranch.

"Maybe you should buy her out," Gunner said.

Charlotte chuckled. "Let me just go to the ATM and take care of that."

"Grab some for me while you're at it." They shared a smile. "No, I realize it would take time. But she'd probably be open to small payments over a long period of time. The more profitable the business becomes, the more the business will be worth and the more it'll take to buy her out."

She hadn't thought of that. "I don't want to skimp on what I owe her."

"That's very kind of you. But she's really not an asset to the business, and it doesn't sound as if she ever plans to be."

"That's true." Maybe she should approach Emerson about it. Charlotte could afford small payments, and it might give her sister financial peace of mind to have a little coming in each month. "I'll think about it. Things are precarious between us right now. She's been a little put out with me since I found Craig."

"I wish she could be happy for you. Even I can tell having an answer has brought you peace. It's something you've been questioning all your life."

"I know, but . . . we've always been so close and she's just afraid of losing me."

If Gunner were in Charlotte's shoes, he wouldn't be so understanding, but he held his tongue. It seemed selfish that Emerson wasn't happy for her sister. But she was young. Maybe he shouldn't be too hard on her.

"It'll work itself out in time," Charlotte said. "Anyway, I can't bring myself to regret it. I like Craig a lot. He's trying really hard to get his life in order, and that's something I can respect."

After that first meeting in the park, Charlotte had met with her father alone. There was no need for a buffer now that she knew he wouldn't reject her. They needed to get to know each other, and that was best done privately.

But Gunner asked regularly how things were going. And if the man ever hurt Charlotte, he'd have Gunner to answer to. Especially when she was putting so much on the line, holding back that information from Gavin and Cooper. Gunner wasn't sure how her brothers would respond to being kept in the dark for months.

But Charlotte was in a tricky spot, and that wasn't his decision.

"Are you looking forward to working at Belle Vista?" She released a self-deprecating chuckle. "Uniform or no, that's quite the step up from this place."

He hadn't given much thought at all to moving on, which was odd as he'd always aspired to work with a Derby horse. "Don't sell yourself short. This is a great place to work. It's been fun, being part of its growth. I'll be sad to go."

It was true, and not just because of the ranch. He thought back to the stable when he'd read so much in her eyes. He'd wanted to kiss her in that moment. Wanted to wrap his arms around her and make her forget Kyle Lemmings. Forget that he was her employee.

Make *him* forget why he avoided such connections.

Absently his fingers found the scars, raised and bumpy, beneath his shirt. Everything could be taken in the blink of an eye. Better not to get attached, to things or to people, than to feel that kind of pain again.

"Let's take him on the trail." Charlotte urged her horse toward the woods where the trail picked up.

As they neared the path, Maxwell whinnied and reared. His forelegs clawed at the sky.

"Whoa!" Charlotte leaned forward at a precarious angle.

Gunner pulled Rogue away from the distressed horse even as he watched Charlotte, his heart beating against his rib cage.

The gelding's legs returned to the earth, and she gave him a kick. The trick worked. The horse leaped away from the woods and back the way they'd come.

Gunner followed the spooked horse until Charlotte brought him to a stop by the creek that ran through the valley. It had only been her expertise that kept her seated.

She was talking softly to the horse as he approached.

"That was some nice maneuvering back there."

She tilted him a sideways smile. "I couldn't end up on my butt in front of my trainer."

"We've all been there a time or two."

She straightened in the saddle as a knowing look settled over her features. "It's the trees. Maxwell's afraid of the trees."

Gunner gave her a nod as pride swelled inside. "Well done, Charlie. Well done."

She'd be just fine when he left. The thought carved a hollow space in the confines of his chest.

Thirty-One

Gunner never should've come back to the ranch tonight. Daisy had seemed fine when he'd left. But once he was home, sitting across the chessboard from Mr. Dixon, he couldn't shake the feeling that the horse needed him. And like a fool he'd come running.

Now he was being subjected to something he'd never wanted to see. But like a rubbernecker at a ten-car pileup, he couldn't look away as Kyle leaned in and kissed Charlotte right there on her front porch.

Gunner felt sucker punched. His feet remained planted in the dirt just outside the old barn. And he didn't look away. Would not let himself off the hook. Because maybe if he forced himself to watch, it would somehow eradicate these unwanted feelings for Charlotte.

Kyle's arm came around her waist and he pulled her close. When she tilted her head, her hair tumbled over her shoulder, glimmering red beneath the porch light.

Why had she left the stupid light on? He could see every detail in living color. If the couple got any closer, they might meld into one person. And seriously, how long would this kiss last?

He clenched his hands into fists. How could his

heart be beating so fast when he was just standing here, rooted to the ground like a dead oak tree?

An eternity later the kiss ended, but he still couldn't stop watching.

Charlotte gave Kyle a soft smile as she reached for the door handle. Her lips moved with some undistinguishable words.

Would you like to come inside?

Thank you for a nice evening.

Please leave and don't come back.

Ever.

Everything in him pulled foolishly for that last option, even though it was wishful thinking. He waited to see what would happen next. He moved his hand over his stomach.

And then she entered the house and closed the door behind her.

Gunner let out his breath.

Kyle headed toward his truck, and Gunner darted back inside the barn. Charlotte had been so distracted by her date that she hadn't even noticed the faint light glowing in the barn or his bike parked right outside. Neither of them had.

His stomach clenched as he headed toward Daisy's stall. The horse was restless and he suspected she'd be foaling tonight. Charlotte wouldn't want to miss her labor, but it was too soon to alert her. Maybe it wouldn't even start until morning.

Anyway, he didn't want to see Charlotte right

now. Didn't even want to look at her. That was wrong. He had no right to be angry with her. The scene he'd witnessed stuck like a boulder in his throat, making him too agitated to go home and sleep.

He paced the length of the chilly barn. The nights had grown cooler and today was the first day of October. Only four weeks until he moved back to Kentucky and took his new position. Until he left this ranch and Charlotte behind for good.

Charlotte wasn't yet asleep when her phone vibrated at almost two o'clock. She'd been replaying her date with Kyle. In particular, the good-night kiss on the front porch. It had become an end-of-date ritual. He would give her a sweet smile and lean down and brush her lips with his. They'd been taking it very slow.

But tonight's kiss went on longer than the ones before it had. Two minutes and twelve seconds. Two minutes and twelve seconds was making out. Two minutes and twelve seconds was . . . progress.

It was progress, right?

There had been no teeth since that first kiss. In fact, since they'd worked out those early kinks, Kyle was mechanically perfect. His lips were soft, his breath fresh. He wasn't sloppy or pushy. He opened his mouth not too little or too much.

Just the right amount. He did all the right things. Said all the right things.

Kyle was an excellent kisser.

She heaved a gut-deep sigh and checked her phone. Gunner.

Daisy is foaling.

She whipped back the covers and jumped from bed. She tried to be quiet so as not to wake Emerson as she navigated the steps. In the foyer she pulled on her boots and jacket. She couldn't wait to see Daisy's foal. But first they had to get her through the birth.

A sudden longing for her mother hit hard and drove deep. It was Charlotte's first delivery without her. She knew what to do, but she wished Mom could be here with her. No matter the time of day or night, her mother had loved helping a mare give birth.

Charlotte pushed aside the bittersweet thought and prayed for a safe delivery as she slipped from the house. Nothing was more natural than birthing, but nature didn't always play nice. Still, she'd managed enough foalings that she wasn't nervous to handle it without a vet. Without Kyle.

She was halfway to the barn when she slowed her steps. Why was Gunner here? The pregnant mare had been fine when he'd left. Fine at night check. A light was burning and when she entered the barn, she spotted Gunner inside the stall with Daisy.

"Hi." Charlotte entered the stall and crossed to the mare. "How you doing, girl? You 'bout ready to meet your baby?"

The horse nickered. Other than a flicking tail and a curled lip, Daisy seemed perfectly fine. But Charlotte knew this horse. She stroked her neck. "Everything'll be fine. Better than fine." Charlotte couldn't keep the smile from her lips. She wasn't the least bit sleepy now that the foaling was imminent. As far as she was concerned, this was the best part of owning a horse ranch.

"She's still in stage one," Gunner said.

Mama was handling the contractions well, but this stage could last for hours. Stage two would begin with the rupturing membrane. The foal would start moving through the pelvic canal and culminate with the birth within minutes of the rupture.

"We should move her tail out of the way," Charlotte said.

"I'll get the wrap."

Gunner exited the stall while Charlotte spoke to the mare in a soothing voice. "You're doing great, girl. You've got this. Soon you'll have your baby after all these months of waiting."

Gunner returned and held the mare's tail while Charlotte wound the nude bandage around it to keep it clean and out of the way during the birth.

She was halfway finished when she realized

that Gunner was too quiet. She flicked a glance his way.

His face was set under the harsh light, focused on the task.

He must be worried about Daisy. "How did you know to come out here?" He'd left just after seven, right before Kyle arrived.

"Just had a feeling."

"Those Spidey senses are working well for you." She glanced at him again with a ready smile, but he didn't even look her way. Something wasn't right. "Is something wrong with Daisy? Something you're not telling me?"

"No, she's doing well." His words were clipped.

"Are *you* okay?"

"I'm fine."

He wasn't fine. His face was stone, his eye contact nonexistent. They'd become closer the past month—how could they not with all the time he'd spent training her? They'd become . . . friends. After all, they talked about much more than just work. He shared stories about Mr. Dixon and told her things Gavin and Wes said while they were hiking and the funny pranks they played on each other at work.

Charlotte shared her conversations with her father and her struggles with Emerson's lack of focus and her inability to accept Charlotte's relationship with Craig. She shared her hope that her brothers would ultimately accept her, and that Emerson would eventually come around. She was so eager to have those bumps behind her.

Charlotte frowned at the bandage. She couldn't imagine why Gunner would be upset with her. He'd been fine when he left. Teasing that he could gauge the humidity level by the condition of her hair. True, unfortunately.

Maybe she was misinterpreting his signals. Maybe he was just tired—it was the middle of the night after all—or nervous about the foaling. This was their first. "How long have you been here?"

"Not long. Awhile."

When she finished wrapping the horse's tail, he stepped away immediately.

Her gaze sharpened on his features: eyes tight at the corners, jaw hard, brow furrowed. "Did I do something to upset you?"

He ran his hand over Daisy's quivering belly. "Of course not."

"Then why are you . . . ? You're angry. Something's wrong."

"Nothing's wrong." His hard tone belied his words.

She huffed. "Gunner, come on. Tell me what I did."

"You didn't do anything."

"Then why won't you even look at me?"

His gaze shot to hers. His eyes narrowed. Lips pressed together.

"See, you are mad. You have a mad tone and a mad face."

"Fine then, I don't want to talk about it."

She clenched her teeth. "Well, that's too bad. You can't give me the silent treatment without telling me why. It's not fair."

"Is that so?"

"It's an unwritten rule. You're supposed to tell me what's wrong, I apologize, and then you're not mad anymore. That's the way it works."

He gave her a withering look. "Drop it, Charlie." His tone was deadly quiet.

"No, I won't drop it because—"

And then he was there. His lips crashed into hers, demanding, delicious. His hands swept over her face. Strong fingers threaded through her hair. He was all over her. Inside her, outside her, and still she couldn't get close enough to him. She pressed in.

A volt of electricity ran through her, making her dizzy and dumb. Within seconds her breaths came in gasps. Her heart fought to burst from its confines. His touch was wild and wonderful. She'd never felt so alive, so charged.

He jerked away.

She whimpered, so far gone she didn't even regret the needy sound.

Their breaths fell heavily in the quietness of the stable. Their shoulders heaved. The air between them crackled with tension. He'd put a good foot between them. It wasn't enough. It was way too much.

His eyes pierced hers, holding her hostage. "It's not like it is with you and me."

Her head was spinning. Her body throbbing. She couldn't think past the residual sensations. Good heavens, what in the world had he done to her? She gave her head a shake, trying to make sense of what he'd just said. "What—? What do you mean?"

"You know exactly what I mean. There's no chemistry between you and him."

From some other corner of the universe, the memory of Kyle's kiss—Kyle's bland, meaning-less kiss—materialized. "You—you don't know that."

He pinned her with an unswerving look.

He could read her as easily as he read the horses. She flushed hot. Had he seen that good-night kiss on the porch? Was that what had gotten him so riled?

So Kyle's kiss had been lacking. She winced at the understatement. On the heels of that explosive kiss with Gunner, it had been downright lame. It didn't even deserve to be called a kiss. Nothing she'd ever had before deserved to be called a kiss.

Kyle didn't set her heart racing. And he definitely didn't make her body buzz like a live wire. But come November when Gunner was long gone . . . Kyle would still be here.

Somehow that didn't seem like enough of a reason anymore. It never had been. Brianna was right. She'd been using Kyle as a buffer, and that was unfair to him. And obviously not working because . . .

Gunner stared at her in silence across the space, his eyes hot and maybe a little dazed. She'd done that to him. And if he'd been angry after witnessing Kyle's kiss, did that mean he was jealous? Some part of her went soft and mushy inside.

His gaze fell to her lips and lingered there for an unbearable moment.

She felt the look like a touch. Her lips tingled with want. She pressed them together, trying to erase the feeling. Hopeless.

Then the sound of rushing water broke the silence.

Thirty-Two

Before the sun even peeked over the horizon, Charlotte awakened, got ready, and headed out to the barn. She used *awakened* loosely as she'd hardly slept last night. After Daisy's membranes ruptured, her labor had been quick and routine. A good thing since Gunner's kiss had fried the wiring in her brain.

They'd worked as a team to bring the foal into the world—Daisy, Gunner, and Charlotte. She'd placed gentle traction on the foal's front legs, and Gunner had cleared the nose.

Moments later the colt slid from the birth canal into the clean straw. He was a chestnut just like Daisy but sported a white blaze. He was beautiful. Charlotte used the stethoscope to check his heart rate and lung sounds—all good.

Daisy got right to her feet and began bonding with the foal. The colt stood on his spindly legs at the thirty-five-minute mark and began nursing soon after. Mother and foal seemed healthy. Charlotte was relieved (for more than one reason) that she didn't have to call Kyle.

But now that it was morning, the vet would need to take a blood sample and check the placenta and colostrum. There was no reason to delay any longer. But since he might not be awake yet, she just sent a text telling him of the foal's routine birth.

You're a coward, Charlotte.

A few seconds later his response came. *Great news. Be right over.*

After last night's kiss with Gunner, she knew what she had to do. But that didn't make it any easier. Charlotte leaned on the stall door and watched Daisy with her newborn colt. The horse was so absorbed with her task, she didn't even nicker at Charlotte's approach. Just glanced over, then went right back to cleaning her foal.

"You did a good job, Mama. Your baby's a beauty."

Daisy went right on about her business. Charlotte never grew tired of watching a foal walk around on those impossibly spindly legs. Of watching the mare nurture her baby. The connection between the pair never failed to warm her.

But the sight of the stall also reminded her of that incredible kiss. As it had a hundred times since Gunner left, her mind reviewed every tantalizing touch, every sound and scent in delicious detail. What had it meant? Had he only been trying to prove she and Kyle lacked the chemistry she and Gunner shared?

Well, mission accomplished.

But the way he'd gazed at her said so much more. There was more than chemistry between them. Somewhere between working with the horses and sharing intimate details of her life, tender feelings had developed. The kind of feelings that made her stomach flutter when he was near. Even at the memory of him . . .

As the realization washed over her, she pressed her palm to her chest. Against her hammering heart. She hadn't meant to, but somewhere along the way she'd fallen in love with her trainer. She'd fallen in love with Gunner.

She measured each shallow breath. How had this happened? And what did it mean? Was he willing to change his lifestyle? And was she willing to take a risk on him? Vince's backside was still in her rearview mirror, the pain of his departure still fresh and raw. Fear surged through her veins. She didn't want to end up in that place again.

It would help if she knew how Gunner felt. But they'd been too consumed with the delivery last night to get around to a conversation. During the birth they'd been all business, making sure the foal was positioned correctly and guiding him out. Afterward, she and Gunner had stood outside the stall watching the pair bond for a while, the wonder of the birth settling like a haze over the stall.

It was three thirty when she'd yawned, and he suggested they call it a night. She followed him out of the barn and toward his motorcycle. Her body was still flooded with dopamine from the foaling, her mind filled with questions stirred up by that monumental kiss.

She had no idea what he was thinking. If the kiss had meant anything. Changed anything. But it had changed something for her. If he would consider staying—and that was a big *if*—how could she not be willing to take a risk? Despite her better sense, she envisioned them working this ranch together. What a great team they'd make. He could partner with her, and if Emerson preferred, they could buy her out.

But Charlotte was getting too far ahead of herself. She didn't even know how Gunner felt about her. What if her feelings were unrequited? What if the kiss had been just attraction on his end? Or sheer loneliness? He was a man with no attachments. A man whose history screamed confirmed bachelor. *Commitment issues.*

They'd reached the bike and stopped. Her heart was still filled with wonder and confusion and indecision. She drew in the night air and let the familiar scents of freshly mown grass and honeysuckle soothe her.

The light of a full moon glistened on Gunner's dark hair and carved out shadows in the hollows of his cheeks. "What a night." His voice was low and raspy. The moonlight caught his crooked grin.

"It was amazing, huh? Birthing foals never gets old."

His soulful eyes pierced hers. "I wasn't talking about the foaling."

Tension sprouted like vines, twining the two of them together, pulling them toward each other. Blood hummed through her veins like a dozen angry bees. Her lips ached for his touch. But just before they came together, a rational thought pushed in, unwelcome but timely.

Kyle.

She pressed her palm to Gunner's chest.

He stopped instantly, waiting.

"As much as I might like a repeat performance, there's something I have to do first."

Their gazes clung. His head tipped back as understanding dawned. He put a few inches between them. "Okay."

And then, because she didn't want him to think she was assuming too much, she added, "Even if this is just . . . you know." *Nothing but a kiss.*

He brushed her cheek with his thumb, firing every nerve cell in the wake of his touch. "It's not."

Warmth flowed through her at the confession, relief surging on its heels. All right. Maybe they were on the same page. Or at least in the same book. The same library?

"We should talk," he said, "but it's way past our bedtimes and we're both exhausted."

"Right. We'll talk tomorrow."

"Today."

They'd shared a grin, then he said good night. And Charlotte walked into the house on a cloud of euphoria, the hum of his motorcycle fading in the distance. Was it any wonder she'd hardly slept?

The grumble of an approaching engine sounded outside the barn, and she straightened from the stall gate. Her heart palpitated in response. But it was a truck engine, not the familiar rumble of Gunner's motorcycle.

Kyle was arriving to take care of the foal and check on Daisy.

Charlotte's stomach bottomed out at the task ahead. Regardless of what might or might not happen between Gunner and her, she had to end things with Kyle. She wouldn't settle for some lukewarm relationship, and she wouldn't let Kyle do that either. It wasn't fair to either of them. She never should've let it go on this long. Why were these things only obvious in retrospect?

"Good morning." Kyle beamed as he entered the barn, his soft-sided vet bag hanging from his shoulder.

"Morning. Thank you for coming so quickly."

"That's the job." He stopped at the stall, observing the foal, while she opened the gate and let him in. "He's getting around pretty well already. Tell me about the labor."

Charlotte filled him in on the details of the birth

while he gave both horses some affection. Then he examined the mare and colt and collected blood samples. Next he took a colostrum sample and used his refractometer, placing a drop on the prism, and read the scale through the eyepiece. "Brix score is 23.5 percent."

"No supplementation then?" Kyle carried frozen colostrum for just that purpose as quality colostrum was an immediate need for a foal.

"Nope. It's all good." When he finished he packed up and stood. "Sounds like everything was pretty routine. Mama and baby seem healthy and happy, but I'll run these samples today and make sure the blood work checks out. I'll give you a call either way."

"Thank you. I'm glad you were able to come so quickly."

"Of course. As you know, the first hours are critical."

Charlotte opened the gate and let him out, then followed him to his truck. "I know, but I hate to wake you at the crack of dawn."

"I was already up anyway. I like to get an early start on the day."

They reached his truck and he turned to her, smiling sweetly.

Oh, she didn't want to do this to such a nice man. Should she wait for a better time? He was working after all. But the memory of Gunner's kiss pricked her with guilt. It would be wrong to string this out any longer than she already had.

"Listen, um . . ." She winced. "Before you go, can we talk a minute?"

His smile slipped. "Uh-oh. That doesn't sound good."

She rubbed her lips together. "I just want to say that I've really enjoyed the time we've spent together . . ."

"That sounds suspiciously like a goodbye."

"No, no, of course not. You're such a great person, Kyle. I definitely want you in my life. You're fun to be with, you're a great listener, and you have the patience of Job. You have so many terrific qualities any woman would love to have in a boyfriend."

"Just go ahead and say it, Charlotte."

She sucked in a deep breath. "I think we're better as friends."

He stared at the ground and nodded slowly. "Right."

Her heart hurt at the disappointment scrawled across his face. "I promise, it's nothing you did or nothing about you at all. It's me. I guess I'm looking for something different."

His face bore a grim expression and he met her gaze. "Before you launch into another cliché, why don't I put us both out of our misery and go, okay?" He opened his door.

She scooted out of his way. She'd hoped this would go better. But nobody enjoyed getting dumped. Even when it wasn't his fault. "Kyle."

He settled into the driver's seat and glanced back at her. His shoulders sank as he released a breath. "Listen, we never made each other any promises. We weren't even exclusive. You don't owe me anything, Charlotte."

"I know, but—"

"And the last thing I want right now is the pity I see all over your face, okay? A man has his pride. I'll get over it."

She winced, then made an effort to clear her face of all sympathy. "Right. Sorry."

"It's fine. I thought things were going pretty well with us, but I guess not."

"I did enjoy our time together, all our chats and laughter." She'd just enjoyed him as a friend would, but he wouldn't want to hear that word again.

"Don't worry, I'll be fine. I just—I'm a little blindsided, that's all."

This had been quick. But had it really? Hadn't she known for weeks this relationship wouldn't amount to anything? She'd caught Kyle unaware just like Vince had when he'd dumped her. She hadn't meant to hurt Kyle, but waiting so long had been cruel. "I'm really sorry, Kyle."

"Yeah, I got that." He pressed the Start button and his truck roared to life. His smile seemed forced. "I'll get back to you by the end of the day with the results of these samples."

"Thank you." She grappled for something else to say, and when nothing came to mind, she stepped away from the truck. The contents of her breakfast curdled in her stomach.

Kyle shut his door, made a three-point turn, and headed down the gravel drive.

Thirty-Three

The mountain of regret and guilt evaporated an hour later at the sound of Gunner's approaching motorcycle. Charlotte hadn't expected to see him since she'd told him to take the morning off.

Adrenaline pumped through her system, speeding her pulse and making her breaths shallow. She'd just turned out the horses and was about to muck stalls. But she set the shovel down and headed outside instead. How would he respond to her in the light of day?

She wrung her hands in anticipation of that talk—it would determine whether or not they had a future.

The sun peeked between the mountain pass, bright and beautiful against a cloudless blue sky. The early October air held a refreshing chill, though it would get up to almost eighty today. And why was she thinking about the weather when a very attractive man was rolling toward her, armed with an irresistible grin? Her heart did a flip-flop.

He stopped the bike a few feet away and shut it down, ushering in silence. Their gazes tangled for a long, delicious moment. She'd really become fond of those eyes. And the way they stared at her just now stole the words from her mouth.

"Morning." His voice was morning-raspy.

She tilted her head and crossed her arms. "You really don't listen very well, Mr. Dawson."

He removed his helmet, then offered a playful shrug. "What can I say? I couldn't sleep."

"Oh yeah? And why's that?" Had he been reviewing their kiss a hundred times too? Speculating about what the future might hold?

"I couldn't help but notice you're not lying in bed either. And you've already fed and turned out the horses, so you've been up awhile yourself."

She mimicked his playful shrug. "The horses wait for no man."

"Or woman. How's our foal faring this morning?" He dismounted but stayed put.

She itched to close the distance between them but couldn't make her feet budge. "He and Mama are doing great. He's been nursing a lot, as you'd expect. Daisy's in mommy heaven. She hardly pays me any mind when I come around. I can't even blame her. That colt's as cute as they come."

"Have you decided on a name?"

"I was thinking about Hunter."

He arched a brow. "Because . . . ?"

"October is the Hunter's Moon, and it was full last night."

"Was it now? I hadn't noticed."

Her cheeks warmed at his flirtatious tone. At the memory of that moonlit look he'd given her just before he'd ridden off into the night. She wished she had the nerve to tell him she wouldn't turn down a good-morning kiss. But he was still yards away, hands stuffed in the pockets of his jeans.

He let out a low, throaty chuckle. "Have I mentioned I love the way you blush?"

"It's so embarrassing."

"You're easy to read, Charlie."

She groaned.

"You don't put on airs. You're genuine. Those are good things, rare qualities."

"Well, I'm happy for you. But you're an enigma, so where does that leave me?"

His eyes sparkled. "Guess I'll have to do more talking."

"More talking would be great." As long as he didn't wait too long on the kissing. Because his lips looked especially tasty in the morning light. And she was eager to see if last night had been a fluke. Because wow. Just the memory of it warmed her all over.

Gunner's gaze roved over her face, then he grinned knowingly. "I won't embarrass you by asking what you're thinking just now."

"Well, thanks for that, but I wouldn't have told you anyway. A girl's gotta have a few secrets."

"What kind of secrets?"

"The kind you don't tell anyone."

"I'm a very good secret-keeper."

"You're the one I'm keeping them from."

He chuckled again as he approached, his stride slow and fluid, eye contact steady and piercing. He stopped an arm's length away. His eyes had a sleepy look about them, and his hair stuck up on top as if he hadn't taken time to comb it after his shower. He gazed at her like she was his favorite dessert and he was just about to ditch his diet. "Now that I'm here, I'm just realizing it'll be torture to be this close and not be able to touch you. When will you be talking to Kyle?"

Well, ahem. She could solve that problem. "Kyle already came and went. I broke things off."

"Why didn't you say so?" He stepped forward, placed his hands at her waist, and leaned closer, his eyes fluttering shut.

She pressed a hand against his chest, stopping him.

"Aw, you're killing me, Charlie."

"I seem to recall something about a talk . . ."

His eyes smoldered. "Now? Right now?"

She barely kept herself from leaning in and collecting that kiss. Her lips itched with want. But the recent pain of her last relationship made her hold her ground. "I think I need to tell you about Vince."

"Sure this can't wait?"

"I'm sure."

He sighed. "You mentioned him at the Robinsons' picnic. Breakup, speeding ticket, emotional breakdown. What kind of name is Vince any-way?"

From the nearby paddock, Midnight nickered. Charlotte had never even heard the horse nicker before. "Well, how about that. Someone wants your attention."

"Not the one I was going for." He flashed a grin, then gave her waist a squeeze and let go. "But you're right. Much as I hate to admit it, we do have some things to talk through. And I'm on the clock. I should probably remember you're my boss."

This was complicated on more than one level. All the more reason to verbalize their concerns before things got out of hand. Who was she kidding? They had already gotten out of hand. "Can you hang around after work tonight?"

"I can manage that."

"I could make us a picnic and we could head up to Wildflower Falls."

He smiled sweetly. "I'll be looking forward to it all day."

If Charlotte hadn't taken off after they'd mucked the stalls, Gunner wouldn't have gotten much done. Ever since that kiss last night, he'd been lost in thoughts of her. And seeing her this morning, all fresh and beautiful despite the lack of sleep, hadn't helped. He'd known it would be that way between them. Explosive.

Had he ever had a kiss like that one? A rhetorical question, because no, he had not. He and Charlotte were like fuel on a fire. But it wasn't just their chemistry. Their time together was always easy and natural. He respected her dedication to family, her business sense, and her passion for horses. She was warm and kind and vulnerable in a way that drew him. Her kiss had been like taking all those wonderful, noncombustible qualities and setting them aflame.

And man, did he want to kiss her again.

If he put aside his hormones a minute, he could agree she was right to be cautious. Their feelings had obviously grown well beyond friendship over the past five months. If he examined his own too closely, he might discover he was wading into the deep end of the pool. He was probably up to his neck already. How had that happened?

It didn't take a genius to see their futures didn't exactly align. He had a dream job waiting in Kentucky and—if he was honest—an aversion to close connections. Could he overcome that? He'd never been tempted to try.

But he was tempted now.

Adding to his issues, Charlotte had been burned once before by that boyfriend leaving her high and dry. That had obviously left a mark. Gunner didn't want to hurt her. Would it be fair to build something together when he wasn't sure if he could give up his roaming ways? When he wasn't sure he knew how to build a real relationship? Or even had the guts to try?

That last part was hard to admit. But it was the truth. He already had real feelings for her. It was just less scary to focus on that amazing kiss than all the rest.

It seemed like a good time to bury himself in work. He grabbed a bridle and carried it to the paddock where Midnight waited. The horse had allowed Gunner to put a bridle on him last week for the first time. Gunner had repeated the process every day since.

Midnight approached, his tail loose and swinging freely. His ears pointed toward Gunner. Good signs.

"Hey, buddy. How's it going?" He stroked the horse's muzzle a minute, then slipped the bridle over Midnight's head. The horse's jaw and nostrils stayed nice and relaxed. They were making headway.

Midnight nickered softly.

"That's a nice new trick you've got there. Happy to see me, are you? I'm glad to see you too."

All signs indicated the gelding was ready for more. Ready to trust. Adrenaline shot through his veins at the coming challenge. Today would be Midnight's big day. He could feel it. "Let's do this, buddy. You ready?"

● ● ●

Twenty minutes later, Gunner free lunged Midnight around the ring, spinning his line to tap the gelding's heels. Gunner kept his posture tall and relaxed, his tone calm and confident. He'd done this a hundred times, but every horse was different. And Midnight had been a real challenge this summer. A long, slow challenge.

But the horse was cooperating well today, all things considered. Every time Midnight followed his instruction, Gunner eased up the pressure.

"Good boy," he cooed when the horse followed his command to change directions. "You've got this." He had Midnight's full attention now. The horse was waiting for the next instruction, the ear closest to Gunner turned his way. He was ready.

Gunner coiled up the lunge line, dropped eye contact, and softened his body language. He closed the hand closest to Midnight and brought it across his stomach, turned his back on the horse. Took a few steps. Even with his back turned, he stayed alert to the horse's movements and waited.

Soon the quiet clomping of the horse's hooves grew louder as Midnight approached. A moment later, the gelding pushed his muzzle over Gunner's shoulder.

Gunner couldn't stop the grin that spread across his face. It never got old, that moment when a horse decided to trust. But this particular victory was especially rewarding. He turned and stroked Midnight's forehead. "Yeah, that's right. Good job, buddy. You're a good boy, aren't you? Just needed a little kindness. A little patience."

Movement in his peripheral vision caught his attention. He wasn't alone. Charlotte stood at the fence line, beaming at him with pride. And he beamed right back at her.

Thirty-Four

The forest's shade offered a welcome reprieve from the hot afternoon sun. From somewhere in the leafy canopy above, a robin tweeted, and in the distance the rushing sound of the waterfall carried through the woods. Brittle leaves crunched under the horses' hooves, stirring up the loamy scent of earth. Charlotte breathed in the pleasant scent of autumn.

She led the way on Firefly while Gunner followed on Rogue. The latter had been unhappy about leaving Daisy behind in the stable. But the new mama was too distracted by her colt to notice her barnyard buddy's departure.

As if by silent agreement, Charlotte and Gunner kept their discussion casual on the ride to the falls. The conversation had turned once again to Emerson's lack of interest in the business. "Did I tell you she asked about finding someone to take her place with the trail rides?"

"Maybe it's time to hire that extra hand."

"I'm not sure it's in the budget just yet. But it's not just the immediate workload that troubles me. This place has always been a family operation, and now it's just me. I don't know if I can do this alone." She swatted a fly away. "But I don't want to think about that right now. Let's talk about your progress with Midnight. I'm so glad I caught the Join-Up this morning. What a magical moment."

"It's been slow work but rewarding too. He's got a lot of potential."

"The first time I saw him, I was afraid he was a lost cause. I've never seen such a traumatized horse. And I've known horses with less severe issues that never came around."

"Most of them just require time and patience."

"You're really good at what you do, Gunner. You don't give yourself enough credit."

"Me? What about you? You've been running this business on your own for months, and you're the only one who doesn't realize it. You don't need Emerson, Charlie. You've got this."

His words bolstered her confidence and warmed her through. "Thanks for saying that."

They entered the clearing and the temperature cooled by ten degrees as the woods opened to the towering falls that cascaded into a clear blue pool. A fine mist hovered above the water, and a rich, earthy scent hung in the moisture-drenched air. She never tired of the sight.

They made small talk as they dismounted. Gunner tied up the horses while Charlotte freed the picnic basket and spread a blanket on the rock shelf beside the pool.

Once they were seated they wasted no time digging into the roasted chicken sandwiches, broccoli salad, and cheese cubes, mostly left-overs from Emerson's efforts in the kitchen.

As they ate, Charlotte was ultra-aware of Gunner's nearness—his thigh pressing against hers, his arm brushing hers. At a brief lull in the conversation, Charlotte struggled for the words to bring up her concerns.

Gunner saved her the effort. "Maybe you should tell me about that loser ex-boyfriend. *Vince.* How'd the two of you meet?"

She stifled a smile at his jealous tone. "Well, I'd say we met at the coffee shop, but we actually went to the same high school. He was three years older, however, so our paths didn't cross much."

"You dated for two years?"

He'd remembered. "Right. We became exclusive almost right away. I'd had enough boyfriends to realize he had long-term potential. He was looking for someone to settle down with eventually—at least that's what he'd said."

"How many boyfriends?"

"I don't know. Several. Nothing terribly serious and nothing that lasted very long. Vince was the only one I ever discussed a future with."

Gunner studied her. "You loved him."

The memory of his sudden departure pinched her chest. "I did. I envisioned spending the rest of my life with him. Personality-wise we were a good match. He had a dependable job, and while he wasn't really the ranch type, he supported my passion to keep the family business. Didn't mind the idea of living here."

"It's a beautiful property. Did he and your mom get along? Did Emerson like him?"

She shrugged. "They liked him well enough, I guess. Never said anything negative about him." Though her mother hadn't been one to push her views on her grown children, and Charlotte had never asked her opinion.

"Did you ever bring him up here for a picnic?" He gestured to the falls.

She slid a smile his way. "Would it bother you if I had?"

He seemed to consider the question. "Little bit. If I'm honest."

"I like that you're truthful. And believe it or not, I never brought him here. He wasn't really the outdoor type. He'd rather hang out at the coffee shop or eat at a nice restaurant—he had great taste in food. He worked at the local bank and made a pretty good living."

"It seems Vince and I aren't much alike."

She chuckled. "You should probably consider that a compliment. At the time I was thinking opposites attract." Their gazes caught and held. "But I'm finding it's also nice to have things in common."

"Tell me about his departure. You said it was sudden."

"Very. It was pretty rough. He got an opportunity at a new start-up business in Atlanta, which he didn't tell me about until he'd already made his decision to leave."

"Nice of him to include you."

"I was completely blindsided. He didn't even invite me to go with him."

"Surely he knew you'd never leave your ranch."

"Maybe so. Still would've been nice to be asked though. As it was, the decision seemed to be Atlanta or me—and Atlanta won. We had a big blowup. Our worst fight ever. He moved the day after he told me."

"No wonder you were shocked. There was no talk of continuing long distance?"

"It was pretty obvious he wanted a clean break." She shook her head, the memory of that bombshell hitting her anew. "I thought we wanted the same things—marriage, a couple of kids, a life here in Riverbend. But in hindsight I can see he'd left some clues. He made offhand references to living elsewhere. Often remarked that there wasn't much to do around here."

"I guess that's true if you're not the outdoors type."

"I just believed what I wanted to believe."

"We do that sometimes."

"Well, now I know that's something I need to be mindful of."

"Which brings us to *us*." He set his plate

325

aside and met her gaze. "Given what you've been through with Vince, I must seem like a big risk. I'm a thirty-four-year-old man without real friends or family." He slid her a smile. "Or furniture."

"That thought does occur. You don't have roots anywhere. How has that worked for you in the past? I can't imagine your mobile lifestyle is conducive to long-term relationships."

"My relationships have been short term and, until now, not very risky."

Risky. She considered a relationship with him chancy, but she didn't realize he also thought of her that way. "Interesting choice of words."

"Real feelings are always a risk, aren't they? Nobody likes to get hurt."

Fair point. "So you haven't had any long-term relationships?"

His eyes softened as he regarded her for a long moment. "I haven't been with anyone who tempted me to."

Her insides gave a squeeze. "A very nice way of putting it."

"It's the truth. This relationship would be a risk for both of us. I guess the question is, are we willing to take it?"

She thought back to Vince and his abrupt departure. Thought of her growing feelings for Gunner. It would hurt even if he left today. She was already in that deep. "I have to ask—

326

how committed are you to an itinerant lifestyle? Would you ever consider settling down in one place—specifically, Riverbend?"

"I've been thinking about that a lot since last night." He gave a sheepish smile. "Longer, if I'm honest. It's the reason I was already awake when my alarm went off this morning."

"I'm glad I'm not the only one who couldn't sleep."

Gunner couldn't drag his gaze from Charlotte's beautiful face. The afternoon sunlight broke through in spots, glistening like sparks of fire in her hair. This was not an easy conversation. They were each vulnerable in different ways. But he appreciated her honesty and owed her thoughtful, candid answers.

Her question was a fair one. "I love your ranch. I love working here. It's peaceful and offers plenty of challenge. Riverbend seems like a great community."

"You've already made friends."

"And that's not really typical for me." Wes and Gavin in particular were fun to hang with, and there was a depth to them he appreciated. They both had roots here—Gavin's deep and Wes's new but growing strong. Gunner could envision long-term friendships and community here in Riverbend. Was that what he wanted? His chest tightened at the thought. Caring about people only to lose them wasn't high on his list of priorities.

"Why do you think that is?"

He lifted a shoulder. "Because I'm always aware I'll be moving on. Why go out of my way to develop friendships that won't last? I make acquaintances, of course. Have amiable relationships with coworkers."

"So Riverbend has been different for you."

"In lots of ways." Starting with Charlotte. Maybe it was time for him to settle down. He wasn't a young man anymore.

But he wasn't sure he could be fulfilled staying in one place. He'd never experienced a real home as an adult. What if he got bored? What if he felt trapped? As much as he wanted a relationship with Charlotte, he had to be honest about that, with himself and with her.

He met her gaze and was immediately drawn into her expressive eyes. He and Charlotte had become closer somehow, as if pulled together by some invisible magnet. He could simply lean forward and kiss her. She was tempting, gazing at him that way. She wanted to pursue this relationship as badly as he did. "This is a new experience for me. I've never felt this way about anyone. I'm wild about you, Charlie."

Her features softened. "I feel the same."

Her face and body language stated that clearly enough. But the words made his heart buck. She turned his world on end. He had to see where this thing led, because how could he not?

But they needed to go into this with their eyes open. "I'm willing to consider staying in Riverbend. But I don't know the future. I can't make any promises."

A smile tilted her lips. "It's too early for promises. I realize that. I just needed to know you were open to the idea."

"You have me open to all kinds of ideas." His gaze dropped to those luscious lips of hers. Finally. He'd been dreaming of another kiss since early this morning. How had it been less than twenty-four hours since he'd had his arms around her? He leaned forward, felt the warmth of her breath on his lips. His heart thudded heavily against the confines of his rib cage.

She placed a palm on his chest, stopping him.

His breath emptied in one long sigh. "You gonna make a habit of this, sweetheart?"

"Sorry." Those worry lines appeared between her brows, and fear shadowed her eyes. "Just promise you won't leave suddenly. That if you decide you can't do this, you'll be honest with me. You'll tell me as soon as you realize."

He wanted to eradicate her every doubt and fear. He wanted to make her smile and laugh and sigh in satisfaction instead. He ran a thumb across her cheek. "I promise."

She held his gaze for a long moment. And then

her lips were on his, soft and searching, giving and receiving.

He pulled her closer, sliding his arms around her at long last. She fit him just right. Familiar somehow, as if he'd held her a hundred times already. But new, too, like he could never get enough.

Her fingers scraped through his hair. A hand gripped his bicep. She had his full attention. He was lost and didn't want to be found. When he deepened the kiss she mewled in response, and the sound sent a jolt through his system. This woman lit him up like a Christmas tree.

The kiss went on and on, stirring every cell to life, making him wish for things they weren't ready for. He should tap the brakes. They shouldn't rush this. He wanted to be careful with her feelings. With his own for that matter.

With the patience of a saint, he drew away, putting inches between them.

Her needy gasp was nearly his undoing.

Her eyes fluttered open, their depths mirroring his own feelings and desires. They took each other in, their ragged breaths mingling in the space between them.

"I guess it wasn't a fluke after all," she whispered.

A chuckle caught in his throat, tangled in a knot of need. "It definitely was not."

Thirty-Five

It wasn't easy. But as if by mutual agreement, Charlotte and Gunner settled into work with an unspoken rule. By day they were boss and employee, and by evening they were more.

So much more.

He made her feel so many good things. The fluttery stomach, the flush of anticipation, the sweaty palms. With him she felt joy and peace and comfort. Until she thought of the future. He hadn't brought up Belle Vista since they'd been together. Had he given up the job, or was he waiting to see how things went between them? Maybe she should bring it up herself, but she didn't want to rush him.

Over the next two weeks, Gunner came for supper several times. And tonight they went to Gavin and Laurel's home. They had a wonderful chili dinner and finished it off with homemade apple pie, the fruit fresh off the trees in their beautiful Harvest Moon Orchard.

After Gavin put Emma to bed, the couples sat around the firepit on their patio, chatting like old friends until the moon rose high in the sky.

The guilt didn't hit Charlotte until she and Gunner arrived at her place. Emerson's car was gone, but that was no surprise. When she wasn't out on a date, she was hanging out with Vivian from the bakery.

Charlotte walked up the porch steps, Gunner on her heels, and turned at the door. The porch light shed a golden light across his lovely features. Sometimes she just stared at him in wonder that he was hers. "Want to come in?"

"We've had a lot of late nights this week—not that I'm complaining. But I caught you yawning at least three times tonight."

"A girl needs her sleep."

"Exactly why I'm gonna get on my bike and let you hit the hay."

"Listen to you, talking like a bona fide southerner."

"I'll leave the sexy drawl to you."

She loved that he adored her accent. It wasn't the first time he'd mentioned it this week. But her thoughts returned to her half brothers and turned sour. "Do you think Gavin and Cooper will be angry when they find out I'm their sister?"

Gunner paused thoughtfully, a frown tugging his brows. "I don't really know them well enough to answer that question. When's Craig planning to tell them about the affair?"

"He gets his one-year chip November second."

"Only a couple weeks to go then."

"But we hung out with Gavin tonight and committed to eating with the Robinsons tomorrow. I'm afraid they'll feel betrayed. Like I lied to them. I am lying to them." She covered her face. "I'm an awful person."

He pulled her hands from her face. "No, you're not. But if you're that worried, you could always tell them."

She felt so torn. "But Craig has so much riding on this. He's been working hard to get and stay sober. He desperately wants a relationship with *all* his kids, and he's determined to get that chip before he tells them. I'm afraid if I told them what their dad did all those years ago, it would only drive a bigger wedge between them. Possibly an irreparable wedge. I can't do that to Craig. And the consequences of that might also come between him and me."

"I wish Craig would just tell them now. Can't he see it's putting you in a bad spot?"

"I haven't really expressed my concerns after that first mention of it. Our relationship is new and fragile. I don't want to rock the boat."

"That's your call. You're in a tight spot, Charlie. But if I can see that, surely your brothers will too."

"I hope you're right."

"They're good guys. Once they find out you're their sister . . . I don't know how they could resist wanting to know you better." A smile played at the corner of his mouth. "I sure couldn't."

Her heart released a happy sigh. "I'm glad you couldn't."

Awareness crackled between them. He leaned forward and brushed her lips with his, holding her gaze through the brief but stirring kiss.

She longed for more but appreciated that he was being careful. Maybe not right now in the moment, but in the long term. Moving too fast would be a mistake. Things could go wrong, and then she'd get hurt all over again. And this time, she was afraid, would be even worse than last time.

Thirty-Six

The last person Charlotte had expected to see tonight was Gavin.

The evening had started on such a high note. She always enjoyed her chats with Craig. They'd begun meeting weekly on Tuesdays at the pizza place where she and Gunner had shot pool the one time. Craig loved their deep-dish Carnivore's Delight, but it had taken him weeks to admit it. He'd always catered to her preference—deep-dish pepperoni.

When she'd discovered this, she insisted they get two pizzas and take the leftovers home. Craig was a selfless man and a good listener. She'd spent many hours filling him in on her life prior to their meeting. His questions seemed endless.

She told him about Gunner, who would've come with her tonight except he had a late meeting with Avery and Lisa to finalize details regarding the fund they were starting for the underinsured. With Trail Days coming up this weekend, the meeting was imperative.

Craig listened intently as she told him how Gunner had brought Midnight around. She was proud of him and wanted her father to like him too. The men needed to get to know one another better.

Craig reminisced about her mother fondly. But in general he avoided talking about his life as an alcoholic.

Midway through their meal he leaned in to the table. "I wasn't a good person back then. I let down all the people who mattered to me—your mom included. I'm not proud of it. But I hope I can do better going forward."

"We've all made mistakes. I'm proud of you for trying so hard."

Like so many veterans he didn't like talking about the war either. But she'd gathered from the little he'd said that he'd begun drinking because of the PTSD he suffered once he was back in the States. He desperately needed therapy and, like so many people, self-medicated instead. She was glad to hear he was getting help now.

He loved talking about Gavin and Cooper. Was hungry to know how they were doing, what their lives were like. Guilt pricked as she fed him information—nothing too personal. Nothing the average neighbor wouldn't already know. It was impossible to miss the way Craig's eyes lit up with pride at every detail she spooned out. And impossible to deny him the pleasure of learning these little tidbits.

Once they'd finished their meals and the conversation died down, Craig walked her out to her truck. The moon had risen and the stars twinkled above on an inky canvas.

They wrapped up their conversation as they came to a stop by her vehicle, situated under a bright safety lamp that lit half the parking lot.

Her father's aging features softened an instant before he leaned in for an awkward hug. This gesture was fairly new as she'd hugged him for the first time just last week. She could tell he wasn't used to displays of affection. He leaned into the hug from the waist and didn't seem to know what to do with his hands.

Her heart softened toward him as she gave him a squeeze. He was obviously in foreign territory, but he was doing his best. She was growing to care about him.

They said goodbye and parted ways. Charlotte remained, watching him walk across the parking lot. His stride and the way he carried himself were already familiar. He walked like a man beaten down by life. She hoped to change that. He'd made a lot of mistakes, but he had many positive qualities and a lot of love to give.

He got into his old Ford and pulled from the lot.

Charlotte turned toward her truck, a smile lingering on her face. And that's when she saw Gavin standing beside his truck, gaping at her, a dozen questions shifting across his features.

Thirty-Seven

The pizza in Charlotte's stomach churned as Gavin approached. The grim look was all she needed to confirm he'd seen her with Craig. The memory of laughing with her brother at Sunday's picnic dinner materialized. They'd built such a good rapport. Was all that about to be ruined? Her stomach threatened to expel its contents.

His long strides shrank the space between them quickly. He stopped several feet away, his head turned slightly to the side, eyes like heat-seeking missiles under the glare of the safety lamp.

She propped up a smile and tried for a casual tone. "Hey, Gavin. What are you doing here?"

"I'm bidding on a project nearby. Bringing home pizza. Do you know who that man was?" He nodded toward the spot Craig's car had occupied.

"Um, yes. I do. You must be wondering what I was doing here with your dad."

He frowned. "More concerned than anything. You shouldn't get mixed up with him, Charlotte. He's not a good person. I know he's my dad, but even if it's business or something, I wouldn't recommend getting involved with him. You can't count on him—except to let you down."

"It's not."

A question flickered in his eyes.

"I mean, it's not business." A car pulled into the lot, its bass thumping as heavily as her heart. "Listen, can we go inside? Have a drink, talk a minute?"

His gaze sharpened on hers. "What's going on? Why were you with my dad? You hugged him," he added as if just remembering.

"Really, if we could just go inside—"

Irritation flashed on his face. "Just tell me what's going on."

The suspicion in his eyes held her captive. She had to tell him now, no matter how it might affect his relationship with Craig—though it didn't seem as if Gavin's opinion of his father could possibly sink lower.

"I have something to tell you that might be surprising. Or shocking. It might be shocking."

He made an impatient gesture that urged her to continue.

"Right. Well, my mom died last year. You know that. And, um, after she died . . . Wait, so you might not know that my dad, Patrick, was actually my stepdad. My mom married him when I was seven. I never actually knew my biological father."

Gavin's jaw muscles twitched.

I need words. I don't want to hurt him. I don't want to hurt Craig. But now I have no choice but to tell him. God? We got a copy?

"And . . ." His tone was impatient.

She just had to spit it out. It was all she could do at this point anyway. "A while after my mom passed, I found some things she left for me in a safety-deposit box. Eventually they led me to believe that Craig was my biological father."

He stared blankly at her for a long minute. "And is he?"

She drew a deep breath. "Yes, he is. We took a test and everything."

His gaze roved over her face, taking in her features the way she had his all those months ago. All those months when she could've told him the truth.

After a minute his features softened a bit. "You're my sister."

The words were said so gently, hope bloomed inside. Maybe all wasn't lost. The Robinsons revered family. And she was family. She gave a shrug like *That's me.*

His eyes tightened with worry. "Charlotte . . . you know he's a drunk, right?"

"*Was* a drunk. He's actually been sober for almost a year, and he's been waiting and hoping that you and Cooper would—"

Gavin's body tensed and his face went hard as stone.

Right. She snapped her mouth closed. Maybe not the time to sell him on his dad. "Anyway. He's sober now."

"Wait." His eyes narrowed thoughtfully. "You're what—midtwenties?"

He was doing the math. She pushed aside her dread and answered his question. "Twenty-six."

A second later he gave a mirthless laugh, shaking his head. "Of course. He cheated on my mom. Don't know why that would surprise me. Why anything he'd do would surprise me. Listen, do yourself a favor and stay away from him. He has a way of—" His eyes sharpened on her again. "Wait. When?"

She blinked. "When what?"

"You said a while after your mom passed, you found that stuff and realized he was your father. When exactly was that?"

Here came the hard part. "Okay . . . so I originally found the contents of the safety-deposit box back in March, but—"

"March."

"I know. But please try to understand. The items she left were kind of vague—newspaper clippings about you and Cooper, a medal, a photo of a man with my mom . . ."

"What kind of medal?"

"What? I don't know. A war medal of some kind, I guess."

His jaw flexed. "The Distinguished Service Cross."

"I—I don't know. Maybe?"

He gave her a flinty look. "My mom's been

searching for that for years. She wanted Coop and me to have it."

Her eyes burned with tears. "I'm sorry. I didn't know. You can have it."

"That's not the point. And you still haven't told me when you realized Craig was your father."

She shrunk at his angry tone. "I was getting to that. I originally thought Jeff was my father. I thought he was your and Cooper's biological father, and then I found out he wasn't, so I did all this research to figure out who he was."

"Why didn't you just ask me?" he spat out.

"Are you kidding me? I had no idea how he might feel about me showing up in his life. Or what if he was married and didn't want his wife to know about me? And what if you and Cooper didn't want anything to do with me because he cheated on your mom with my mom?"

He swatted the air. "You still haven't told me how long you've known." He pressed his lips together and pinned her with his intense stare. "It was before we built your barn, wasn't it? You hired us because you wanted to snoop around and get your answers without telling us who you were."

"I needed that barn!" She swallowed against a mountain-sized knot. "But yes, I also wanted to get to know you. Is that a crime? You're my *brother*."

"That's why you were staring at me like that."

Her cheeks heated. "Please understand where I was coming from. I wasn't trying to do anything underhanded. I was just trying to see if you might—"

"We welcomed you at our family suppers. I welcomed you into my home. At my *table*. You know my wife and daughter. What more could you have possibly needed to know before you told me the truth?"

"It's not just me now. I only met your dad—our dad—a couple months ago. He didn't want—"

"*Two months?* You met him two months ago." He shifted away, ran a hand through his black hair.

She took his arm. "Just listen, please. Craig wanted a full year of sobriety before he told you and Cooper. He wanted you to know he was serious about quitting. I know you're terribly angry with him, but he's been working hard, and he's really hoping to have a relationship with—"

"You don't know anything about Craig or my relationship with him! You weren't there when he didn't come home or when I heard my mom crying at night. You weren't there when he didn't show up for baseball games or award ceremonies or birthday parties because he was too busy getting drunk. Or when the police hauled him away from our elementary school because he was hanging around, peeing on the brick walls and embarrassing himself in front of all our friends.

You don't have the first clue." Gavin turned and paced away from her. He stopped and braced his hands on his hips, his shoulders rising and falling.

A vise tightened around her heart. She couldn't even imagine growing up with that kind of father. "You're right. I don't know what that was like."

"My mom's been through enough. And now I have to tell her that in addition to verbally abusing and abandoning her, Craig also cheated on her. Had a child with someone else. A child who has ingratiated herself with our family and who's been creeping around us for months all the while knowing that we're related."

Charlotte winced. It wasn't like that. He was making it sound so much worse than it actually was.

But was he really?

The question gutted her because he was right. She'd gotten caught up in his wonderful family and hadn't wanted to lose them. Despite her best efforts to hold it back, a tear trickled down her face. Her chin wobbled. "I'm sorry, Gavin. I'm sorry I waited so long to tell you. I didn't mean to get so close to your family, but you were all just so welcoming, and I couldn't resist getting to know you better. I was trying to honor Craig's wishes, and it all just got away from me." She swiped away another tear. "I know how it appears, but please believe me when I say I didn't mean to hurt you or anyone else. That's the last thing I wanted."

He heaved a sigh. Gave her a grim look. "You can't just expect me to be okay with this, Charlotte. You've known we were siblings for *seven months*—and from over here it feels like you chose Craig over Cooper and me. That doesn't feel very good."

Regret unfurled in her chest. "I'm so sorry, Gavin."

He held her gaze for a long, painful minute. "I am too." Gravel scraped beneath his feet as he turned and headed toward his truck.

As Charlotte watched him go, a bone-deep cold swept over her, chilling her from the inside out.

Thirty-Eight

It was the kind of day when Gunner preferred to stay busy. The kind of day when downtime only meant old memories crashing into the present day. He'd always coped with the anniversary of his parents' death by staying busy. If he was busy, he couldn't think about the horrible fire and its aftermath. Couldn't feel that awful void he tried to pretend wasn't there. Or remember the way he'd felt when his grandpa delivered the terrible news.

When he was four or five, he'd been at a friend's house, in their swimming pool. He and his friend stayed in the shallow end, tossing a small football. But soon they were playing on their own. Gunner tossed a penny and dove down for it. Several times later he came up for air but couldn't find any. His feet couldn't find the bottom either. He'd drifted into the deep end.

Panic surged. He flailed his arms, kicked his feet. He reached air, drew a breath, but sank again, breathing in water. His lungs felt as if they might burst. A sense of doom nearly swallowed him whole. He was drowning. Just when he thought he was done for, his friend's mom fished him out of the pool.

That's how he'd felt when his grandpa told him

his parents were gone. Gunner was back in that pool, flailing, kicking, drowning. He still felt that horrible panic when he remembered that day in the hospital and all the days after as he counted his losses.

Which was exactly why he preferred not to think of it at all.

And as it happened, staying busy on Charlie's ranch was easily done, with so many tasks to distract him. He was even glad for the after-hours meeting at the Robinson house. And he didn't mind when it ran later than expected.

It was going on eleven when he said good-bye and mounted his bike. They'd gotten a lot done. Avery was organized and efficient—she'd already formed a nonprofit, HealthServe, which would make Trail Days' gift and future contributions tax-deductible. Lisa was the creative one. She had lots of ideas about how to spread the word about the charity so that many people would benefit. She'd already given it a prominent spot on the Trail Days website and on all the flyers they'd posted locally.

On his way home, hugging the tight curves of the road, he once again pushed back thoughts of the anniversary and focused instead on feeling grateful. It did feel good to give back. This small community had such a big heart. The people cared about each other, pitched in when help was needed. They came through when disaster struck.

No wonder Charlotte wanted a life here. Who could blame her?

He hoped the dinner with her father had gone well. She seemed to enjoy their chats and was growing attached to him. As much as he would've liked to check in with her, it was too late to call. She usually went to bed around ten thirty, and he didn't want to wake her. It would wait till morning.

The past couple of weeks with her had been amazing. He couldn't seem to get enough of her. For the first time since he'd lost everything, he could see himself settling down somewhere. Making a family. Making a life.

Charlie.

His heart swelled two sizes in his chest at the thought of her. He enjoyed working with her. She was an excellent boss, neither demanding nor lax. There wasn't a task on the ranch she considered herself too good for. She got right in there and mucked out the stalls with him—a big difference from his previous bosses.

But their relationship had progressed well beyond boss-employee. The evenings he spent with her had deepened their connection. And when they were apart he found himself thinking of her, wanting to be with her. He couldn't wait to get his arms around her. To get his lips on hers. She was . . . she was everything to him. And he couldn't deny the truth any longer.

He was head over heels in love with the woman.

A feeling of euphoria swept over him at the thought. But before it could carry him away, a sense of doom nearly squeezed the air from his lungs.

He gave his head a hard shake. No, he wouldn't give in to negative thinking. Of course love was a risk. But he'd push through the barrier. He'd focus on the positive.

Gunner opened his eyes to inky blackness. His bedroom was hot and alive. Heart hammering, he jerked his Superman blanket over his head. But he couldn't escape the loud roar or the sound of shattering glass. He couldn't even breathe. Smoke caught in his burning throat and he choked out a ragged cough.

From somewhere far away, his dad's voice broke though the chaos. "Gunner!"

He pushed down the covers. Peered through the darkness to where the hall glowed a strange orange-red. The colors moved and shifted.

The house is on fire.

The realization flooded his veins with fear.

"Dad!" He squeezed into the corner of his bed. "Dad! I'm in here!"

"Gunner! I'm coming!"

A crash sounded from somewhere outside the darkness. Sparks flew. The flames growled and hissed like a ferocious lion. He threw the covers over his head.

Go away. Go away!

He curled into a ball, made himself as small as he could. If he could make himself small enough, maybe he would disappear.

"Daddy!" he croaked out.

His body trembled. His chest was wracked with coughs. *Daddy! Help! Somebody help me. Please!*

In a flash he was waking up in a foreign bed. He lay under a crisp white sheet. Beeping noises assaulted his ears and the smell of medicine filled his nose. His throat burned and his eyes stung. Fear raised the hairs on his arms.

His grandpa appeared at his side. "Hey, buddy boy. You're awake."

"What—what happened?" he croaked.

Grandpa's eyes turned down at the corners, filled with tears. He put his hand over Gunner's. "You don't remember the fire?"

Gunner's thoughts flashed back to the roaring and hissing and the paralyzing fear.

"There was a fire at your house, son. I know you're hurting, but you're going to be okay."

Gunner recalled his dad's voice, calling through the fire. "Where's Mom and Dad?"

Grandpa opened his mouth. Shut it again. His Adam's apple bobbed.

A terrible dread bloomed inside. Gunner had the urge to put his hands over his ears.

But a quiet beeping rose from the hospital clamor. Grew louder.

Gunner's eyes flew open. Dawn's early light filled the room. It was silent except for that incessant beeping. His alarm clock. The bed quaked with the force of his heartbeats. His lungs struggled to keep pace, and sweat beaded his forehead.

A dream. It was only a dream.

He shut off the alarm and fell back in bed. He closed his eyes against the light, trying to shake the remnants of the nightmare. But it hadn't just been a dream, had it? The fire had been real. He had lost everything that night. Some people said they'd lost everything, but they hadn't. Not really. Gunner, at the tender age of nine, learned what it was like to lose even the pajamas on his own back.

They said he'd passed out in his bed. His dad died trying to save Gunner. A beam fell on him in the hallway. The firefighters found his mom collapsed on top of him. They carried the couple from the burning house, but it was too late.

They were gone. His parents were gone.

Inside he flailed and kicked and fought for breath. He was drowning in a pool of despair, and no one would save him this time.

He'd lain in that hospital bed for over a week. Learned his parents had been killed by faulty wiring and flammables in the garage. And when the hospital released Gunner, when he moved miles away to live with his grandpa in Kentucky, the rest of the losses piled up like a stack of dirty dishes.

His baseball card collection—gone.

The stubs from every movie he'd attended with his parents—gone.

His new Adidas tennis shoes—gone.

His blue Huffy bike—gone.

The pajamas Mom got him for Christmas—gone.

Even his friends and his school and his favorite park were gone because they were four hundred miles away, and he would never see them again. Each loss was a weight to his sinking body. But the loss of his parents sat like a boulder on his chest, their absence pressing him to the pool floor.

Everything he had was gone somehow. The only thing left was him. And he didn't know how to exist without all the rest.

His grandpa had taken him shopping, but Gunner didn't care about new clothes. Or a new bike. Or replacement baseball cards. He didn't even pick them out because they didn't matter. Why would he let them matter when they could be taken in the blink of an eye? Losing hurt too much.

Now Gunner rolled to his back and flung an arm over his face, trying to erase the nightmare from his memory. He thought he was done with that wretched memory. Or that it was done with him. It had plagued him for so many years and then faded away like the mist over a pond on a cool fall morning.

But now it was back.

The nightmare made it all fresh and raw again. Memories rolled through his mind. His mom had always stayed home with him. She was wonderful. She handled the day-to-day running of the house. On the side she made special-occasion cakes—tiered wedding cakes, covered with cascading flowers, and birthday cakes in every theme imaginable. His favorite was the Spider-Man cake she made for his seventh birthday.

His dad had put in long hours as a plumber, but he was the one Gunner worshipped. When he was home he was the fun dad, taking Gunner to Twins games, watching Saturday morning cartoons with him, and fishing with him.

Only after Gunner was all grown up did he realize his mom had gotten the short stick where his regard was concerned. That thought always made him ache with regret. Had he ever told her what a great mother she was?

He sucked in one deep breath after another, trying to remind himself that he wasn't drowning. Trying to shake the paralyzing fear that he was doomed.

He let thoughts of Charlie flood through

instead. Let them take up all the space the nightmare had filled. Let them soothe him.

But something dark and slippery persisted. It sprang up from the shadowy corners of his mind. From the storehouse of each and every cell that remembered something he'd briefly and stupidly forgotten the past two weeks: Anything could be snatched away at a moment's notice. And the pain of losing it could last a lifetime.

Thirty-Nine

Even sleep-deprived and miserable, Charlotte could see from yards away that something was off with Gunner. She'd overslept. And when she'd awakened at almost eight to the memory of hurt and anger on Gavin's face, she wanted to pull the covers over her head and fall back into the oblivion of sleep.

But there were horses to care for. Besides, she needed to tell Gunner everything that had happened last night. Get his advice. How would she fix things with her brothers? By now she was probably persona non grata with the entire Robinson family.

She'd tried to call Gunner twice last night, but his battery must've gone dead. She hadn't bothered leaving a message. She'd called Craig instead and told him what had happened after he left the restaurant. He handled the news with grace, but Charlotte could hear the disappointment in his voice as he assured her everything would be okay. His kindness in the face of adversity brought tears to her eyes.

But now as she approached the barn where Gunner was mucking out stalls, she could see something else was awry. His shoulders were tense as he stabbed the shovel into the hay. His brows pinched together and a frown tugged his lips.

Surely he wasn't upset about her late start. "Good morning."

He barely glanced her way. "Morning."

All thoughts of her own troubles fled as a niggle of fear squirmed up her spine. "Sorry I'm late. I must've turned off the alarm and gone back to sleep." She grabbed a shovel and went to work in a nearby stall. "You should've called. You didn't have to do all this yourself."

He pitched a load of soiled hay into the wheelbarrow. "No problem."

She watched him for a moment, that fear blooming in her chest, compressing her lungs. "Is something wrong? You seem upset." The last time she'd said that, they'd been about to deliver a foal. About to have a kiss that just knocked her socks off. She had a terrible feeling this discussion wouldn't end the same way.

He emptied another load, then set down his shovel and faced her. His resigned look made her want to rescind the question. Made her want to return to her house and crawl under the covers.

He came around the partition and stood at the open gate of the stall she was cleaning. He stared at some point near her feet. "Listen . . . I think we need to talk. Maybe we should sit down somewhere."

Her spine stiffened in defense. She leaned

her shovel against the wall. "Sounds serious." He was gonna break up with her. It didn't take a genius to recognize the signs. After all, she'd done the very same thing to Kyle less than three weeks ago. She braced herself for the coming impact. "I'd rather just talk right here." Where the familiar scents of hay and horseflesh could comfort her.

"All right." He absently rubbed his stomach, his gaze lighting everywhere but on her. "I've really enjoyed getting to know you, especially the past couple weeks. It's meant a lot to me. *You* mean a lot to me. And this might seem sudden, but— You asked me before to let you know if—"

"You're leaving." Her tone was somehow flat despite the fact that her heart was splintering into a million pieces.

He finally made eye contact.

And now that he had, she couldn't seem to pull her attention from the deadness she saw there. It was as if someone had shut off all the lights, locked all the doors.

"I'm sorry."

The backs of her eyes stung. That familiar lump swelled in her throat. She didn't understand. She thought back to last night when they'd parted ways. Everything had seemed fine. They'd kissed goodbye and he pressed a sweet kiss to the top of her head before getting on his motorcycle and heading down the drive.

"What happened? Did I do something wrong?"

He pushed his hands into his pockets. "It was nothing you did. I just . . ."

She might not know what had happened, but she knew what the problem was. It was the very thing she'd feared when she decided to risk her heart anyway. "You don't want to settle down here with me."

His eyes softened. His posture lost that starched look. "It's not you. It's nothing to do with you. I can't settle down. It's just not in me, that's all."

He was choosing his vagabond lifestyle over her. It meant more to him than she did. That was hard to swallow because nothing meant more to her than him. And she was getting really tired of being everyone's second choice.

"I'll stay through the end of the month like we agreed."

She blinked at him. And work together for eleven more days? See him and not be able to touch him? Talk to him and not be able to hold him or laugh with him or kiss him silly? She was already shaking her head. "No. That won't work."

"At the very least you'll need time to find some help. And there's Trail Days this weekend. I'll do my part."

"I'll figure it out. I can't do this. Work together and just act like—" Her voice wavered pitifully. She pressed her lips together.

"I'll stay out of your way. Come on, I don't want to leave you in a bind."

In a bind? Didn't he know he was ripping her heart from her chest? Leaving her short-staffed was the least of what he was doing to her. He was abandoning her, and she didn't want him hanging around, watching her fall apart. She didn't even know if she could hold it together long enough to see him off today.

She pressed through the pain. Pushed back the tears. Swallowed the lump in her throat. "Thank you for telling me how you feel. But I think it's better if you just leave now. I'll make out a final check—"

"Charlie . . ."

"—and forward it to your new address, or I can drop it by your place later, whichever you prefer."

He tilted his head. Resignation showed in the downward tilt of his eyes and the slump of his shoulders. "I'll leave if that's what you really want. Keep the money though. It's the least I can do, leaving you in the lurch." Their gazes lingered for a long, painful moment. "I want you to know this isn't easy for me either. I wish . . ."

She waited for him to finish. Hoped for something that would ease the terrible ache building inside. Crushing her.

Gunner shook his head.

That was all she was getting. The thought of

running the ranch without him seemed so empty now. So lonely. The thought of losing him made her legs tremble under her weight. It took all her will to straighten her spine, lift her lips into some semblance of a smile. "All right then. I guess this is goodbye."

The shutters over his eyes pulled back, allowing her a glimpse of his pain. "I'm really sorry, Charlotte. I never meant for this to happen."

Charlotte.

Her formal name had never felt like such a slap in the face. "Good luck to you, Gunner." She turned to leave just in time. The tears she'd held back burst like water from a breached dam. Still, feeling his hot gaze on her, she kept her posture erect, her strides confident as she headed toward the house.

Forty

It was the longest day in history. Every hour, every minute passed with the growing realization that Charlotte had lost Gunner for good. That she was running the ranch on her own. She couldn't think past today. The burden of now was heavy enough on its own.

All was quiet on the Robinson front. But she wouldn't kid herself. Gavin had told them all by now, and they were undoubtedly angry and disgusted with her. She couldn't even blame them.

It was well after dark when she did the night check. She took a few extra minutes with Midnight. He'd bonded so well with Gunner. She would've eased the transition had she seen this coming. She reached out slowly and stroked his face, comforted that he let her touch him at least.

"It's all right, boy. You'll be okay without him. You'll see."

Her feet were heavy and sluggish as she headed back to the house. Her stomach gave a rumble. She'd forgotten to eat lunch. Had tried to stay busy to stave off thoughts of Gunner. It hadn't worked.

She should eat something. She headed into the empty house, wishing Emerson were around so the place wasn't so quiet. She scooped out some homemade mac 'n' cheese and put it in the microwave. Midway through the cycle a knock sounded at the door.

Her pulse shot into overdrive. Had Gunner changed his mind? She gave her traitorous heart a stern rebuke. More likely it was the Robinson clan come to tell her off. She'd sent Lisa an email this afternoon, canceling the Join-Up demonstration Gunner was supposed to do at Trail Days. She hadn't heard back.

Her legs wobbled as she headed for the door. With sweaty palms she reached for the handle and pulled it open. She'd been partly right. Just past the screen door, Cooper stood under the glow of the porch light, still wearing his sheriff's uniform. His grim expression made Charlotte's heart bottom out.

What did you say to someone who'd just found out he was your brother after months of—how had Gavin put it?—ingratiating yourself into his family? She settled for a simple "Hi."

"Hi." His tone was neutral. But he had that strong jaw that flexed when he was angry just like his brother.

"Would you like to come in?"

"Maybe you could come out here instead."

He backed away as she slipped outside. He seemed too wired to make use of her porch chairs. So she just stood by the door, folded her arms over her chest, and waited for him to tear into her.

A cricket chirped from somewhere under the porch, and a soft nicker carried from the barn. A breeze ruffled the hairs that had escaped her ponytail over the course of the day. She didn't have to look at Cooper to know he was staring at her. His attention felt like a hot spotlight.

"You have his cleft chin," he said finally, his tone full of reluctance.

Her gaze swung up to find his expression still guarded, despite the admission. His corded neck led down to the rigid line of his shoulders. His arms hung at his sides in a ready stance, as if he were about to draw his holstered gun.

She shook away the absurd thought. "You have his eyes. It was the first thing I noticed about him."

His lips formed a tight line. "Trust me, I know. I've spent my whole life trying not to be my dad. That's the one thing I can't change."

"I guess Gavin told you everything."

"I'd rather hear it from you."

It was the least she could do. And so she told him, starting with the items she'd found in the safety-deposit box and ending with Craig's wish to collect that one-year chip before he approached his sons. "I know I should've told you both sooner. I should've told you before I even met Craig that first time."

Hurt flashed in his eyes. "You should've."

"I'm so sorry for the pain I've caused. And if your family is reeling right now."

He gave a mirthless chuckle. "Oh, they're reeling. Mom's shaken over an affair she never knew about, Gavin feels betrayed, and Avery's upset on all our behalf."

Charlotte squeezed her eyes shut, wishing she could make it all disappear. But she couldn't. This was all happening because of her and she had to face up to it. "I'm so sorry." She opened her eyes and forced herself to meet his gaze. Forced herself to ask the question. "And you, Cooper? How are you feeling about all this?"

He regarded her for a long moment, emotions shifting on his face. "Did you ever hear how Kate and I got together?"

She blinked at the abrupt change of topic. She recalled some Robinson family scandal several years ago involving the two of them, but she hadn't been privy to the details. She'd been too busy with her own life to pay it much mind. "Um, no, not really."

"I'll give you the short version. Back when I was running for sheriff, I met Kate when she had a car accident. She was in imminent danger and we bonded quickly. Afterward, I couldn't stop thinking about her—I was smitten. But then I found out she was Gavin's girlfriend—the one who'd helped pull him from a ditch of despair after his divorce."

"Oh no."

"It wasn't good. I tried to stay away from Kate, but we kept getting thrown together—and I could tell she had feelings for me too. Long story short, we slipped up, got caught. It wasn't pretty. It was very public, humiliating even, for Gavin. He was ticked—and rightfully so.

"I'm only telling you this because I'm someone who's made his own share of mistakes. I've hurt people I love in the process. So these days I'm a little more inclined to give others the benefit of the doubt." He crossed his arms over his chest, looking formidable in that uniform. "Don't get me wrong—I'm upset that you hid the truth from us. You should've told us months ago who you were."

She swiped away a tear. "You're right. I'm sorry, Cooper. I never meant to hurt you or any of your family. I hope you believe that."

"I do. And sorry helps. But of course it doesn't erase the consequences."

She winced. Why, oh why had she waited so long to tell them? *Fear,* her gut screamed. Yes, she'd been afraid. Just as she'd been afraid to tell Emerson about the contents of that folder. It seemed Charlotte had a problem being open and vulnerable with the people she cared about. She'd never even gotten around to telling Gunner she loved him. Maybe it would've made a difference. But that boat had sailed.

Cooper shifted. "I'll get over it eventually, Charlotte. Gavin'll come around too. Give him some time."

Hope fluttered like butterfly wings in her belly. "You really think so?"

"Something you'll learn about Gavin: he's got a temper, but it flares up and dies off pretty quick." His dark-brown eyes sharpened on her. "Especially when it comes to his family."

Family. He was including her in that word. She sucked in a deep breath as the tears started all over again.

He made a pained face. "You're gonna have to stop that. I don't do well with tears. You might remember that from the time I pulled you over."

She recalled the helpless look on his face when she'd broken down in tears and choked back a chuckle as she wiped her face dry. "Right. I'll try to remember."

"And this business between our dad and Gavin and me . . . you might want to stay out of it. There's a lot of water under that bridge."

"Fair enough."

"Let's give this a little time." He straightened from the railing and fished his keys from his pocket. "I'm sure we'll see each other around."

"I'll be at Trail Days." How she'd manage it all, she had no idea.

"All right. I'll see you there then." He made his way down the porch steps.

"Thanks for coming by, Cooper."

He gave her a nod before he was swallowed by the shadows of the night.

Charlotte slipped inside, her thoughts and feelings a big jumble. The conversation had left her hopeful. Hopeful that the Robinsons might forgive her. Cooper could only speak for himself. But still, that was something. She might be able to build a relationship with one of her brothers at least.

She went to the kitchen, feeling somewhat dazed by the roller coaster of emotions today. Her appetite was gone now and her stomach had ceased growling, so she left the mac 'n' cheese in the microwave and started on the dirty dishes instead.

It didn't take long for her thoughts to return to Gunner. Was he still in Riverbend or had he left already? What did it matter? He'd made it clear their relationship was over. They didn't want the same things out of life. She longed for roots, and he didn't want to be tethered by relationships or towns or jobs.

Or her.

Tears prickled her eyes, and this time she let them fall unhindered. She'd shed more tears today than she had since her mom had passed.

"Oh, Mom, I miss you so much."

Charlotte wanted her there. Wanted to fall into her arms and sob. Her mom would understand how she was feeling. She'd loved and lost and lived to tell about it. And given how Charlotte was feeling just now, she wasn't sure how.

She didn't hear Emerson's arrival until she burst through the kitchen door. "Guess what? Vivian wants me to open the new bakery in Greensboro!"

Charlotte used her dry wrist to swipe away the tears. What did Emerson just say? She was leaving Riverbend? Leaving the ranch? Suddenly the thought of losing the extra help paled in comparison to living three and a half hours from her sister.

"Did you hear me, Char? They want me to open the bakery and manage it by myself!"

Face now dry, Charlotte turned and tried for a smile. "Wow, that's wonderful, Emmie. What a great opportunity. I'm really proud of you."

Emerson's smile slipped. She slowly closed the distance between them. "Hey, what's wrong?"

Charlotte drew a shuddering breath and opened her mouth to say she'd just had a bad day. She didn't want to rain on Emerson's parade. But nothing came out. Nothing at all. Instead the words tangled up, forming a knot in her throat. Tears filled her eyes again and began trickling down her face.

Compassion filled Emerson's eyes, softened the planes of her face. "Tell me what's wrong. I know it isn't my news. You look like you've been crying for hours."

In fact, she had. She dried her hands on the towel, tossed it aside, and met her sister's gaze. "So much has happened in the past twenty-four hours. The Robinsons found out who I am and . . . Gunner left." Her words died off as sobs wracked her body.

"Oh, honey." Emerson drew her into her arms and held her tight. She rubbed her back, murmuring soothing words. "Everything will be okay."

But nothing felt like it would ever be okay again. And now she was losing Emerson too.

Her grip tightened on her sister. "It hurts. It hurts so bad."

"I know. I'm so sorry this is happening."

"He doesn't want roots. He doesn't want *me*."

"He must be crazy then."

"But he isn't," Charlotte said. "He's wonderful. He's kind and patient and honorable . . ."

"Don't forget sexy."

Charlotte gave a strangled laugh that died off in another sob.

"Oh, honey. I hate that you're hurting. Can you tell me what happened?"

"I don't even know. We didn't argue or anything. He just told me first thing this morning that it was over. We had an agreement that he'd tell me if this wasn't working for him instead of just taking off like Vince did."

"But he did take off."

"He offered to stay until I found a replacement. But I can't work with him, feeling this way about him. You know it hurt me when Vince left . . . but this feels so much worse."

"You love Gunner."

"So much. Oh, Emmie, I didn't know how much until today. And now it's too late."

Emerson rubbed Charlotte's back for a while. Until the sobs died down again. Then after Charlotte drew away and blew her nose on a paper towel, Emmie asked, "Do you want to talk about the other? The Robinsons?"

Might as well get it all out there. She had to talk to someone. So she told Emerson about the run-in with Gavin last night and finished with Cooper's visit.

"It sounds like there might be some hope, at least where Cooper's concerned."

Charlotte sniffed. "I guess. He was really pretty understanding."

"Maybe the rest of the family will come around. You didn't mean any harm." Emerson took Charlotte's hand and gave her a pained look. "Char, I need to say something: I've been kind of a brat about Craig and the Robinsons. I should've been more supportive. I should've been happy for you."

"And I should've been honest with you from the start. I understand why you were worried. We've always been so close."

Emerson's eyes went glassy. "I felt threatened by them. I was afraid of losing you."

Charlotte dragged her sister into her arms, holding her tight. "Oh, sweetheart, that could never happen. You're my family and you always will be no matter what."

"I know that in my head. It's my heart that's having trouble."

And no wonder. Emerson's mother had abandoned her after all. And then their mom had died suddenly. "I love you, honey, and so did Mom."

"I know. I was just feeling a little bitter about how she handled the ranch in the end, but she didn't mean to slight me. She just loved it so much she wanted to preserve it. I can see why she confided in you. She was always so hopeful we'd run it together. And now she's gone and sometimes I feel like I'm losing you too."

Charlotte drew back and palmed her sister's face. "I will never leave you, Emmie."

"I'll never leave you either."

Charlotte gave a wry grin. "Except to run a bakery clear across the state?"

"Let's not think about that right now. What do you need from me? I can take a bit of time off from the bakery—I have some PTO. I can pitch in around here the next couple weeks. Isn't Trail Days this weekend?"

Charlotte's stomach dropped. She had a booth, and since they'd begun offering lessons, she'd advertised pony rides also. Plus, she'd have to see Lisa at the event and would probably run into all the Robinsons at some point. "I don't even want to think about all that right now."

"You won't have to. I'll handle the pony rides, and you run the booth. We've got this."

Her heart turned to mush. "Really? Are you sure Vivian won't mind you missing work?"

"She'll understand that family comes first."

Charlotte grabbed her sister in another hug. "Thank you for this. And thank you for listening. I can't tell you what it means to have you in my corner."

Emerson leaned back and met her gaze. "Always. We'll get through this together. That's what family does."

Forty-One

The scent of grilled hamburgers and smoked brisket should've cheered Gunner up. But he hadn't looked forward to this last meal with Gavin before he headed out of town.

"You're leaving?" Thought lines formed between Gavin's brows.

Must be a family trait. What would happen between Charlie and her brothers when Craig finally got around to telling them the truth? Gunner hated that he wouldn't be here to support her when it all went down. "I'll be heading to Lexington tomorrow. My new job starts there the first of the month."

"But I thought since you and Charlotte were together . . ."

"Yeah." Gunner glanced down. "That didn't work out." Such a generic thing to say. But he wasn't going into all the painful details. He didn't need sympathy—it was his own doing, after all.

"This doesn't have anything to do with . . . ?"

Gunner's gaze darted to Gavin's face. "With what?"

"I was pretty rough on her the other day. I mean, she shouldn't have done what she did—I'm still upset with her. But I hope that didn't somehow cause problems between the two of you."

Gunner blinked at him. "Wait. What are you talking about?"

"She didn't tell you? I caught her out with my dad Tuesday night. *Our* dad, as it turns out."

Oh no. It had already come to a head. On Tuesday night—and Gunner had broken up with her the next morning. A fist tightened around his gut. So much for supporting her. She'd never said a word. Then again, he really hadn't given her the opportunity. Was she going through this all alone? Emerson was no fan of Charlotte's new family, and Brianna had her hands full with her grandma.

"—and all that time she kept it from us."

Gunner had missed a few things while his mind was spinning.

Gavin's gaze zeroed in on him. "But you already knew that, didn't you? You've known she was our sister for months and you kept it from us too."

Gunner held up his hands. "I didn't like it, but it wasn't my place to say anything."

Gavin fell back in his seat, lips pressed into a firm line, fixed stare steady and formidable.

"She really struggled with this decision. Come on, she was in a hard place. Craig wanted to be sober a year before he approached you and Cooper. The last thing he wanted to do was to reappear in your lives and surprise you with his love child. And Charlotte had just found the biological father she'd always wondered about, and she didn't want to ruin her relationship with him."

Gavin waved his words away. "I already know all this."

"Well, maybe you could cut her some slack then. She was navigating difficult terrain."

Gavin studied Gunner for a long moment. Then his lips tipped in a knowing smile. "You realize you're in love with her. It's all over your face, man."

The words were a punch to the heart. "Charlotte's a great girl. If I were ever gonna settle down . . ." No reason to go down that road. "She deserves someone she can put down roots with. But that's not me."

"Maybe if you stopped moving from town to town long enough, you'd find out differently. You fit in here."

Gunner shook his head. "I'm not like you. I'm just not built for the long haul." Something inside him reared at the thought.

"Don't know what you're missing."

"I'll have to take your word for it."

The teenage server chose that moment to set down their plates. "Here you go, guys. Two brisket specials, extra barbecue sauce. I'll be back with refills."

"Thanks." The savory smells assaulted Gunner's senses, making his stomach turn.

"Let's dig in," Gavin said. "If I can't change your mind about leaving, maybe Lonnie's brisket will."

The next afternoon Gunner's feet dragged as he returned to his cabin. He'd visited Mr. Dixon one last time to say farewell. Paid him till the end of the month even though he was leaving early. Gunner had also assured him some monthly financial support would be coming his way soon via HealthServe.

It was the only positive thing Gunner had to focus on right now.

Well, that wasn't true. He was about to hop on his bike and set off for someplace new.

But the thought only left him achy inside. Being untethered to anyone or any place used to make him feel free. Invigorated. Why did it now make him feel lonely instead? And when had that shift occurred?

He forced his thoughts in a new direction. Toward that dream job awaiting him at Belle Vista. Thankfully, he'd never gotten around to telling the manager he wouldn't be coming. Maybe Gunner had known all along it would never work with Charlotte. With anyone.

He shook away the depressing notion and focused instead on his upcoming job. Working with a winning Derby horse was a real honor. He waited for the punch of excitement that thoughts of Belle Vista used to bring. But it didn't come. He had to face facts: ever since that first kiss with Charlotte, his dreams had begun to shift.

But now it was time to get his head on straight.

He entered the quiet cabin, his gaze falling on the empty duffel bag he'd left on the bed. After the breakup he'd told himself he'd stay till Saturday. He'd leave once he was sure Charlie wouldn't need help with Trail Days. Maybe he'd just been kidding himself. Maybe he'd just been delaying the moment when he put Riverbend and Charlie in his rearview mirror.

Anyway, he hadn't heard from her at all. Not that he'd really expected to.

The last three days had passed slower than a mare's gestation. He'd done some biking on the winding mountain roads. Played a lot of chess with Mr. Dixon. He'd even rented fishing gear from the outfitters shop and spent a day casting his line into the river. He'd thought a lot about his mom and dad that day.

The window air conditioner hummed loudly as he gathered the contents of a drawer and dumped them into the duffel bag. Time to hit the road. There was nothing left for him here. He didn't have to be at Belle Vista for another ten days. He'd take his time, stop in Gatlinburg and Knoxville and any other place that caught his eye along the way. He'd arrive in Lexington with plenty of time to find a place and settle in.

He put the last of his things into his duffel. Glanced around the cabin. It had taken only five minutes to clear the room of all his possessions. That's what happened when you traveled light. The thought usually pleased him. Made him feel a little superior, if he was honest. But today the realization fell flat.

A knock sounded on the door. His head snapped that way. *Charlie?*

His pulse raced at the possibility of her just on the other side of that door. *Stupid.* She was working at Trail Days. She'd have no reason to come here. Probably figured he was already long gone.

Still, he couldn't quell the foolish glimmer of hope. Until he opened the door. Wes stood on the stoop. His dark-blond hair was windblown, his facial muscles tense. The man's gaze shifted past Gunner, then returned to his face. "So it's true. You're leaving."

Gunner left the door open as he turned back inside. "Word travels fast."

Wes followed him inside and pushed the door shut. "This the way you usually do it? Just pick up and go when the mood strikes?"

"I was gonna stop by and see you on my way out of town. I have a job lined up—everybody knew that."

"But then you and Charlotte got together and everyone assumed you'd rethought your plans."

"Myself included. But I guess it just wasn't meant to be." That same feeling he'd had earlier pinched inside at his proclamation.

Wes shelved his hands on his hips. "What happened? You guys seemed really happy together."

They had been happy. Making her laugh was the best kind of reward. Having her in his arms was a feeling just this side of heaven. His stomach twisted at the thought of leaving her. He would only have memories to keep him warm on the lonely winter nights to come.

"Did you have an argument or something?"

"No."

"Then what? Why aren't you sticking around? Making things work out? I thought you liked it here."

"I do. I'm just—I can't do it, the whole settling down thing. I start feeling, I don't know, all cooped up inside."

Wes studied him for a long moment, his gaze penetrating like a hot laser.

"What?" Gunner turned and zipped his duffel bag.

"Are you sure that's the problem? Because that doesn't account for the panic I see in your eyes. Look, I know you lost everything when you were a kid. You never went into the details, but that must've been pretty hard. Maybe that screwed you up. Maybe it explains this free-and-easy lifestyle of yours."

The words hit their target. Gunner gritted his teeth. "I don't need you to analyze me."

"Somebody has to. You're a thirty-four-year-old man who can fit everything he owns on the back of his bike. A guy who's uncomfortable with the idea of home, close friends, family. Everything in your life is temporary. That sounds to me like a guy who's afraid of losing again."

"Yeah, well, losing everything bites. Maybe I don't want to risk that again. That doesn't make me a monster."

The tension at the corners of Wes's eyes eased. "It must've been traumatic. But do you really think you're just gonna leave town and forget all about Charlotte?"

What if he couldn't? His chest tightened. He pushed through the anxiety. "It's always worked before." His heart refuted the thought. He'd found places he'd liked. Places he could stay. People he could embrace as friends. But he'd never been in love.

Wes gave a wry chuckle, shaking his head slowly. "Buddy, you are kidding yourself."

Okay, now the guy was ticking him off. Gunner snatched his duffel off the bed. "Glad I could amuse you. It's been real, but I should get going if I'm gonna make it over the mountains before dark."

Gunner exited the cabin with Wes on his heels,

locked the front door, and tucked the key under the pail on the porch.

Wes grabbed his arm. "Hey, I'm sorry. I didn't mean to be insensitive. I've never walked in your shoes. It's just—I've been where you are right now, heading out of town with other plans, leaving the woman I love behind. And, friend, let me tell you—you're making a mistake."

"I'm not you, Wes."

"You're more me than you know. Do yourself a favor and rethink this. You and Charlotte have something special. That kind of connection doesn't come around every day."

It had taken thirty-four years for it to come around at all. If Gunner was lucky, it never would again. His gaze sharpened on Wes. He was a good guy, trying to be a friend. "I appreciate what you're trying to do. But I have to go."

Wes's countenance drooped with resignation. He nodded slowly. "All right. Okay. I wish you the best, buddy. I really do." Wes gripped his hand, pulled him in till their shoulders bumped, thumped him on the back a couple of times. "Keep in touch, man."

With every mile Gunner drove, it seemed an elastic line stretched taut between Charlie and him. The tension pulled at him. He took the road out of the valley, waiting for the line to snap. He hugged the mountain curves, waiting for it to snap. He left Riverbend, left Madison County, waiting for it to snap.

He was still waiting forty-five minutes later when he came to a stop behind a line of cars. Road construction. Great. Just what he needed. He stopped his bike and set his feet on the hot pavement, hands gripping the handlebars so hard they ached.

Thoughts of Charlie had plagued him as he rode, the memories forming a knot in his throat. The first time he'd seen her, ogling Gavin through binoculars out the barn window. Riding Rogue across the pasture, auburn hair flying behind her. Laughing at herself when she tripped over nothing but air. Kissing him so passionately the night Daisy foaled. Holding him so tightly as she fretted over the conundrum with Craig and her brothers.

He wanted all the images of her out of his head. He also wanted to memorize every detail so he didn't forget a single thing. He gave his head a sharp shake. What was wrong with him? He'd lost his mind.

No, he'd lost his heart.

"Do you really think you're just gonna leave town and forget all about Charlotte?"

Wes's words reverberated in his brain. How had Gunner allowed this to happen? He'd been so careful all these years to keep his guard up. But there'd been no keeping Charlie at a distance.

She'd just sucked him right in and made him love her.

And here he was, in that place he'd always feared: having too much on the line. And now he was walking that familiar, dreaded path of pain he'd sworn he'd never walk again.

The realization hit him like 120 volts, shocking his system. Waking him up. He was leaving Charlotte because he was afraid of losing her. But by leaving he was just losing her now instead of later. Just because the pain was self-inflicted didn't make it hurt any less.

He worked the insight around his brain, turning it every which way. It was a new thought. But it made more sense than all the previous ones. His pulse raced and his palms sweated on the handlebar grips.

Leaving was pointless.

Leaving was *stupid.*

He could suffer definite heartbreak now or go back and perhaps lose her later. Or maybe have a long, happy life with her. Why hadn't he seen that before?

He recalled his last words with Charlie and guilt hammered him. He'd left her. He'd disappointed her. He'd hurt her. She might not even want him back now, and he couldn't even blame her.

But he loved her, didn't he? So he had to try.

Gunner turned the bike's front wheel and

throttled forward, leaving his left foot out as he made a U-turn into the other lane. Once the bike was pointed in the right direction, he throttled again and eased off the clutch.

He was heading home.

Forty-Two

It seemed like every family in North Carolina had decided to attend Trail Days. And half of them wanted pony rides for their kids. Charlotte had abandoned the booth hours ago to assist Emerson. The long line extended across the green and into the game area.

Charlotte had no idea what time it was, but she was pretty sure supper had come and gone. Her empty stomach complained. The delicious aromas of funnel cakes and blooming onions hung in the October air.

She hadn't had time to eat since the caramel apple she'd grabbed for breakfast. That was when she'd made eye contact with Gavin, who was crossing the green with Wes and Avery. It was the first time she'd seen him since they'd had words on Tuesday. A moment later the group was gone. Had she dreamed the whole thing?

She didn't have time to dwell on the thought as she'd nearly ran smack into Kyle Lemmings. "Sorry!"

He steadied her with his hands. "No worries."

She hadn't seen him since their breakup almost three weeks ago.

His hands dropped as an awkward silence brewed between them.

"I was, um . . ."—Charlotte held up her caramel apple—"just grabbing breakfast."

"Looks good. Do you have a booth this year?"

"I do." Had he heard about her breakup with Gunner? She wasn't about to bring it up.

"Me too." He gave her a tentative smile as his gaze zeroed in on her. "I hope it goes well for you, Charlotte."

Relief bloomed in her chest. "Thanks, Kyle. I hope the same for you."

She smiled at the memory as she greeted a set of parents, took their ticket, and handed them a ranch brochure that promoted their lessons. She tried not to think about what she'd do if that part of the business exploded. She was already in over her head.

After adjusting the little girl's helmet, she boosted her onto Firefly and sent them off around the makeshift ring. They'd started letting parents spot their own kids a long time ago. It wasn't ideal, but there was no other choice.

She'd called Brianna this morning to see if she was available today, but her friend had long hours at the coffee shop. Brianna had shown up at her door last night with a gallon of rocky road ice cream. She'd begged a neighbor to stay with her grandma so she could come over and commiserate with Charlotte. It had meant so much to her.

"Here's our ticket," a woman said.

Charlotte turned to greet the parent—and found Gavin and Jeff standing nearby. She balked, speechless for full seconds.

Gavin couldn't seem to hold eye contact with her.

Her spine stiffened at his guardedness. This was the first time she'd seen his stepfather since the news had broken. Cooper never said how Jeff was responding to all this. But he couldn't be enjoying the upheaval she'd caused in his family. Nonetheless, his smile seemed friendly enough.

"Hi," she said.

"Hi, Charlotte." Jeff frowned pointedly at Gavin. Nudged him in the gut.

"Um, my mom sent us over to see if you needed some help." His tone was somewhat begrudging.

She wished she were too proud to accept the offer, but she didn't have that luxury. "I'll take whatever help I can get."

"Where would you like us?" Jeff asked.

"Can one of you man the booth? Pass out brochures and attempt to field questions? Most of the answers are in the brochure."

"I'm on it." Jeff scooted off, leaving her standing awkwardly with Gavin, who was clearly only here at Lisa's request.

"I can take tickets, I guess."

"Okay." Charlotte handed him a stack of brochures. "Give these to the parents, please."

She turned and greeted the older woman whose grandson wanted a pony ride.

Even with the extra help, the line was still slow since she had to put on helmets and get the kids onto the ponies. Her arms were getting so tired. To say nothing of her back. Some of these kids were not so small. What a day. When she got home, she would take a nice, long shower and flop into bed.

A half hour later Charlotte sent Firefly on another ride around the ring. How much longer could she go on? Across the ring, Emerson looked ready to drop too.

"Reinforcements have arrived," Cooper announced as he approached with Laurel and Avery.

"We're here to help," Avery said.

Laurel touched Charlotte's arm. "Where do you want us?"

Charlotte blinked, touched by their obvious care. Almost all the Robinsons had shown up to help her—and were apparently not angry, except for maybe Gavin. Her heart bucked. Her eyes stung with tears. She cleared her throat. "I'm so glad to see you. Cooper, can you help kids onto the horses? My arms are about to fall off."

"Got it." He turned to greet the next kid in line.

"What about us?" Laurel asked.

"Can you spot the kids? The parents are doing it, but I'd feel better if—"

"We're on it."

Charlotte put the helmet on the little girl, then Cooper scooped her up and onto Ginger. Laurel chatted with the little girl as they headed off around the ring.

It seemed like minutes, not hours, later when the fair lights came on. Twilight was already upon them, and the line was finally starting to die down now that folks were heading off for food or leaving for the day. The air had chilled a bit with the setting sun, but that didn't account for the improvement in her mood. There had been such great camaraderie since the Robinsons had shown up to help. She'd felt like she was a part of something.

Charlotte made eye contact with Emerson across the ring.

Her sister's expression said, *Can you believe this?*

Charlotte's gaze drifted over the Robinsons, who were tackling their jobs like they were invested in the ranch. Even Gavin exchanged pleasantries with the customers in line. Of course, he hadn't spoken to Charlotte except when necessary. The thought was like a hole in the bottom of a bucket, draining away some of her joy.

By the time she assisted the last child in line, it was dark and several minutes past closing time. She made her way to the booth where Jeff was stowing brochures in a box.

She stopped across the table from him. "Thank you so much for your help, Mr. Robinson. You were a lifesaver."

He slid her a smile. "It's Jeff, remember? And I was happy to help out. Passed out quite a few of these. I have a feeling your business is about to have a growth spurt."

He was right. She paused a moment and let that sink in. Even though she might feel overwhelmed by the growth, all of her efforts to save the ranch had worked. *We did it, Mom. It's a full-time operation once again.* Oh, there'd be a lot of hard work going forward. But for Charlotte it was a labor of love. A business she hoped to carry on to the next generation.

Laurel appeared and threw her arm around Charlotte. "You were wildly popular today, lady. I'm pretty sure we gave half the county pony rides."

Charlotte glanced around the area. "I can't believe I have to do this for another whole day. I don't even know if I'll be able to move in the morning."

"Don't worry." Avery approached. "We'll be here to help. I would've been here earlier, but the clinic needed me. I swear fairs bring out the crazy in people. A teenage boy ate sixteen corn dogs, a three-year-old stuffed a balloon up his nose, and a fistfight resulted in a fractured jawbone and a head laceration. The woman in the middle ended up leaving both guys high and dry."

"What's this about a fight?" Cooper asked as he met them at the booth.

"Never mind," Avery said. "You're off duty today, Sheriff Robinson."

While the two of them bickered, Laurel leaned in and said quietly, "I'm sorry about Gunner."

His name brought a pang of loss. "How did you know?"

She lifted a shoulder. "Small town."

Avery approached. "Well, it's been real, but I need to talk to Alex about a funnel cake. I've been dying for one all day."

"You're on a first-name basis with the funnel-cake guy?" Cooper asked.

"Well, duh."

"I wanna know the funnel-cake guy," Laurel said.

"I'll introduce you." Avery crossed her fingers. "We're like this."

Gavin approached then, having been standing silently outside the circle.

"Is there anything else you need before we go?" Avery asked.

"I don't think so. Em and I can trailer the horses. You guys were a godsend today. Thank you so much. And tell Lisa thank you too."

"Will do," Cooper said. "We should probably go see if Mom needs help with anything."

"After the funnel cakes."

Cooper rolled his eyes at Avery.

The group said goodbye and turned toward junk-food alley.

"Gavin," Jeff called. "Hold up a minute."

Gavin approached the table and stopped across from Jeff, a safe distance from Charlotte. Wouldn't want to get too close to the enemy.

Jeff regarded Gavin with a frown and gave a deep sigh. Then he fished something out of his pocket, set it on the table, and waited expectantly.

Charlotte frowned at the two pennies. "I don't understand."

Gavin glanced her direction, his expression a little too smug for her liking. "You should pick them up."

Jeff scowled at his son. "Oh, trust me, this one's for both of you."

His jaw flexing, Gavin held eye contact with Jeff. Finally his expression turned somewhat sheepish, and he scooped one of the pennies off the table.

"What's this about?" Charlotte asked.

"Dad doesn't give unsolicited advice to us kids," Gavin muttered. "When he has something he's just bursting to say, he sets out his two cents. If you want to hear it, you pick them up."

Her gaze toggled between the men. She peered down at the remaining penny. Oh, why not? If nothing else, she was curious.

"Good move," Gavin said.

Jeff faced off with his son. "We'll start with you, son. I know you're hurting and your mother is hurting. But you're putting all the blame for this on Charlotte. It's not her fault your dad had an affair with her mom. It's not her fault she was born or that she wasn't told who her birth father was. And once she did find him—correct me if I'm wrong, Charlotte—you tried to get to know Gavin and Cooper, wanted to feel things out before you stormed into the family with an announcement that may or may not have been welcomed." He waited for Charlotte's confirmation.

Her heart quivered in her chest. "Yes."

"Things get a little out of hand with that, sweetheart?"

She breathed a shaky laugh, eyes tearing, and nodded.

He set his hand on Gavin's shoulder. "Charlotte didn't mean you any harm. She didn't mean to hurt your mom. In fact, I think she was trying her best to avoid that. She was in a bad spot and she made a judgment call."

Jeff's gaze slid to Charlotte. "As for you . . . I understand Craig is sober now, and you've been getting to know him the past few months?"

She nodded, unable to speak past the boulder in her throat.

"That's a wonderful thing for you. I'm glad it seems to be working out. But you should understand that while Craig has a fresh start with you, that's not the case for Gavin and Cooper. They have a long and painful history with Craig. He let his sons down for many years, and because of that, there's a world of hurt and distrust there. That's not going away overnight."

She peered at Gavin and caught a glimpse of vulnerability in those blue eyes. Caught a glimpse of the little boy who'd waited for his dad to come home. The child who was embarrassed by his father's drunken antics. Who ached for his abandoned mother. "No, sir."

"My sons know I'm a huge fan of forgiveness. Just as God forgives us, He expects us to forgive others. But Gavin and Cooper have to resolve their own feelings about their father and the past at their own pace. They may never choose to have a relationship with Craig. And that's their decision."

She nodded again, glancing at Gavin. He was staring at her. His face had softened.

"That doesn't mean they can't have a relationship with you." He turned his attention to Gavin. "I can't tell you how to feel or what to do. But as far as your mom and I are concerned, Charlotte is your sister—and that makes her family."

A tear spilled over. She swiped it away.

"All right." Jeff pushed away from the table. "I've said my piece. Your mom is probably up to her eyeballs in cleanup, and I'm gonna hunt her down and give her a hand. Good night."

"Good night," Charlotte squeezed out.

Silence hung awkwardly between them for a long moment. Charlotte wanted Gavin in her life more than she could say. But it wasn't her call.

He shifted. "I probably overreacted the other day. I do that sometimes."

"It must've been quite a shock to find out you have another sister."

"It was. But Dad is right—about all of it, actually. He usually is. It's pretty annoying."

She breathed a laugh. "Is this where we find common ground by complaining about family?"

Gavin sobered. "No. This is where I apologize. I was tough on you. All I could think of was my mom and the hurt this would cause. I should've tried to see where you were coming from. I'm sorry for that."

She melted at his gentle tone and remorseful expression. "And I'm sorry I waited so long, didn't tell you months ago. I'm sorry for hurting you and your family." Her eyes filled with tears again.

He held his arms open, tilted his head. "Come on, bring it in."

She stepped into his embrace and his arms came around her. Big, protective-brother arms. It was a feeling she'd never quite had before.

"Another sister," Gavin mumbled a moment

later. "You and Avery are gonna gang up on us, aren't you?"

"I've always wanted a big brother to annoy."

He gave a wry laugh. "Great."

Her grin widened as she drew away from him, and a movement in the corner of her eye caught her attention. Her smile wilted and adrenaline flooded her system, leaving her rigid and trembling.

Forty-Three

Charlotte's grip tightened reflexively on Gavin's arm. She blinked just to make sure it was really Gunner standing under the fair lights in his T-shirt and jeans, looking tense and tired and tempting. The image didn't go away. She homed in on his rigid shoulders and the uncertainty in the planes of his face.

Gavin stepped in front of her. "What are you doing here? I thought you left."

"I need to speak with Charlotte."

Hope kindled inside her, but fear doused the flames. Her pulse kicked into a higher gear as the two emotions warred with each other.

Gavin turned to her. "Is that what you want? 'Cause I can toss this guy out of here if you want me to."

"Hey." Gunner frowned. "I thought we were friends."

"She's my sister."

His words warmed her through. "It's okay, Gavin. You can go."

He studied her features. "You sure?"

She had to know what was going on. What Gunner wanted to tell her. But she was afraid to know. Afraid to hope. Afraid to believe. But she had to push through the fear. "I'm sure."

A long, scowly moment ensued between the men. Finally Gavin looked at her. "Text me if you need me."

"Thanks."

The sound of his footsteps faded away, but she saw only Gunner. He approached with that lazy stride she'd become so familiar with, then stopped. His gaze roved over her face as if he was trying to read her thoughts.

Good luck with that. Her brain was a jumbled mess. And the rest of her was even worse. "Wes said you'd left."

"I did." His Adam's apple bobbed as he swallowed. "But I came back."

"I see that." Her heart skipped a beat, then scrambled to catch up. "Why?"

He stepped closer. Started to reach out to her, then dropped his arm. "I was wrong, Charlie."

Charlie. The nickname shouldn't melt her into a puddle. Shouldn't make her stomach flutter or her knees go weak. But it did.

"I shouldn't have—" Gunner gave his head a shake, closed his eyes. "I need to tell you something that happened when I was a kid. I should've told you before. It had a big impact on me."

Her gaze sharpened on his earnest expression. "Tell me."

"I haven't said much about my childhood. Honestly, it's hard to think about, much less talk about. It started out good. I grew up in this nice community in Minnesota. I had neighborhood friends, a great park nearby, a school I liked. My mom was a stay-at-home mom. My dad was a plumber."

"You mentioned before he worked long hours."

"He did. But he was a good dad. We were close. And my mom was the best. She—she was always there for me. We had a pretty great life."

There was a *but* coming. The death of his parents, she assumed. Dread pinched her chest. "What happened?"

He glanced away, off into the darkening night just beyond the fair lights. Off into some other time and place. "One night when I was nine—it was mid-October—I woke up in the middle of the night and the house was on fire. I was so scared. I heard my dad calling for me, but I couldn't move. I was frozen. Then there was this loud crashing noise and . . . that was the last thing I remember. Days later I woke up in the hospital. My grandpa was there. He told me my parents were gone. The house was gone. Everything was just . . . gone." His jaw flexed.

Oh, she ached for him. She touched his arm. "How awful. I'm so sorry that happened to you. You must've been hurt too. You said you were in the hospital."

He looked at her again, fully in the here and now. He took her hand and placed it just beneath his shirt on his stomach. Holding eye contact, he moved her fingers along a ridged network of raised skin that covered most of his abdomen.

She sucked in a breath as her eyes filled with tears. All those times he'd absently touched his stomach . . . He wore a constant reminder of that night. "Oh, Gunner."

"It doesn't hurt anymore. I'm fine physically. But the trauma left other kinds of scars."

"I can only imagine."

"I had nightmares for years. I'm just beginning to realize the full impact of that night." His eyes grew intense, piercing hers. "It's hard to admit this, but . . . the thought of caring too much about anything or anyone scares me. If I care too much—it might all disappear again."

Her thoughts sharpened with clarity. "That's why you don't have belongings. Why you don't have meaningful relationships. Why you don't have a home."

"If I never have it . . . I can't lose it."

Her insides softened until her heart was just a big, achy lump. "Oh, Gunner. That's no way to live."

"I know," he said softly. "It's not freeing or invigorating. It's just empty and lonely. I've been lying to myself. And I don't want to live that way."

"What about Belle Vista?"

"I don't care about that job anymore. I haven't cared about it for a long time." His eyes seemed to see all the way to her core. "When I found you, Charlie, I found my home."

A tear spilled over. It was what she'd longed to hear. "I want that too."

His warm breath fell over her mouth just before his lips brushed hers. She savored the feel of him, the taste of him, as he pulled her close. Chest to chest. Heart to heart. She reveled in his gentle caress even while that familiar buzz inside grew from a dull hum to a heavy drone.

She'd never thought to have him in her arms again. Not since he'd walked away from her. The thought pressed in. There was still an unanswered question. Something that had bugged her for four days.

As if feeling her shift of attention, he pulled away. His gaze roved over her face, no doubt seeing every tense muscle, every furrow, every emotion that flickered in her eyes. "What's wrong?"

"Sorry . . ."

"You don't have to be sorry. You can tell me anything."

"Can I ask you anything?"

"Of course. What is it?"

She put a few inches between them. Created a little breathing room. "Can you tell me what happened before? Why did you break up with me out of the blue? Was it something I did or said or—?"

"No, honey. It had nothing to do with you.

The day before we broke up was the anniversary of the fire. Of my parents' deaths. It had been haunting me all day."

She felt a catch in her throat. "Oh, Gunner. Why didn't you tell me?"

"I didn't even want to think about it. But I had a nightmare that night—my first in years. It was pretty bad. It shook me up." The remnants of that dream still flickered in his eyes. "I got scared and I acted out of fear."

She touched his face. "I get scared sometimes too. I'm afraid of getting left behind. I'm afraid of being vulnerable."

"And here I am, this guy who runs from job to job, town to town. I made you think it was safe to care, then I left you in the dust."

"But in the end, you chose *me*. Besides, some wise guy once told me love is always a risk."

He cradled her face. "You are so worth that risk. I love you, sweetheart. So much. I'm not going anywhere."

Had sweeter words ever been spoken? Had a man ever looked at a woman with such adoration? Such reverence? "Oh, Gunner. I love you too."

The kiss that followed might have lasted minutes or hours. They might've been standing in a busy fairground or on a quiet street corner. Time and place were irrelevant when she was wrapped up in Gunner's arms. In Gunner's heart. And she intended to keep it that way.

Epilogue

Charlotte slid into Gunner's arms, and they began swaying to the tune of "God Gave Me You." White lights twinkled above the makeshift dance floor. The air was crisp with autumn, and the trees were clothed in fall's splendor.

Charlotte laid her head against Gunner's chest, and even with the music floating on the breeze, she could hear his heart keeping time with hers. Feel his strong arms around her. Smell the leather and spice scent that was uniquely his.

She was so blessed. She just wanted a minute to take it all in.

The last year had been busy and exciting. Following Trail Days, the Stables at Wildflower Falls had experienced a hearty growth spurt. They'd expanded their riding program and now offered lessons six days a week. She'd hired two additional hands to care for the horses so she could manage lessons and trail rides. Gunner had his hands full with the training program, which had also grown as his good reputation spread.

And as it turned out, Emerson had decided to stay in Riverbend Gap after all. When Charlotte mentioned the idea of a chuck-wagon supper, it inspired Emerson's inner chef. They now offered the supper on Fridays and Saturdays, and her sister was constantly tweaking the menu. The schedule allowed her to keep her job at the bakery where she'd recently been promoted to assistant manager.

On Sundays the sisters often found themselves at the Robinson house, where they engaged in the cornhole wars. Nobody complained when they were paired with Charlotte or Emerson, even though they were novices. After the games they sat down to delicious potluck suppers that were filled with bright chatter and lively banter. When the Robinsons welcomed you into their family, you and those you loved were warmly received.

There had been a lot of excitement in November. Laurel went into labor late at night and progressed so quickly that she ended up having the baby at the town clinic. Avery delivered her niece—Madelyn Mae Robinson—who was born at 3:15 a.m. After a short stay Laurel and Gavin brought the infant home to a very excited Emma.

And at the end of March they learned the lively clan would soon grow even larger—Avery and Wes were now expecting. A new member of the Robinson family would be born at the end of the year. There was much celebrating about the upcoming arrival of another baby—Avery and Wes's first.

And how were things faring between Charlotte and Gunner? Well, on a perfect April day, wildflowers blooming in riotous color, Gunner dropped to his knee and proposed to Charlotte by the falls where they'd shared their first picnic. The memory of that day was one of her favorites. It was romantic and special and also kind of sweet that he was nervous.

She smiled now as she swayed to the swelling chorus, remembering the way his hands had trembled when he presented the engagement ring.

"Everybody's staring at us," he whispered into her ear.

"Well, it is kind of our moment."

"But I want to kiss you."

Laughter bubbled up inside as she leaned back far enough to meet his gaze. "You just kissed me not even an hour ago. The vows, the rings, the kiss. Sound familiar?"

"It was a great kiss." He dropped his eyes to her lips, giving her that sleepy-eyed look she'd come to love. "But it made me want more."

"There'll be plenty of time for *more* later, when you take me away."

He set his forehead against hers, putting them so close their breaths mingled. "Tell me more about *later*."

"Well . . . after we make it through the dance and the cake and more dancing—"

He groaned.

"—we'll jump into your new Silverado and head over the mountains to Gatlinburg, where we'll cozy up for three glorious nights in our honeymoon chalet."

A little smile played around his mouth as his arms tightened around her. "That was such an awesome idea."

"It was *your* idea. So was this." She drifted her gaze over the small crowd of close friends and family. Over the photos of their parents on a memorial table they'd set up. "One of your better ones, I'll admit."

In a tradition that was old to the Robinsons but new to Charlotte, she and Gunner had said their vows in the Robinsons' backyard under the shade of a gilded oak tree. Emerson served as her maid of honor, and Wes stood up for Gunner in the simple ceremony.

"Did I mention how beautiful you are tonight?"

"Several times." Though his expression when he'd first seen her had said it all. She ran her hand down his lapel. "And you, my love, are a very handsome groom."

The song was winding down and the father-daughter dance was next. Charlotte's gaze caught on Craig, where he sat watching from a table with Gavin, Laurel, Cooper, Katie, and the kids. It would be premature to say her brothers' relationship with their father had been repaired. But they were all making a tenuous effort. And Craig, now almost two years sober, had been careful not to push them. Charlotte was proud of them all.

The last of the lyrics trickled out, and the melody's final strains hung in the air as the clinking of glassware rang across the yard.

Gunner's eyes twinkled at her. "Looks like I'm gonna get my way after all, Mrs. Dawson." He leaned down and pressed his lips to hers, instantly sweeping her away. But since they had an audience, the kiss was far shorter than either of them would've liked.

When he drew away to raucous applause, he whispered in her ear, "To be continued."

Acknowledgments

Bringing a book to market takes a lot of effort from many different people. I'm so incredibly blessed to partner with the fabulous team at HarperCollins Christian Fiction, led by publisher Amanda Bostic: Patrick Aprea, Kimberly Carlton, Caitlin Halstead, Jodi Hughes, Margaret Kercher, Colleen Lacey, Becky Monds, Lizzie Poteet, Kerri Potts, Nekasha Pratt, Savannah Summers, Taylor Ward, Jere Warren, and Laura Wheeler.

Not to mention all the wonderful sales reps and amazing people in the rights department—special shout-out to Robert Downs!

Thanks especially to my editor, Kimberly Carlton. Your incredible insight and inspiration help me take the story deeper, and for that I am so grateful! Thanks also to my line editor, Julee Schwarzburg, whose attention to detail makes me look like a better writer than I really am.

Author Colleen Coble is my first reader and sister of my heart. Thank you, friend! This writing journey has been ever so much more fun because of you.

I'm grateful to my agent, Karen Solem, who's able to somehow make sense of the legal garble of contracts and, even more amazing, help me understand it.

To my husband, Kevin, who has supported my dreams in every way possible—I'm so grateful! To all our kiddos: Chad and Taylor, Trevor and Babette, and Justin and Hannah, who have favored us with three beautiful grandchildren. Every stage of parenthood has been a grand adventure, and I look forward to all the wonderful memories we have yet to make!

A hearty thank-you to all the booksellers who make room on their shelves for my books—I'm deeply indebted! And to all the book bloggers and reviewers, whose passion for fiction is contagious—thank you!

Lastly, thank you, friends, for letting me share this story with you! I wouldn't be doing this without you. Your notes, posts, and reviews keep me going on the days when writing doesn't flow so easily. I appreciate your support more than you know.

I enjoy connecting with friends on my Facebook page: www.facebook.com/authordenisehunter. Please pop over and say hello. Visit my website at www.DeniseHunterBooks.com or just drop me a note at Deniseahunter@comcast.net. I'd love to hear from you!

Discussion Questions

1. Following her parents' passing, Charlotte found herself wanting to fill the void by locating her biological father. If you were her, would you make the same decision? Why or why not?
2. Discuss why Charlotte's mom withheld the identity of her father. Do you think she was right or wrong?
3. How did you feel about Charlotte's decision to get to know her biological siblings before telling them who she was? Discuss.
4. When Charlotte was backed into a corner, she finally told Emerson about the folder their mother had left behind. How did you feel about Emerson's response?
5. Could you ever live a vagabond lifestyle like Gunner? Discuss how his past contributed to that way of life.
6. Charlotte goes to great lengths to fulfill her dream of running the ranch full-time. What dreams have you worked hard to fulfill? Are there any you've left on the back burner? Discuss.
7. The Robinsons have such a warm way of welcoming people into their lives. Is there someone in your life who welcomes you that

way? Are you that kind of person for someone else? Discuss.

8. Charlotte's biological father made many
   mistakes in his past, mostly due to his
   alcoholism. Did you feel empathy for him?
   Why or why not?

9. Charlotte withheld the truth from Gavin and
   Cooper for her biological father's benefit.
   Did you feel that was the right thing to do?
   Why or why not?

10. Charlotte had difficulty being open and
    honest with those she loved. When was the
    last time you avoided conflict with someone
    you care about? How did that work out?

About the Author

Denise Hunter is the internationally published, bestselling author of more than forty books, three of which have been adapted into original Hallmark Channel movies. She has won the Holt Medallion Award, the Reader's Choice Award, the Carol Award, the Foreword Book of the Year Award, and is a RITA finalist. When Denise isn't orchestrating love lives on the written page, she enjoys traveling with her family, drinking chai lattes, and playing drums. Denise makes her home in Indiana, where she and her husband raised three boys and are now enjoying an empty nest and three beautiful grandchildren.

DeniseHunterBooks.com
Facebook: @AuthorDeniseHunter
Twitter: @DeniseAHunter
Instagram: @deniseahunter

Center Point Large Print
600 Brooks Road / PO Box 1
Thorndike, ME 04986-0001 USA

(207) 568-3717

US & Canada:
1 800 929-9108
www.centerpointlargeprint.com